THE ALTERED RISE

The Sentinel Quartet
Book Two

MEGAN MORGAN

Clickworks Press · Baltimore, MD

First publication: Clickworks Press, 2022
Release: CWP-ALT2-INT-E.M-1.0

Sign up for updates, deals, and exclusive sneak peeks at clickworkspress.com/join.

Ebook ISBN: 978-1-943383-94-8
Paperback ISBN: 978-1-943383-95-5

For Erik, who believed

VARCOVE
QUELLAN OCEAN
Port Ellicott
Redholme
HIGH CRESCENT MOUNTAINS
Harfield Manor
Irion Valley
Palisade
LOW CRESCENT MOUNTAINS
Valance
The Crag
Dunes
Mt. Ashling
Brook's Cove
OTARION
ADVON
BLUESTONE RIVER
Storach
Lake Country
Mt. Tahon
THE RING
Tunnel to Estecost
Owl Canyon
Esanad

THE ALTERED RISE

001

WILLIAM JUMPED THE stairs leading down out of his cramped, silver camper. He'd rather land heavily in the bone-dry sand than risk the clanging, swaying steps. The door slammed shut behind him. He shifted the wide straps of his pack on his shoulders, felt the weight of its contents slide against his back. Then he tromped off across the desert. The sand and rocks glowed in the rising sun. Birds sang high-pitched music. Insects burred and buzzed.

Ahead stretched the canyon. An abrupt gap in the landscape, from where he stood. But it widened as he walked towards it.

William could have parked closer to the edge, but it felt too precarious, those steep pitched walls plunging down, down to the riverbed far below. Layers of earthy color banded the sides, meandering along with the curves of the walls. To think that the minuscule ribbon of brown river below had chiseled out all that rock boggled the mind almost as much as the existence of the chasm itself. The whole thing defied his sense of space and time. That it was beautiful as well seemed like an unjust abundance of riches for one landmark.

He came upon a metal ring in the ground a few feet back from the edge. He dropped his pack to the sand where Tristan had drilled the anchor a couple of weeks before when William first arrived. His cousin had guided him through the process of setting up.

William pulled out the climbing gear, checked each part for damage, then tied in to the hook, ropes slithering around as he made complicated knots, metal rings clanking.

He saw the sparks of energy flying off as the ropes passed over each other, generating just the tiniest bit of warmth. Cameron Kardell was to blame for that. Even now he could see in his mind her dark eyes boring into his, clear and certain, always unwavering. Up in the mountains, in the white snow and the dark trees, she'd magnified his latent abilities to see and manipulate energy. Now the golden glow of energy was inescapable. No amount of suppression could diminish it. And the amount of fire he could now cradle in his hands because of her. He swallowed hard.

He'd come to the desert to escape her. An impossibility in Advon, where she stood at the High General's shoulder during meetings.

Did he hate it most when she stared straight ahead, or was it worse when she looked right at him, seemed to see right through him? Divining the way he tried to hate her, and failed. How he wanted to. He should. He must. She'd killed Erika.

Part of the problem, of course, was that he wasn't convinced it *was* her fault. Erika had gone messing around in something none of them understood. Cameron had just *reacted*, hadn't she? After Erika killed all those people, Cameron *had* to stop her. They'd all made mistakes, they'd all tried to fix them. Cameron had just fixed hers in the most permanent way.

It wasn't as if he played no part in Erika's fate.

William tied off the last knots. He listened to the gentle rhythms of the desert. A flame-hawk already screamed above him as it hunted for lizards, wings cutting the sky, tail-feathers blazing red in the sharpening light of the sunrise.

You think too much, Harfield.

Knowing he should resist, but unable to, he pulled a creased and frayed piece of paper from his shirt pocket. He unfolded it with fingers that were stronger and more callused than they'd been at the beginning of the summer, when he'd unfolded it for the first time. The writing within was a scrawl that he'd had to learn how to interpret, because the writer certainly wasn't going to improve in spite of his complaints.

> *Remember: you are more than a mind. Our path isn't on any map. Our answers aren't in the pages of any book. And Erika wouldn't want you to throw your life away on a fool's errand. But if you must go, you stubborn ass, at least be careful.*
> *—CK*

The flare of his nostrils as he read it was only slight. She had a way of sneaking scraps of paper into his pockets and desk drawers, with her wild theories and infuriating advice scratched on them. He read this one now, as if he could inoculate himself against the instinctive reaction he always had to them, to her presence.

He refolded it, and then slipped it back into the pocket where it lay, right over his heart. A strange place to keep the words of his sister's killer? Perhaps.

Enough delay. Today, he was either going to get stories, or he was going to get the data core.

Ropes in hand, the backpack tied so it would dangle between his knees, William leaned backwards over the edge. Tristan had lectured him on keeping the brake behind him, so he never forgot that, at least. He shuffled down the rock face, letting the rope slide out until he was far enough down to kick off. The rope buzzed as he let it out, his body swinging out over empty air, dropping down until he increased pressure on the brake. He swung back into the rock to kick off again. Wind whipped through his hair.

He reached the ledge where a hard layer of rock underscored a softer band which had crumbled away, leaving a lip jutting out from the canyon wall. It was maybe a twentieth of the distance from the rim to the canyon floor. His feet slipped over the stone that had weathered off the rock above. Fortunately, the distance to the door was not much.

They were always in rock, which made a certain amount of sense. They were usually very well hidden. William had watched Tristan clear a lot of bramble away before he could move in to open the door. They'd developed a rhythm over the summer. William found the locations of bunkers and labs. Tristan swooped in to help him gain access to them. Then William spent weeks trying to figure out how to either find something useful, or find the next bunker.

It had been a very long, frustrating summer for William.

A black panel stood beside the door, just like in Lab Nine. William pushed his hand against the surface, it glowed green, and the door slid open.

The sand he tracked in each morning lay on the floor. The walls were a cool blue, rather than the white of Lab Nine. William wasn't sure if that meant something, or if it was an aesthetic choice. Either way, the pale shade was a welcome change from the red-hued landscape outside.

The white room he walked into was small, with an activation panel set into one wall, and many screens set above it. William dropped his bag and put his hands on the panel. It glowed green, and a voice drifted down from over his head. To remind him who was in charge, here.

"Welcome to Historic Database Five, Subject Seven-Three-Two. How are you this morning?"

"Me, I'm fine. How are you enjoying your last hours?"

The voice was quiet for a long time. Whatever it was that did the thinking had trouble with sarcasm and vague hints.

"You still intend to remove the data core?"

"You got it. Unless, of course, you'd like to give me access to the information I need."

"You are free to ask any question you like."

William laughed. "What is this place?"

"You're in a historical archive for the Skylark Program."

"And can you tell me any of that history?"

It paused. In the silence William could almost hear gears turning, cylinders pounding, pathways coming to dead ends. Then, "I'm sorry, but I'm afraid you—"

"—don't have access to that information. Yeah. And where could a Twenty-Four run their activation sequence?" Cameron couldn't do much other than see other Altered when her powers were dormant. The serious stuff was one-time-use only, a single life-altering beacon in the darkness, impossible to reignite until they found another lab where she could activate them once again. William saw the wisdom in this.

"I'm sorry, but I'm afraid you don't have access to that information."

"That's where you and I have a problem. I need to know these things." It was impossible to tell a machine that he burned for answers to a thousand questions, why they might make a difference. He knew, if he'd only had more pieces of this puzzle that had become the predominant thing in his mind, he would not have ended up holding his sister's lifeless body in his arms as snow drifted down into her blank eyes.

He took his hand off the panel, slung his bag over his shoulder.

"You won't leave here with the data core," said another voice. William stopped at the door. He shuddered and the hairs on his arms lifted. That wasn't the archive talking. That was an entirely new voice, speaking in a human rhythm that the machine simply couldn't achieve.

"Who are you?" William said.

He breathed in the stillness. The only sound was the creaking of his overburdened backpack straps. The small gurgle of his stomach digesting breakfast.

"I'd hate to lose another one. Your set has potential."

William stared at the ceiling. Cameron had said they were being watched, their lives interfered with on a level they couldn't comprehend. He'd wanted her to be wrong.

"Who are you?"

"I am an artificial intelligence, designed to facilitate access by members of the Skylark Program to historical information contained within this archive."

The clipped AI voice had returned. Whoever had been speaking before was gone, or at least had gone silent. The eyes, though, they were still there, weren't they? Watching him, like a specimen in a tank. Maybe nudging the pieces of his life around, controlling its trajectory.

William made a rude gesture into the empty room, then walked back out into the hallway. Down to the next door on the left. It stood open, and a glow emanated from within. William had grown tired of breaking into the room over and over again. Finally, he'd opened it and then forced electricity through the wiring so it would never close again.

Quite a destructive streak you've developed.

The room beyond the broken door was not like the first. All that glow came from a column in the center of a circular room. In that it was like Lab Nine. But this column had no banks of computers. Instead, the center part of the column was open. Where the top and bottom should have met, in seemingly open air, was a glass sphere. Or at least it looked like glass.

He dropped his backpack again. He reached out to touch the sphere, and about two inches away from it his hand stopped moving forward. There was a slight tingling in his fingertips, but otherwise he could not feel the barrier keeping him back.

"What is that?" he said, with as much wonder as he had the first time. And as he had so many times since, he raised his palms out to either side of the orb, pushed them as close to it as he could. He gathered the energy.

Electricity crackled and raced along the surface of the barrier, up and down the column, tracing even across the ceiling above his head. William swallowed hard, breathed deeply, tried to put his mind somewhere else. Still, remembered smells of burning hair and flesh tainted the odor of ozone. The silver flashes of light turned his stomach into a heavy weight.

He concentrated on what he needed to do. Crack the barrier. He'd been so close so many times. He just needed to hone the energy down, bring it to a point, *focused.* A pound of force spread across a square foot did much less damage than a pound of force brought down to the size of a pinpoint.

The lines of electricity withdrew from the ceiling, backed down the column, and then slowly, slowly, tightened up around his hands, growing ever brighter. The energy pushed back harder. William's arms shook with the effort of keeping the power contained. Sweat beaded on his forehead.

And he saw—just for a moment—the field around the orb flickering.

So close.

He took a deep breath and spread his fingers. He saw the ghost of his sister across from him, her face lit by the silver light. He would know why. He had to. Inches from his hands, was a piece that he needed.

The air in the room got colder, but still perspiration stung his eyes.

He pushed the energy in, sending lances of lightning towards the orb. Yes, there, it broke through—

The room exploded with sound. A force struck William in the chest, hard enough to knock him off his feet.

Some minutes later, he woke up on the floor, gasping. His fingers tingled. His chest ached. His breath misted in front of his face. He'd drawn so much energy from the room that it was near-freezing.

He pushed himself up, forcing screaming muscles to move. The electricity had never rebounded on him like that before.

The core still hovered there within the force field. The metal column was scorched above and below, but otherwise he'd accomplished nothing.

He wanted to scream in frustration, but all he had strength for was a groan.

So now what? Try again? He didn't even want to stand. He was drained, a weariness that must have been building for weeks, unheeded, settling at last in his flesh and bones. He'd have given anything just then to see another human. Tristan would have sufficed. Even Cameron he could have dealt with. Just someone to take his hand and pull him back up onto his feet.

An abrupt thunk interrupted his thoughts. William looked up. The core rolled across the floor. He scrambled to his feet and grabbed it, as if afraid that it might get snatched away at any moment. It was warm in his hands, the surface smooth, but within it ran networks of threads, finer than spider web. For such a functional object, it was beautiful. How he was going to get it to work, he had no clue. A question for another time.

He pulled one of his old, worn shirts out of his bag. He wrapped the soft fabric around the orb.

Metal grated. Something moved at the corner William's left eye. He turned. A panel in the wall had slid back, and from it emerged a new horror. It was a four-legged piece of machinery with a horse-like gait, made stranger by the lack of anything like a head on its pale body. It was all metal joints, with some smooth material in sweeping shapes overlying the skeleton. It stood no taller than William's waist. It might not have appeared immediately threatening if he hadn't experienced the dangers of Lab Nine.

"Return the memory core," the voice said from above. An appendage unfolded under the machine's carapace, an arm that ended in a grasper, all hinged squeaking metal. William watched in fascination as the three 'fingers' opened, an invitation for him to place the core within its grip. How did it work? It wasn't alive, was it?

He leaned closer—and then the hand made a grab for the core. William took a step back. It took two clanking steps forward.

What could it do, besides walk and grab? What secrets lay beneath the smooth pale carapace?

How fast was it?

There were perhaps several ways to find out, but only one was a good option under the circumstances. William turned to his bag, dropped the core inside, wheeled for the door—

The mechanical guard already blocked the doorframe. A second appendage had appeared, this one ending in a blunt metal pipe rather than a hand. It now looked more crab than horse.

"Okay. You better not hit me with that," William said, as if it would make any difference. Then he took a step forward, gathering energy, casting a broad net. He'd already used up so much getting the core free. He had to reach very far out to find any.

The thing crouched, the pipe arm jutting forward. The bending of the jointed legs suggested a great deal of power, waiting to be used. William called fire into his hands. The thing withdrew.

Then the four legs moved, and the pipe jabbed William in the shoulder. Not that hard, really, but the collected energy scattered. The fires went out. The machine's grasper went for his backpack.

William tried to leap aside, but his feet tangled. It was this sudden stumble that probably kept the core out of the thing's grip. He regathered the scattered energy as he gained his feet. Maybe the electricity that worked on the core would work here, too. He went forward again, this time with lightning out in front of him.

When it touched the machine, it did indeed skitter up the arms, which trembled and froze, followed by the legs. The thing clattered into a heap.

Another ball of pain shot up the back of William's thigh, and again he lost his grip on the energy. At the same time his backpack jerked backwards, the straps cutting into his shoulders, his whole body going with it. Another one. He barely stayed on his feet as his pack jerked back and forth. The machine's legs splayed out, braced against the floor for leverage. William pulled more energy, from so far away that he felt like he was up on the very tips of his toes, reaching for a shelf in his lab, far over his head.

Then he threw lightning over his shoulder. The thing jerked him one last time before releasing. William leapt over the first machine, which had started moving its legs again.

Out in the main hall, he found two more of the machines between him and the door out. Hell. He was so tired.

Maybe he should just hand the core back. He probably wouldn't even be able to retrieve anything off it, anyway. He could go home. He didn't have to do any of this.

The voice from above said, "Return the core. Failure to do so will result in the use of deadly force."

Ah, yes. That was why he was doing this.

"Like hell am I giving you anything," William muttered. Not that he had any strength left for fighting.

What he'd give to see Kardell. But she wasn't there.

So, when one of the machines in front of him rushed forward, two heavy stick arms cocked back and ready to strike, he relied on what little instinct he possessed. As well as its rusty gait. He threw himself into the wall. With his shoulder braced, he kicked out hard, landing a blow against its shoulder joint. It was heavier than he'd expected. Rather than crashing to the floor, it stumbled slightly. It whirred as its legs struggled to move fast enough for it to balance. One leg swung out too wide, and it fell, its stick-arms replaced by graspers, which reached for him.

William backed up.

A rush of air preceded the next burst of pain in William's body, this time in his left shoulder. He gasped and reeled, then choked because a fine dust filled the air. Whatever had struck his shoulder had disintegrated into near-powder on impact. A sleek metal tube stuck out over the carapace of the second door guardian, aimed at William. Clacks filled the air as a second projectile locked into place.

He needed another way. He didn't have one.

Unless . . .

But he'd never tried that before. It was undoubtedly dangerous.

The machines crept forward. He didn't have the strength to keep fighting them off one by one. It was either take the risk, or die down in the archive.

William knelt and put his hands on the floor. He saw the fissures running through the rock all around him. He had no idea how they might shift. He could only guess.

One of the machines had dropped some sort of heavy cylinder out of its carapace. William heard a hum, saw a flash of light. Rocks flew up from a hole in the floor, inches from his hands. As bits of shrapnel pelted the walls, the floor, his arms, he brought his hands into a fist, and drove them down into the floor, plunging energy into the fissures, the largest ones, ones that criss-crossed the rock between him and the machines. Deep cracks in the rock below him, that could bring the entire side of the canyon crashing down into the river below, if he hadn't been careful enough.

He hoped he'd been careful enough.

A crack rent the air. And kept going. Kept growing. William watched, half elated, half horrified, as first the floor and then the walls of the hall in front of him split in a hundred places. The machines scrambled as the world in which they stood disintegrated.

The door at the end of the hall twisted sideways, plunged away. Light shone in the hall for a moment, before a rush of rock blocked out the sun. The avalanche grew, ate away another five feet of hallway. Dust roiled through the air.

Maybe this hadn't been the best idea. William hastened back as rock crushed the machines, and then swept them away. The sides of the canyon had become a river of rock.

The ground under William's feet trembled. He looked up. The ceiling above was cracking.

He ran to the end of the hallway, as the air filled with dust and sound. There he crouched in the corner, his arms shielding his head and neck as well as he could manage. Could he maybe stabilize the rock around him? There was suddenly raw energy everywhere, in a way he'd never experienced before.

So he drew it in. Pulled every ribbon of light nearby towards him, winding it in like fishing line, like yarn. After what seemed like half a lifetime, the avalanche slowed.

William looked up. Dust choked the air. Fine rocks fell out of his hair. He could see through the haze that he stood on a tiny ledge of the hallway floor. The rest of the archive was gone. A distant rattling of rock suggested that it still slid down the walls of the canyon.

Above him, the rim of the canyon was just visible through the dust.

Fortunately, any weariness he'd felt before was gone. He resettled his backpack on his shoulders, and climbed. For twenty minutes, he scrambled and groped along freshly exposed rock seeking one familiar thing. After that, it was the same trek up that he'd been making for weeks.

When he crested the rim, he saw the blood-red motorcycle at once. A Sentinel's bike.

Cameron?

William's breath stuck in his throat for just a second. It couldn't possibly be her. The High General kept High Guard Kardell close. Even armed with this knowledge, he fumbled a little untying the knots and stowing the equipment back in the bag.

Whoever it was, it appeared they had taken the liberty of going inside the trailer. He hoped he hadn't left too many dirty clothes lying around, although at this point he didn't think any of his garments could be called clean.

The door banged open before he was halfway there. A figure nearly filled the frame from one side to the other. William couldn't hold in his smile as Armel shouted, "Please tell me there's something to eat in here besides this freeze-dried crap!" An owl that had been roosting in a bush by the front door took flight.

"I'm afraid not," William yelled back.

Armel cursed. "You look terrible, by the way. What is that on your face?"

"It's a beard," William responded, finally able to speak in a normal voice. Armel's eyes widened as he regarded William.

"Oh yeah, I guess there are people in the world allowed to go without a shave sometimes." Armel jumped down, and thumped William on the back, nearly knocking the breath out of him. "How has your summer been?"

William shrugged as he went into the trailer with Armel behind him. "Interesting."

He pulled a couple of the pre-packaged meals from a cabinet, and started heating the water necessary to make them edible. He'd once tried to consume one of them cold in a desperate attempt to combat the heat, but it wasn't worth it.

"You should come home. For a lot of reasons, but mostly because I don't think it's been good for you to be out here by yourself."

"There's still a lot to be found here . . . " William trailed off, knowing very well that wasn't true. The archive lay at the bottom of the canyon. The only remaining answers about who had done this rested in the orb in his bag.

"My wedding is in a month. You're my best man, Will. You kind of have to be there."

William saw it, then, her hand in this. "Kardell suggested you come to bring me back, didn't she? Because she knew I wouldn't dare miss your wedding."

Armel looked a little torn about his answer, but he nodded. William filled up each packet with the hot water. They sat on the table, traversing slightly up the spectrum from 'strange-smelling-powder' to 'glop-that-passed-as-food'.

Armel's eyes were knowing. "She didn't mean to hurt you. I understand it's hard, I really do, but everything she's ever done was to protect people."

William nodded. He sank onto the bench across from Armel, staring at the table. "I know that. In my head, anyway." He was not looking forward to the wedding. He'd have to stare at Cameron the whole ceremony, since Owena had won the fight over whose side Cameron would stand on. He would have to dance with her.

You've danced with her before. That wasn't so bad.

But wasn't the pleasantness of it precisely the problem?

Armel looked at him, filled with faith. Faith in William. In Cameron, too.

William sighed. "Sure, I'll come back to Advon." It would take a stronger constitution than his own to disappoint Armel. He wasn't sure even Cameron could do that.

William reached out for a pouch, stirred the contents. It wouldn't get better, and it might get worse. Armel sighed as he grabbed the other.

"I call the bed," he declared at last.

William shook his head. "The only other place to sleep in here is this bench."

Armel grinned. "But you're a lot smaller than I am, and getting smaller, apparently."

They argued about it for the rest of the evening, in between swapping news on what had transpired since William left Advon. Armel seemed to be one of the few people in the city living in a sphere of hope, while war swirled all around him. Some things didn't change.

002

Cameron held her curses, as she always did in the High General's presence. Not that he cared. High Guard Brecht shouted a string of obscenities beside her as he spun his blade threateningly at the secessionists eyeing them. She felt High General Ellis's eyes on her, knew he sought points of strength and weakness, places he might gain a foothold. She would not give any.

She swept her blade down, smooth with a snap at the end, hard enough to cut muscle and crack bone, which it did. The young man who fell at her feet would, fifteen months earlier, have been under her protection. Now, he was a secessionist, holding a firearm given to him by Varcove.

Neighbors and friends, not so long ago.

A small but poignant pain, unrelated to any injury, traced its way up the inside of her ribcage, like a centipede, hungry for her heart.

The High General said from behind her, "Good work, Kardell. We're almost ready."

She nodded, short and tight. She didn't dare speak, and betray her fury that he'd brought them all out here. To 'assess the war effort, give a bit of morale to the troops'. Bullshit. He'd been too claustrophobic to sit in Advon watching metal soldiers shuffle around on a map.

Now people from the North, *their* people, died. So their leader could go on a field trip.

The sky burned, striped with scarlet, plum, and navy. As darkness folded in on the myrtle trees, Cameron and the rest of the High Guard did what most of them did best. They eliminated threats to the High General's life.

A bead of sweat traced down Cameron's face, following the line of her scar. It prickled her skin. She took cover, what little there was behind the spindly trunks. Above them all, a windmill hummed, massive arms sweeping the air. A few pops of gunfire punctuated the evening. The sound oriented Cameron to the last of the scouting party's gunman.

She sprinted from her cover. This was not like the solstice party, when she'd run at a sniper who would take many seconds to reload. The Varcove handgun would be deadly again in seconds.

But, it was that point of the evening when most of the light had leached away. The world became shapeless, movement harder to track, colors faded. Twisting between the myrtles, she would be hard to pick out, let alone hit.

"Sta! Sta!" the scout cried. Cameron was within a couple of steps, seeing their face pale in the trees. She raised her blade. Another step, she was sweeping it down. The sandy soil released her feet reluctantly. She adjusted her motion. Her blade struck.

Was that blood on Ellis's hands? Or hers?

She looked back over her shoulder at High Guard Brecht, breathing heavily.

"That's all of them, Kardell. Let's go."

Any other group of Sentinels would have had to stay and take care of the fallen scouts' bodies, lying there under the trees, under the turbines, but not them. Another team was on its way for that. Instead, they climbed into the massive vehicles that carried the High General and his retinue away from the danger.

"They've overextended," High General Ellis said as the car jerked into motion. "If they're all the way down to Northsands."

None of the High Guard spoke. They stared out the windows, catching their breath, remembering all the meetings about how the secessionists and Varcove had prodded further and further into Cotarion, haphazardly, but always managing to get more and more control of the nation's precious turbines. Its power.

Cameron cleaned her blade. Darkness folded around the car, which rocked along a dirt road, which became gravel, which turned to pavement. Their wheels turned to Advon.

It felt like years crushed into a few hours. Cameron sat in a bar called Henry's Dilemma. She sat at a table near the side wall, where she had a good view of both the front entrance and the back door, not too near the crowded bar. She defended the table from those who approached hunting for a place to sit, until at last Armel and Owena arrived. The couple didn't hold hands quite all the time, but they walked close together in a way suggesting that hand-holding was imminent. William Harfield drifted along in their wake. Cameron swallowed frustration.

"The shoes look nice on you!" Owena cried as she slipped into a chair across from her sister. Armel had already split off to order their drinks, a good tactical decision because he was so large that the busy bartender could not possibly miss him. William slumped into the chair next to Cameron. He tried not to look at her, though he couldn't seem to help stealing glances.

"Thank you for letting me borrow them." The shoes pinched Cameron's toes and she thought them ugly, but she kept that to herself. As she did so many things, now.

She turned to William. "How have you been, Doctor Harfield?" An unnecessary question. The skin under his eyes was dark, his cheeks hollow from the weight he'd lost, and the stubble he'd grown along his jaw in an attempt to hide it only made him look scruffy. His eyes lacked a spark, their emerald green faded. The new calluses on his hands didn't exactly look academic in nature. What had he been doing out in the desert for so long?

"I'm fine," he answered, looking everywhere but at her. Armel slid a beer in front of him. He finally looked up, and grudgingly said, "You look nice."

His gaze lingered on her scar. She could almost hear him thinking about Erika, about how his sister should be here, *would* be here, if not for Cameron. He looked away again quickly. His voice was brittle with false levity as he asked Owena about the wedding plans.

Cameron glowered at Armel. He shrugged sheepishly, but then he widened his eyes in supplication. She looked again at William Harfield's sad state, pressed her lips together, and nodded slightly. If anyone could pull the scientist out of his dour mood, it was Armel, though Cameron saw a lot of work ahead of her future brother-in-law.

The pub filled up, faster than Cameron had ever seen before. Her nerves thrummed as the noise in the room swelled. Someone bumped into the back of Cameron's chair, speckling her and Harfield with beer. William raised his eyebrows as he wiped the splashed liquid off his shirtsleeve.

"The band is a lot more popular these days, I see."

Cameron nodded. "Yes."

William swallowed some beer. "You like all this? It seems to be not your usual sort of thing." Then he took another long drink.

Cameron wrapped her hand a little tighter around her beer. "Sometimes even I have to get away from the work."

Someone bumped the back of her chair again, hard enough to make her jump. She closed her eyes and gritted her teeth. Just breathe through it. This was good practice. It was good to be out around people, to remind herself that not every bump or jostle was a threat.

"That sounds like something Erika would have said. To both of us."

She couldn't remember the last time William had said that name in her presence. Without shouting it, at any rate. "Yes. I'm sure she'd approve of Ethan and concerts in bars. And she'd be proud of you."

A storm of sorrow and satisfaction raged in the scientist's gaze. He tipped his head in acknowledgement before turning away.

The bass player struck a few deep notes. A breathless quiet filled the pub. The stage lights blazed on, and a few people cheered. The entire band made a series of noises, enjoying the anticipation of the crowd. Then Ethan, his hair falling in his eyes, stepped up to the microphone.

It wasn't so much that he became a different person when he was performing, but there was a spark there that he didn't have when he wasn't in front of the crowds. He was nervous, his expression uplifted. She recognized the way it all seemed to take hold of him, the years of practice and the comfort with his own hands and his words and his songs. All of that for this. Cameron watched. Pretended that she could be somebody else. Somebody who didn't think of the falling of a sword.

Ethan's words were rushed and soft as he spoke, "Hello there, thanks for coming out to Henry's Dilemma tonight. We're excited to be here, and we hope you are, too." There were some shouts from the tables. "We're going to start off with *The Star Home*. Thank you."

Cameron knew as soon as they started playing that tonight would be a good show. The rhythms were right, the sound in the room dynamic. And the crowd was with them, as well, which Cameron had been surprised to learn was vitally important. The audience became a part of the show, Ethan had explained to her, and she had seen it for herself. An uninterested crowd was a difficult force to combat, but when the people in the seats were invested, the band had more freedom.

At the end of the first song, William smiled at Cameron. "They've really gotten good! I mean, they were always good, but now they know it, you know?"

Cameron laughed, the sound of it lost as the next number began.

Three songs in, Ethan looked out through the burning lights to the table where Cameron sat. His smile was so sure that even she was entranced. He had a way of catching her attention and holding it. He leaned closer to the mic. "This is a new song that we've been working on for a while now, and we hope you like it. This is for my sweetheart."

Whatever face Cameron made at this announcement, Armel thought it was so funny he snorted into his beer. Owena hid her expression by taking a drink. Cameron turned away, kept her eyes up on the stage, so she didn't have to see them.

The first chords sounded, and Cameron was immediately relieved. She could tell it wasn't going to be anything too unbearably romantic. Ethan grinned knowingly as the music swelled up. Then he leaned close.

They told me you are poison
But your eyes are warm and dark.
They told me you're made of steel
But the night is cold and stark.

Armel was making strange sounds behind her. Cameron tried to ignore this. The words of the verses washed over her. She should be pleased, shouldn't she, that her boyfriend had written a song about her?

I will raise this cup and drink
And you'll be the death of me.
I'm standing on the brink
So please, be the death of me.

I invite you to be the death of me.

The crowd liked it, she could see that. The air was much too warm, and the people were much too close all around, but Ethan's eyes were on her. He appeared to become something slightly different under the influence of her expression. He smiled as the music swelled up, then quieted again. He sang, just as he did in their room, low, for her.

The trees shake with rain,
The storm has shown me plain
That you'll be the death of me.

I invite you to be the death of me.

The last note hovered in the air for a long time before the pub erupted with noise. Then Ethan jumped down off the stage to push through the crowd. People let him through, because he'd enthralled them, and could get away with almost anything for a few moments. Cameron stood, half her muscles poised to flee this noisy place, half of them ready to strike. At least the song hadn't laid any expectations on her, but it was still a song that he'd written for *her.* She wasn't used to this sort of thing. Which, of course, was exactly the point.

He pushed through the last few people. Grinning, he wrapped his arms around her and kissed her, thankfully before she had a chance to say anything. It didn't last long. He was riding a wave of energy much greater than his own. For just a moment he wanted to wrap her up in it too.

When he broke off the kiss, he grinned and said, "I knew I could write a song you liked." Then he dashed back to the stage before she could answer. Cameron sat quickly as the next song started. Anyone who'd been staring at her looked away, back to Ethan, because he was the only person in the room worth staring at.

Armel laughed like he might never stop. Owena shouted exclamations over the noise of the music and the crowd. Cameron, well, she wasn't exactly sure who she was just then.

Another bump at the back of her chair. She held in the reaction, held in the urging of all her instincts to spin around and strike. She closed her eyes, breathed.

When she opened them again, she could see William staring at her on the periphery of her vision. She looked over, with the music rising and falling in her ears. Concern was written on his face, in the furrow of his brow. But he didn't know what to say or do.

Cameron lifted one shoulder in a resigned shrug. His brow only furrowed more, but he nodded and turned his eyes back to the band.

The rest of the concert seemed to pass quickly, but the time it took for the crowd to disperse after it was over seemed a small eternity. Cameron kept well out of the way while people talked to Ethan and the band, glad not to be noticed. Owena and Armel stayed with her for a long time, but eventually she insisted they go home. William remained for just a couple of minutes after that. It seemed he had something he wanted to say, but he never found the words, because all he said before he left was, "Well, that was nice. Goodnight."

She watched him go, frowning. Armel was good with people, but she wasn't sure her friend understood what William needed. He struggled with more than just the loss of Erika. William hadn't exactly allowed his sister to run away again when they found her in the Low Crescents. He'd fought her, had been near to killing her.

Cameron went up to the stage at last, and congratulated the band on a great show. They were all so excited after the performance that they accepted her words without any of their usual reserve. In their eyes, she was temporary, just one in a string of Ethan's girlfriends. Perhaps the worst of them, considering the scarlet uniform.

Ethan kissed her again, more gently now, clearly worn from the performance, but he was smiling, still radiant. "Did you really like it?" he asked.

"Yes, I really did," she said.

He chuckled a little and released her from the embrace. She picked up the equipment she'd carried from their apartment, in part as a signal she was ready to go, but also to prevent any further displays of affection in public. Ethan quirked an eyebrow. He picked up his guitar and bid his band-mates goodnight.

The streets of the city seemed very quiet after the bar. Ethan asked her a few questions about how the show seemed from the audience. Her answers attained, he said, "From my side, that's the best show we've done so far. The energy was really good on the stage."

"Harfield said he thought you've gotten very good. No, wait, he said you've always been good, but now you're confident of it, or something along those lines. He liked the show, was the point."

"Yes, I saw him. Has he always been so sad?"

Cameron shrugged. "He's always been thoughtful. Not as much as the past couple of years, though."

"I just wonder, because Armel and Owena are always so happy, and I know he's especially good friends with Armel."

She smiled in the darkness. "I believe that Armel is currently on a campaign to cheer Doctor Harfield up, which is part of why he brought him to the show tonight. He must have thought your music worth the price of my presence."

"Now, what could be wrong with the presence of my girlfriend?"

"A lot of things, Ethan."

She said it lightly, but felt underneath lay the darkness and the chill of that day in the mountains. It began and it ended with Erika. Cold staring eyes that had once been fierce.

Cameron swallowed. "So, when is the next concert in a basement bar?"

They talked about upcoming gigs all the way back to their apartment. Cameron kicked off her shoes as soon as they were through the front door. When they had both put down everything they carried, Cameron kissed Ethan as she probably should have in the pub, savoring the sweetness of his embrace, his arms as they wrapped around her. She put aside Harfields and scarlet uniforms. Ethan's breath quickened, and after that they didn't speak much more.

003

No glasses were empty at this party. No dark thoughts or worry shaded a single beautiful face. In the fashionable district of Advon, the war was still a long way off. For some traders, business had increased. The young man throwing the party had his mother's boats full of metal sailing up and down the Bluestone River to thank for the large house. The trade stocked his soirees with the effervescent cider and Shivring whiskey that attracted flocks of the shiniest young ladies and preening young men. The music blared, the lights sparkled, the conversation ebbed and flowed. But Tristan could not enjoy it.

It wasn't that the tall, young women were somehow less interesting or desirable than they'd once been. In fact, he met a few that evening who were remarkably intelligent, several of whom appeared to be kind, and worse, one who was downright cunning. Yet it was a rather uncouth and reckless memory to which his mind turned. She who cut him with words, who wrapped him in heat, who walked in and out of his life.

His glass was still nearly full. He took a sip. He laughed with the men to either side of him, listening well to their words. The changing tides of trade, the small tugs of war, what it meant as the weight pulled at the fabric of Advon.

After an hour, a laugh floated above a pause in the music. If he'd been superstitious, he would have thought that he'd conjured her up by thinking about her. He was not, so he cursed his bad luck. He put down his drink and turned.

There in the middle of the room stood Melanie Stillwater, dressed in her usual ensemble, everything clinging, every hemline curtailed. Her pale hair shone. A man stood with his arm around her waist. She looked everywhere in the room but at Tristan.

He took the cue. Tristan drained the glass in front of him, stepped right out of the conversation he'd been having, and slipped away. The woman he'd been talking to might have turned a few seconds or a minute later to notice he was gone; he wouldn't know, as he did not look back.

A moment later he was out on the street. A few moments after that he was a block away among a different group of revelers. Lamps flashed above him. The crowds thinned. The alleys darkened.

Tristan heard the boy walking behind. He didn't bother to turn and look at that, either. Instead, he rounded the next corner, and folded himself the shadows of a doorway. The gangling, teenage frame jerked when he realized Tristan had vanished. Tristan's hand leapt out of the dark and grabbed the boy's sleeve.

Niko swallowed his yelp. A wide-eyed street urchin, recruited by the organization. And apprenticed to Tristan.

This had made Tristan grumpy.

Niko was small, though he was almost seventeen. Tristan supposed that malnutrition was to blame. He was stronger than he'd been, but sloppy. Picking pockets, even well, didn't prepare a desperate boy for spying and assassination.

"What did I tell you about following me?" Tristan snapped when they were on a quieter street.

"That I shouldn't unless I could do it without being seen. But the thing is, Mr. Rush, you haven't taught me anything about how you sneak around, so I don't see how I'm supposed to learn it—"

Tristan shuddered every time he heard 'Mr. Rush'. It was horrifying, but he didn't want to correct the boy, for fear of appearing interested "Look, I don't care what you do, as long as you stay out of my way. I didn't ask for an apprentice. I'm not a teacher. I never wanted to be. So my advice is, bide your time and twiddle your thumbs until you get shuffled to your next instructor."

The boy stuck his sharp-edged chin out in defiance. "But I requested to be placed with you. I fought to be here."

Tristan smirked in the boy's face. "Well, that was a stupid thing to do then, wasn't it? Now *go*. I have work to do." He strode away, but Niko wasn't giving up this time. Tristan heard the patter of his feet on the sidewalk behind his heels.

"I saw the tape from your final exam," Niko said.

Tristan didn't turn, but he could picture the skinny figure trotting along behind him, all elbows and knees. When he didn't respond, the boy continued.

"I don't know anybody who can move like that. And the way you threw that dagger at the target behind you, without even looking, it's like you knew exactly where it was by listening. But nobody's that good." Niko waited for Tristan to answer, but like hell was he responding. "The thing is, I *can* do some of that stuff."

Tristan turned back to look at the boy. The sincerest of faces shone back at him in the lamplight. A child who'd sold his soul without realizing it, for warm clothes and a full belly.

What were the chances that someone like him would fall into the same organization? It seemed unlikely. Except, of course, the skill set that came with Tristan's ability was tailored to just this kind of job.

"You ever hear and smell things that nobody else could?"

The boy nodded. Tristan listened to his heart, trying to catch the rhythm of a lie. He watched the boy's pupils, too, for the expansion and contractions. This street was dark, since the city couldn't afford to keep as many street lamps lit. It had been good for people in Tristan's line of work. "And what about in the dark?"

Niko scuffed one foot on the ground. "My old crowd kept me around mostly for how I see in the dark."

Tristan reached out a hand, gripped one of Niko's, and brought it up to chest height. The whites of the boy's eyes were bright against his coppery skin. "Don't let me move your hand, if you can." Then he pushed, lightly at first, testing. The boy's hand held steady for a long time as Tristan increased the force. At last, Niko could push back no more, but Tristan had come close to using his full strength to get the boy's arm to give way. He stared at the street-urchin-turned-assassin. Then he threw one of his daggers, so the spin would carry it to the boy's chest hilt-first.

Niko caught it, just before it hit him. Tristan laughed as Niko's eyes went wide with shock and anger. Then he snatched back the dagger.

"The Agency doesn't know just how good you are, do they?" Tristan returned the dagger to the secret pocket in his jacket.

"You don't survive long on the street by being different. I saw how quick the strongest boys got taken down. Got good at hiding, for the most part."

Tristan thought of Red's sworn vendetta against him. "Assassins aren't much different." What should he do? He hated coming up against a situation that required him to make a decision. Worse, this one involved another person.

When he was this kid's age, he would have killed to know more, to be told what to do next with those reflexes, that strength. He couldn't explain everything, though. Some secrets weren't his to divulge. And it was one thing to find out at twenty-four that you were somebody else's experiment. It was another thing when you weren't even old enough to have a beer.

Probably best to stick to the basics.

"You can come with me. But you have to do what I tell you. No questions for now, got it? If I feel like telling you something, I will."

Niko smiled, his white teeth flashing. "Yes sir, Mr. Rush."

"Don't call me that."

Niko trotted along behind him. "What should I call you, then?"

"Don't care. Anything else. And I said no questions." He was already regretting taking an interest in the boy, just as he regretted bringing Mel to Advon. How was it that *he* was the one collecting other Altered? Cameron was the one who could see them. William was the one who knew how it all worked. Tristan wasn't equipped to help anyone. "Do you know your parents at all?"

Niko shook his head. For the first time Tristan noticed that the kid wore a Hectic Sound t-shirt a lot like one of his.

"Did you already sign an agreement?"

Niko nodded this time, and Tristan sighed. Once the Agency owned you, there was no going back. Their contracts were notoriously airtight, their enforcers were as good as death itself.

"Anybody ever talked to you about what you can do?" Tristan strolled down a broad street, which lay hushed at night because either side was lined with shops that had closed hours ago. One of the buildings held a family health clinic. Tristan decided to approach from the back of the building.

Niko shook his head again.

"Okay, listen carefully. I'm going in for some records, and I can't tell you what the procedure will be, because I make it up as I go. So, you just follow my lead."

The boy pursed his lips. "You mean, you don't have a plan before you go in?"

"Never made much sense to me, when you never know what you'll find when you get in there."

"But it took three months for you to poison Mr. Quell, you had to have planned that." Niko said this in hushed, but radiant tones.

Tristan stepped around puddles in the back alley, which was lightless. "That stuff is different, and we'll discuss it later." He pulled on a pair of gloves.

The closest window was just a little too high for a standing jump. The alley wasn't very wide, though. So Tristan turned his back on the target window, ran at the opposite wall, leapt, pushed off it with one foot back and up at the window. He perched there on the ledge, which was very narrow. How to unlock it?

"There's a window the next story up that's already open a crack, you know."

Tristan kept applying pressure to the window, wiggling it to loosen the latch. "I know. The security in those offices is better, though." A clack announced his success. He slid the sash up and slipped into the dark office. He watched Niko make the jump up, a little clumsily, but he managed. Tristan had never considered how important all that time he spent practicing and showing off to his cousins really was. This boy would need some instruction.

"You're really loud, you know," Tristan whispered as he unlocked the office door and went out into the hall. The place reeked of bleach and other cleansers. The floor was the beige ceramic tile specific to medical facilities.

"Why do you think I requested you? I wanted you to teach me that."

Tristan found the door to the records room. There he withdrew his set of lockpicks from yet another pocket. He worked two slender pieces of metal in the lock, easing the tumblers up one at a time with one, holding everything steady with the other. He didn't know how to teach someone *quiet*. It had come naturally to him. In a world rich with noise, he'd liked to move silently. He didn't ever remember practicing.

As he levered a tumbler into place, he considered that it was a question of balance, of just the right amount of force needed to meet a surface. Then there was the absorption of any excess power in the landing. He stuck to quiet fabrics when he dressed, too. He spent hours in stores every time he had to buy new shoes. There was so much involved in maintaining that quiet bubble around him that he didn't know where to start.

The last tumbler went up. Tristan turned the door handle. He almost shut the door on Niko before he remembered that someone was with him. There was a copy machine in one corner, and he hit the power button, filling the space with its hum.

The records room had no windows, making it so dark that Tristan needed a moment before he could make out the letters on the cabinets. He found the one with 'S' names, and picked the lock on the set of drawers while Niko drank it all in as if nothing could be more fascinating. There was only one Sitka, and it was in the second drawer down. Cameron's mother had changed her name both times she married.

The copier was warm and ready, so he ran off each page for perusal later. He folded up the copies in his jacket, then returned the originals to the drawer, and turned off the copy machine. He gave the room a quick scan to ensure everything was still in place, then left. This time he really did forget Niko. The boy glared at him as he crept out of the records room after having the door shut on him.

"Was that all?" Niko asked as Tristan slipped back to the office by which they'd entered.

"This stuff is bread and butter, Nicky. And it isn't as easy as it looks. This is one little crumb in a long trail I'm following. It might not lead to anything at all, or it might take me to treasure. The pot of gold. Never know. Think you can shut this window behind you?"

Niko nodded as he looked at the alley below. "That's a long way down."

Tristan grinned. "That's nothing." He demonstrated by leaping out. He landed lightly, absorbing the shock with a slight bending of his ankles and knees. Niko didn't wobble on the narrow ledge as he pulled the window shut behind him. Then he jumped out.

The crack when he hit the ground was redolent of bone breaking. Tristan stared in confusion as the boy's face went white with pain, and Niko bit down on his pain. His left leg was definitely at an odd angle.

But the boy was strong. And he'd caught the dagger. And he'd made the jump up, and navigated through the dark rooms!

None of this changed the fact that the leg was broken.

Tristan saw only one option in front of him. He reassured Niko as well as he could, threw the boy over one shoulder, and went in search of Melanie.

She'd returned to her apartment, Tristan could tell because he heard her voice through the door, as well as that other man's. He winced at a particularly telling sound, then pushed the doorbell. He did not let up until he heard footsteps.

Melanie threw back the door. She stood in front of him, her face red with more than just anger, though that was definitely involved.

"Tris, what the hell?"

He noticed a distinct absence of jasmine. She must wear the scent just for him. He wasn't sure how he felt about that.

"Really sorry, but I have a patient for you. This is Niko, and he has a broken leg. Niko, this is Melanie Stillwater. Be polite, say hello."

The boy waved. Melanie rolled her hazel eyes, but Tristan knew she hadn't had much opportunity to practice her skills recently. She wasn't about to turn down an opportunity to show off her Alteration.

"Put him on the couch. I'll be there when I've kicked out my guest." She muttered some particular epithets at Tristan as she went back into the bedroom.

Tristan had to throw an awful lot of pillows and magazines off the couch before he could put Niko down. Then for his own benefit, he removed all evidence of Melanie's courtship rituals, including the pair of half-emptied wine glasses. He tried to keep his mind on the question of why the boy's leg would have broken. Tristan had jumped from some significant heights, and never had a bone betrayed him. Maybe the boy wasn't Altered at all.

Melanie shut the door at last on the confused young man. She returned with her hair tied up on top of her head, more appropriately dressed for the task. The glare she gave Tristan somehow balanced venom and sorrow. It was to Niko she spoke.

"Thank you for waiting. Now, how did you come by this broken leg, and what is preventing you from going to the doctor like a regular person?"

"Jumped out a window," Niko gasped as Melanie gently removed his shoe, winced as she rolled his pant leg up to his knee. The bruise was a dark purple, the swelling grotesque.

Tristan supplemented. "We were on a job. And I think he has the same abilities that I do. Except that jump didn't break my leg." It occurred to him that he might have discussed his abilities with someone who was not, in fact, Altered. How stupid. What would they do, if that were the case? Why hadn't he thought to check with Cameron, first?

Melanie frowned as she ran her hands over the area where the bone was broken. "Niko, have you ever found it difficult to get enough to eat?"

The boy gave a dry laugh. "Story of my life, Miss Stillwater."

She gave Tristan a look of exasperation. "Have you ever noticed that you eat a lot more than most people?" He shook his head. She sighed. "Then it probably never occurred to you that someone who hasn't had access to a diet as good as yours might not have the same bone density. Go to the kitchen while I work. Try to stay out of trouble."

The disappointment in her tone was enough to cow him. He retreated while she worked, and perused the papers he'd stolen. It was primarily stuff he didn't understand, having little knowledge of the care women received while pregnant. But the physician's name was there, which was all he needed to move forward.

When looking over Seren Lee/Sitka/Kardell's medical records was no longer of interest, he studied Melanie's kitchen. It was sort of cluttered, but every space in which she lived tended to fill up with many layers of decorative items. As much as he loved her, that had nearly driven him mad at the end. Just now a ceramic rooster stared at him from the counter by the stove. Next to it was a line of jars painted blue and white. Little towels hung from every available hook.

Melanie didn't take long fixing Niko's broken leg. When she was done, she came into the kitchen for her glass of water, which Tristan had already filled. She took it, smiled. He looked away.

"You should probably be more careful," she said. "And that boy definitely needs to be better fed than he is."

Tristan nodded. For something to do, he held out the papers to her. "Do you see anything here that isn't normal?"

She glanced over the records, pretending to be clinical about them even as a spark of interest lit her eyes. "Well, this test here, it's definitely not anything I've seen run before. Codes have changed a bit since then, but that might be worth checking out."

She handed them back. Finally, Tristan said, "Thank you for your help. But listen, I need you to stop coming by my place like you did a couple weeks ago. I can't handle it anymore."

Melanie leaned against the edge of the counter. He always wanted to get closer and see how much of her iris was brown and how much was green, but he resisted. He swallowed hard.

"Is it all really so bad, Tris?"

"You stayed with me," he responded. "For almost two years. And you didn't fall in love with me, but I did love you, Mel. I still do."

Her face had gone careful, as if she felt something she would rather not show him. She knew as well as he did that he might be saying this now, but the next time she came to his door, he would fling it wide.

He turned away from her lovely face again, went to the couch to collect the sleeping Niko, and carried him through the pitch-black city to his tower.

004

DAYLILIES LINED THE paths in the Military Quarter in late summer. The shade of the trees and the green of the lawns soothed William after so long in the desert, although Advon was unpleasantly humid. People greeted him as he passed, some of them appearing genuinely glad to see him. A lot of them asked if he was well, their tone suggesting they suspected that he might not be.

Well, damn. He'd even shaved that morning.

His office was exactly as he'd left it three months before, which was mostly good, except for the half-empty coffee cup on his desk. He frowned at the white patches floating on the surface of the liquid before moving the mug to a bookshelf, then unpacking his bag. He checked through the thin stack of paper on which he'd printed his report to the High General. An orb full of data that he didn't know how to access. How was he going to justify that?

He slid open the top drawer of the desk. His heart swooped oddly at the scraps of paper it held. Notes. From Cameron. Dozens of them.

How many times since he'd left had she walked in here, placed her hand on the handle he now held, dropped in a note? By some insane instinct he reached his hand up to the pocket lying over his chest, the one he'd carried through the desert. In doing so he realized it had become more soothing a gesture than not. That it reminded him of a solstice when they'd run together through woods bathed in fire, towards danger. Her hand in his. And she'd drawn him through safely.

In placing his hand there, over his heart, it was like he'd placed her hand there, too.

He swallowed hard.

"It was adrenaline. Don't be stupid."

William pulled the note out of his breast pocket and dropped it on top of the pile before shutting the drawer again, harder than he'd meant to, making pens and collected stones rattle.

He picked up the mug with the mold floating on the surface, and walked down the hallway to a small kitchen area where he and his fellow advisors made lunch or coffee or just wasted time hiding from High General Ellis.

Ophelia Sands, a fellow member of the High General's Council, stood with Councilor Yeats. Sands gave William one of her trademark warm smiles. Yeats glared.

"Ah, the terrier is back," Councilor Yeats said, as if in admonishment. William just smiled politely and nodded his head, not pausing on his way to the sink.

Sands smoothed her light lavender scarf. "It's not as if he was traipsing about for pleasure. How are you, little Harfield? You still have sand on your boots."

"I'm sure there's still a scorpion in one of my pockets somewhere, to be honest. But it can't be anything like being here." If given the choice between stinging crawling things and politics, he knew which he'd rather have.

"It's been much duller without your yapping," Sands said with a toothy smile. "But may I say, you look like you've been run absolutely ragged."

Yeats rolled his eyes. "Do stop doting on him. Just because you and his father—"

Sands stopped him with a glare so cutting that it apparently stilled his voice in his throat.

"Still indulging in rumor-mongering, Yeats. In a time of war? How very wasteful of you. I would have hoped by now that you might have turned your attention to more substantial matters than whom is sharing a bed with whom."

This was more than enough to cow Yeats, who said goodbye. He shuffled off, surely to review the state of Cotarion's roads and bridge repairs.

William dried his mug. I see you're still managing public relations disasters with your usual grace, Ms. Sands."

She smiled again. "I've needed every ounce recently. The High General doesn't make it easy. But let's save that for meetings. How are you, really? Because you look like someone who spent six months in the desert."

He shrugged. "But who doesn't, these days?"

"Well, I certainly don't. By the way, Sheff was excommunicated last month."

William clutched his mug a whole lot tighter. "What? Why?"

It was with her bright eyes fully on him and an almost challenging set to her chin that Councilor Sands responded. "She questioned the High General's most recent trip out to view the lines one time too many. And so she will no longer be seen here in Advon, or anywhere else in Cotarion. You understand, I hope, why I would mention this to you, in particular, Little Harfield?"

She left with a flutter of scarf. William dropped his forehead into his hands. He'd been back for half an hour, and he already wished he could leave again. If Kardell was on duty when he met with Sean Ellis, he was guaranteed to say or do something very stupid.

Tristan was right, he'd fallen into a pit of snakes. Why had he taken the job? He remembered the warm glow of compliments at his intelligence, the hope that at last his father would be proud. He certainly wouldn't have had the freedom to go to the historical archive if he didn't work for the High General. The price didn't seem worth it, at present.

He checked his watch. Did he wish the meeting were closer, or further off? He occupied the remaining time ensuring his papers were, indeed, all in order before sorting through months of mail. Most of which, it turned out, he could safely toss in the wastebin beside his desk.

When he could avoid it no longer, he picked up his satchel, heavy with the orb that he'd avoided thinking about for days, and which now felt very worthless. He'd risked his life for the damn thing. Now, he saw no way of getting anything from it. There were other labs to look into, all their locations gleaned from Tristan's far-flung searches for mysterious and hazy guidebooks, but William didn't have much hope. Many had collapsed, or didn't have enough power to permit access to any information.

Every step he took to the High General's office brought his heart higher into his throat. What was he going to say? How would he explain the waste of resources when war raged?

High Guard Lin stood outside the office door. She regarded William with pity. This did not comfort him.

He was glad to see, when Lin opened the door to the office, that Cameron Kardell did not stand behind the High General. Sean Ellis ate an orange, which was nice, because it did not crunch like many of the things he snacked on. William took his seat, and laid his report on the smooth surface of the desk. He wondered if the High General had looked so worn when he'd left. Perhaps the weariness had crept up so slowly that William hadn't noticed it until now. He imagined that the burden of leading a country in war against itself must be heavy.

To his surprise, Sean Ellis dismissed his guards, then turned through the first few pages of William's report. "Did you find anything of interest?"

William shifted in his chair. Had the room grown hotter? He fumbled with the straps on his leather bag. Some sand fell onto the carpet. "I wasn't able to get the voice to tell me anything, but . . . "

With both hands, he lifted out the orb. It thunked onto the High General's desk. William looked up at the man's face, trying to interpret the expression there.

Because the High General had gone quiet. He swallowed the segment of orange, and put down the rest. He stared at the orb, which looked dull in the dim office light. His face remained inscrutable.

"You should not have been able to retrieve this, young Harfield."

William swallowed. "Shouldn't I?"

The general looked up at him, the faintest trace of a smile in one corner of his mouth. "Oh, no. Most definitely not. I've certainly never seen one outside of an archive."

"Is it all right that I brought it here?"

"All right? This is a treasure beyond any hope or expectation I had. You have no idea the value of what you've brought me."

William furrowed his brow. "You know what this is?"

"Yes, I do. This orb holds the history of what those Skylark bastards did to me. And did to you. And maybe clues to what they'll do next."

Of course, part of William said. Of course the High General was Altered. Of course he knew all about the Skylark Program, of course he knew about the memory core. He wouldn't have let William go out lab-hunting if he hadn't seen the value in it. But all that meant that Cameron had seen the truth years ago, and never breathed a word. She'd warned him many times that Sean Ellis was dangerous, but never had she said he was Altered.

"Oh, I see. I thought you would have figured it out by now. Well, I didn't mean to send you into shock."

William swallowed. He hated how easily everyone could see what he was feeling at all times. "How useless is it? Surely now that it's away from the archive we can't do much with it."

The High General smirked. "Oh, Harfield the Younger, you have no idea how little you know. I believe it is time to expand your horizons. You'll come back in a week, and I will show you the very smallest morsels of the greatest war humanity has ever known."

"What do you know about all of this? Do you know who—"

"No. I'm not going to tell you any background material. If it was discovered I divulged certain pieces of information."

That was strange. The High General's face changed. There was a gleam in his eye less like a sharp knife and more like the glint in a rabbit's eye as an eagle swooped over. Was Ellis actually afraid of something? There was some satisfaction in that, but also, if that man was frightened, how much more so should William be?

"Why tell me at all?"

The High General still looked haunted. "I have a remote hope that equipping you with information might improve some things. Very small. Very far off."

"You knew all along. That's why you put Erika and Sentinel Kardell in the High Guard, right? And accepted me into the Council." He hadn't had any qualifications. Everyone had dismissed his appointment as the result of his father's power. He hadn't questioned it, at the time.

The High General nodded. "Yes, I knew. I could see you all for what you were right away. One of the few advantages of being a Twenty-Four. I can guess, then, that The Maker has not spoken with you."

William shook his head, which was starting to hurt. Why hadn't Cameron told him? Sean Ellis was like them, and they were working for him. If he wasn't the one who'd given them these abilities, what could his purpose be?

"Surprising. It will be soon, then, you can't go much longer without having your Alteration completed. After a certain age, it becomes difficult to adapt." William rubbed his temples. A thousand thoughts shouted for attention, so he caught none of them.

"Kardell already completed my code, almost three years ago." He should stop talking. He was definitely saying more than he ought to. He remembered Sentinel Kardell's whispered warning, *He's dangerous.* She had probably put her own job at risk to tell him that. He should remember it.

But now it was Sean Ellis's turn to look surprised. William had never seen his face so pale as he said, "Are you sure of that?" He leaned forward, his eyes bright as he waited for the answer.

William chastised himself. He'd definitely said too much. "I'm not sure of very much at this point, sir."

Sean Ellis smiled in a way that made William feel less like a terrier than a sheep. "You retrieved this orb using your abilities, didn't you?" William, miserable now with worry, didn't say anything, but the High General showed a few more teeth. "That's a yes. And still The Maker has stayed quiet. That is interesting."

William collected himself enough to say, "So, The Maker is . . . "

"Exactly what it sounds like. Although I really shouldn't say anything more about it."

The High General turned the orb over in his hands, staring. It was unfair that he should mention The Maker, as if he knew the person well, then drop the subject. Finally the High General sighed, tucked the orb away in his desk drawer, swapping it for a folder that he handed to William. "I want your ideas on these new reports before you leave this evening. I hope you have something good, I need leverage in the upcoming negotiations. And in a week—I'm sure you worked hard to obtain this orb. You deserve to see at least some of what's on it."

With that, William was dismissed. He returned to his office with the information he had been given. He shut his door.

He turned through the pages without seeing them. Sean Ellis was Altered. He knew who'd done this to them. If he weren't the High General, William would go right back to his office and demand to know who it was. But Sean Ellis *was* High General.

Why hadn't Cameron told him? Had she been afraid of what William would do? Did she mistrust him, somehow?

He closed his eyes, rubbed his temples, and forced his mind back to the papers in front of him. Pen in hand, he scribbled in the margins. This helped to solidify his attention.

After a few hours, he thought he would be ecstatic if he never saw the words 'wind turbine' ever again. He spent part of the afternoon talking to the engineer who worked on the Council, who looked constantly close to tears these days. Neither of them felt better about the power supply or their strategies for dealing with it at the end of the meeting.

By the time William finished his second meeting with Sean Ellis, the sun was setting and his head ached. There was no further mention of The Maker. William did not dare broach the subject. He sensed that the High General savored this, doling out morsels of information, then leaving William to ponder.

He walked home through the evening air. He didn't know how much to say, or to whom. He knew Tristan had been getting excellent jobs from high places recently, so he was probably in contact with Sean Ellis, but William still didn't think he would be free to mention something like this.

Maybe the High General was using this as a test. If that was the case, he probably shouldn't say anything to anyone at all.

How much did Cameron know? She had less freedom to ask questions than he did, but more opportunity to watch. But considering her loyalties, it was probably a bad idea to talk to her.

Cesar waited for him when he went in the front door. The dog danced and whined a greeting.

A battered piece of luggage sat in the hallway, holding together in spite of much abuse. William recognized it, and bit back a groan of frustration. He did not want to deal with this, not after the day he'd had.

"Mom! Are you here?"

"In the dining room, sweetie!" Teague Harfield poked her head out of the door at the end of the hall, and gave him a cheerful smile that looked like it might break at any moment. "I picked up some takeout on my way over here. I got your favorite noodles."

"Great, I'll just take Cesar out, and then, uh, we'll talk."

William grabbed the leash, and ran outside and around the block before she could stop him.

Tristan appeared next to him as soon as Cesar found a good place to stop. How he knew, William didn't know, but he was glad his cousin did. His sleek, cat-like presence, usually irritating, was a comfort just now.

"Don't worry Billy, I'm here with you. Now, what is she going to ask you for?"

William frowned. "My apartment."

Tristan nodded. "And what did Erika always say?"

"Granddad left it to me. Mom had a house, and she lost it gambling. That's not my fault. Don't give in. But Tris."

"No!" Tristan cried, gripping him by the shoulders and shaking him. "No buts. Your mom is an adult, and she can take care of herself. She's had her chances. You dig in and hold on for all you're worth, got it?"

William nodded, his stomach tight with nerves. Then he laughed. "I've had a hell of a day, and now I'm getting advice from my assassin cousin on how to keep my mother from taking my house from me. Isn't family supposed to make life easier?"

Tristan grinned. "Not in my experience. Oh, do you know how to build someone's bone density?"

"Um, stuff with calcium. Milk, kale, that sort of thing."

"What's kale?"

William explained, in detail, the differences between kale and other varieties of greens, then said, "Wait, why are you asking?"

Tristan had been waiting for this. "I found a kid who has the same abilities I do! He's my apprentice, actually. But apparently he didn't get enough to eat on the streets, so I'm trying to get him back in fighting form. Mel seems to think there's still time to make his bones stronger."

Feeling that he wasn't keeping up at all, William said, "I thought you weren't talking to Melanie anymore."

Tristan was turning to leave, and walked backwards to say, "You know how these things are. Good luck, Billy. Remember what Erika said!"

William was left nodding. He hadn't appreciated the isolation of the desert nearly as much as he should have.

He went back to his home. *His* home. His grandfather had left it to him. Yes, it was bigger than he needed, but someday he might have a family. Maybe. It was her choice to live apart from his father. Of course, he couldn't really blame her for that.

She'd set out some plates on the dining table. The silverware wasn't in the right positions, but tables had been set for her most of her life, so he respected her attempt. She smiled at him again as he sat. She looked good, better than the last time he'd seen her. She was tall, more handsome than pretty. Tristan had definitely gotten his cheekbones from that side of the family. Teague looked . . . strange. Comfortable.

"I thought you should know, first of all, that I'm not here to ask for your apartment. And I'm sorry for the times I did. It wasn't right."

And now when he smiled back it was easy, but his voice told them both he lied when he said, "I wasn't worried about it." He spooned his noodles from the takeout container to his plate. They had been his favorite when he was twelve, but he hadn't eaten them much since. She took some for herself. Asked him how he was. She commented that he'd lost weight, notes of concern in her voice.

"You know, I've been thinking a lot since Erika died, about a lot of things. I spent some time with your Aunt Charlotte and Uncle Jim at the farm, thinking they would know what it was like to lose a child, but they dealt with it so differently. They never talk about Beth, or Chris, or Tiff, or the baby."

"Sam," William said quickly, knowing Tristan would have hated for anyone to forget.

"Right, Sam. They didn't even ask about Tristan. It's like they *want* to forget, but I don't. I thought a lot, and I decided. I've been so miserable, for so long, about what I lost. The house, the money, that whole life, that I forgot about everyone else. So, now I'd like to be a better mother to you, and maybe be there for Tristan, too. Because you boys are what matter now."

William chewed. He tried to think of the gaps in his life that his mother might fill, and he didn't know what they might be. She'd been so unreliable for so long that he'd stopped counting on her years ago. She wasn't exactly great at the advice Erika had once dispensed. It was impossible to tell what the result of this resolution would be. So he just nodded. "That sounds good, Mom."

"I'm starting by doing what I should have done a long time ago. I'm divorcing your father."

William guessed, from the worried way she looked at him, that she thought this would come as a shock. He hadn't dealt well with talk of their divorce years ago, but since then he'd seen the reality of their situation. They lived apart, had separate lives, and were divorced in all but name.

"Okay." William didn't know what else to say. This response increased his mother's worry.

"You think that's all right?"

He nodded. "Sure. I think it will be good for you."

She smiled, full of warmth and hope. "Well, good! So, the problem, of course, is that . . . "

"You can stay here for a while."

Her smile broadened. "Thank you, that's very nice. I hate to be in the way, especially, you know, if there's a girl. Or boy."

"Not at the moment. Work keeps me busy."

"I hate to see you getting involved in this political stuff, it's not good for you, especially the way things are."

He tried to explain to her how little he really did, but eventually he let the matter drop. He thanked her for the food, then washed the dishes, and cleared out his guest room for her. She ruffled his hair before retiring for the evening.

William grabbed the leash again. Cesar was only too willing to stroll the streets of Advon while William thought about Sean Ellis. The hints about The Maker. About the things Cameron hadn't told him. About what Erika would have done.

OOS

THE ZIPPER TUGGED around Cameron's waist, yet fabric gapped so much at the top she had to hold it down. It clung tight to her hips and knees, so even a single step became a trial. Owena pursed her lips as she walked all around Cameron. The seamstress ran her fingers between the fabric and Cameron's skin. She pinched it together here and there, trying to smooth the fabric puckering over Cam's legs.

Finally the seamstress said, "How long until the wedding?"

"Three and a half weeks," Owena responded. She looked far more elegant in an old pair of pants and a gray shirt than Cameron looked in a shiny, expensive gown. Cameron watched her sister pace around, her reflection passing from one mirror to another as she moved. There was no comparison between the half-sisters. Owena's hair curled into a dark nimbus around her head. Somehow she made consternation look elegant. Even Cameron thought her own expression grim.

They all had to know that even with alterations, this dress was never going to work on Cameron. She opened her mouth to say as much, hoping to get this over with as quickly as possible, when Owena clapped her hands together, making her bracelets jingle. Her bright blue eyes lit up with an idea.

"Cameron is the Maid of Honor, so why should she have to wear the same dress as the Bridesmaids? There's no reason why she shouldn't stand out, in my opinion."

The seamstress released the fabric she'd been pinching, causing the front of the gown to sag. Cameron raised her arm to hold it down. Her eyes went wide in three different mirrors.

"You mean, you want me to try on more dresses?"

But the seamstress, enthused at this idea, was already helping to free Cameron from the dress. Owena jangled off to peruse the racks.

Cameron had just managed to peel off the first dress, suppressing a string of unladylike curses as she forced the damn thing down over her thighs, when piles of wispy fabric sailed over the side of the changing room. "Try the purplish one first," Owena ordered as Cameron hanged all the finery on the available hooks. This was her sister's domain. She pulled on the next candidate.

At least this one wasn't so tight around her legs that she could barely move. And the grayish-purple color looked much better against her skin than the icy blue. The bodice portion was shaped to give her the appearance of both waist and bosom, which seemed to be the effect her sister desired. When she stepped out, Owena gasped and smiled. The seamstress looked greatly relieved.

Cameron stepped up in front of the mirrors. She tried to put her mind elsewhere as Owena and the seamstress went back through the process of suggesting improvements.

What was Ethan doing? Probably he'd arrived home from some catering job, and was plucking a new song out of his guitar, one chord at a time. She liked that better than his performances, the quiet strumming that filled their place in the afternoons, his voice reverberating along with the strings. His hands curled around the instrument, shaping themselves into notes and notes and songs.

She might have a little time to see him before her shift, if this didn't take too much longer. If not, there was always the morning, after she finished work, and before he left.

Would they would get along so well if they saw each other for more than a couple of hours a day?

She wanted to read Doctor Harfield's report, which had been passed on to her by Sean Ellis. He hadn't said much, but apparently the fact that they were both *different* was something he was now willing to acknowledge. He'd probably gotten tired of waiting for her to say something. All self-restraint he exercised always came to nothing when he grew too impatient to wait any longer. Then whatever he'd withheld would come bursting out.

Owena called her attention back to the moment at hand. "I think this is the one, but you should try on the others, just in case." So much for time with Ethan. Cameron went back into the dressing room, and the swaths of purple whisked over her head, to be replaced by a bright green dress. The color was declared more flattering, but the shape less so. The third dress was all-around bad, the rusty orange color dulling out the color of Cameron's eyes, the ruffles laughably girlish. Four dresses later, Owena decided the purple gown was the best of them, setting Cameron free. Owena thanked her for putting up with the fittings.

"My little sister is happy. Someone deserves to be these days, right?"

Cameron had just enough time to jog home, change into her uniform, and kiss Ethan. His eyes were sad, but he tried to hide it, since he'd already realized that her time with Owena had gone too long. Cameron paused at the door as she said goodbye to him. There were a lot of words heavy in her mouth. Ethan wanted a life. A real life. Not a Sentinel who breezed in and out of the door as her duties beckoned.

And what did she want?

To know what she was. What she'd been made to be.

When she checked in with the Master of the High Guard before her shift, she found Thea Clemens more discomposed than usual. Cameron took the seat across from her. Clemens, thankfully, knew her well enough by now to launch into the news right away.

"The leaders of Varcove and the secessionists have agreed to meet with the High General and discuss terms for peace. The High General will leave Advon the day after tomorrow, and all the High Guards will go with him. You will be ready?"

"Yes ma'am." She would laugh if, after so much work and anticipation, she missed Owena and Armel's wedding. If Cotarion and Varcove actually came to an agreement she could be gone for weeks. She knew the High General would not make any concessions without a fight, and the secessionists hadn't gone through all this to lay down arms without some benefit.

Thea Clemens grimaced. "I am going to count on you to be prepared for anything. I've collected information on the leaders who will be involved in the talks, which you will pick up and study after your shift. Make sure your sword is sharp."

Cameron grinned and hazarded a joke. "My sword is always sharp."

The Master of the High Guard arched one eyebrow. "I'd tell you to be careful of getting overconfident, if that weren't a factual statement. Can you check the newbie's gear before we go?"

"Yes, ma'am."

"Very good. As I'm sure you can guess, this development has put the High General in an odd mood. He's making a press statement this evening, so be prepared for his usual torment of those who defend his life." She made a face which suggested she knew she shouldn't say such things, but Cameron tried to nod reassuringly. Sean Ellis had been getting under all their skins recently. Even the Master of the High Guard needed the occasional opportunity to express exasperation.

The High General dined alone when Cameron arrived. He looked over the positions of his forces, and read stacks of reports. He picked at his meal every now and then, but mostly he nudged troops around on the map.

He looked up when she entered, and watched her take her position, his gaze more pensive than usual. The turn of his lips, the lines between his eyebrows, suggested he was worried. He prowled around the maps on the table, then said, "Kardell, come look at this."

She'd been afraid he would ask that. The look on High Guard Brecht's face suggested this had already happened more than once. Cameron went to the table to study the maps, while Sean Ellis stopped his circling directly across from her. He watched her face while she considered.

Finally she said, "Both sides are in good position, but Varcove is better supplied in weapons, and the secessionists will have a major advantage as the weather gets worse in the higher elevations. But the more they push our forces back, the stronger our position. Our supply lines will get stronger, theirs weaker."

Sean Ellis nodded. His voice was low when he said, "The ammunition and weapon supply we stole last May is almost out. Then we'll be back to the old stuff."

Cameron understood the implications of that well enough. The Cotarion Armed Forces had scored a major victory early in the conflict by stealing a massive shipment of the advanced firearms Varcove was sending to the secessionists. Without those weapons, the advantage was all the enemy's.

"We've had some success reverse-engineering the firearms themselves, but their gunpowder formula has been a little more difficult. And production is slow. By next spring we might be able to meet them, but we learned last winter that Varcove doesn't mind fighting in the snow." Sean Ellis took a deep breath. "Our vehicles are better, at least, and overall our soldiers stronger. They still haven't managed to produce their own turbines." His eyebrows were tight and low. "The question is, what do they want?"

Cameron didn't know the answer. She understood the secessionists' position, having seen how some of the smaller towns suffered. But she didn't know why Varcove had agreed to help them. Sure, Varcove's forces could fight their way into Cotarion, but they couldn't hold it for long. Varcove had better weaponry, but a much smaller population, and much worse infrastructure.

Sean Ellis braced his hands against the table edge. "If I don't make peace, Advon might be theirs by spring. But I get the impression from their tactics that they don't want that. They're holding this border, harassing our forces with something that seems like an attack, but then they retreat. I think they're just pushing our resources. They're going to make a steep demand, I think." The High General looked up to her. "You know I had a clash with a few Varcove troops, about fifteen years ago."

Cameron shook her head. "No, sir, I didn't."

He frowned. "I was young. My unit was checking a border crossing, and so was a unit from Varcove's forces. It was routine, it happened all the time. Both sides had translators and we were all just supposed to ride up, declare the crossing satisfactory to both parties, swap news, go home.

"But their leader was the Prime Minister's son, and he recognized me as the High General's nephew. He made some remark, something unkind about my grandfather. And I—well, has anything ever made you very angry, Kardell?"

Cameron had to think about this. Most of the things that caused her to be very angry were the things that *she* did. "A few times, sir."

Sean Ellis smiled without humor. "Well, I have been known for my temper in the past, and on this occasion it got the better of me. I met him in the field of verbal spars. The shouting escalated, until I called his mother a whore, more or less. We were each on our own side of the border, practically nose-to-nose. He pulled out his pistol, leveled it at me, and told me to run home.

"Some of the comments our translators probably shouldn't have filled in. But he was the Prime Minister's son. I was the High General's nephew. We were both accustomed to having our way. And I really didn't like having a gun pointed at me."

He nudged a little piece of stone that represented a hundred men. "You know, they hardly ever train with edged weapons in Varcove. In close quarters, most of them don't know what to do. I knew that the only way he would be able to shoot me in time was if his finger was tight on that trigger. It wasn't. So, I struck him with my sword. Hard enough to knock him down. His men came at me; some of them, the ones that weren't trying to help him. I told mine to stand down. Probably the only smart thing I did that day. And Varcove took me prisoner.

"The Prime Minister's son died that night. They would have killed me if not for my blood ties to the High General. As it was, it did not go well for me. Eventually, my uncle negotiated for my release."

His frown now was severe. "I didn't respect my uncle much, because he wasn't what I thought of as a strong leader. But he got me out of there, not by show of force, but by negotiating. I hated the way he treated his High Guards like friends, but now I see how few people there are to speak with, when you're High General." He paused for a moment.

"Before they released me, the Prime Minister swore to me that he would get revenge for his son's death. My uncle sent me south to deal with raiders. The Varcove Prime Minister's term ended, and he became head of a weapons manufacturer. Now his daughter is Prime Minister." He pushed up his sleeve. He had a scar on his forearm, the shiny ghost of a burn vaguely in the shape of a B. "Barren was his name. They wanted to be sure I remembered." His gaze held Cameron's. "This might be personal."

She swallowed. "That's a long time to hold a grudge, and going to war over one man is extreme."

He pushed his sleeve back down, then sat in front of his plate, and picked at a few select morsels. "Varcove has never officially declared war against us, though. The Prime Minister has insisted this whole time that the government never sanctioned any assistance to the secessionists." At last he shrugged. "I'll know, soon enough. For now, I will worry more about what to say to those damn cameras."

Cameron returned to her position. The High General reviewed the prepared statements for the evening. When his meal had officially ended, he joined a group of speechwriters and public-relations specialists, who coached him through the primary focus of his comments. They attempted, not for the first time, to tell him not to speak so aggressively, especially since he was talking about making peace, but aggression came naturally to Sean Ellis. They suggested a few changes to his appearance. In some cases he took the recommendations, although he always did so himself. There had been an incident, about a year ago, when one of them reached out to straighten his jacket. No one had dared touch him since. Cameron considered the burn on his arm, the many years of combat experience, the attempts on his life.

But there was no list that made the suffering of his people acceptable.

By the time he walked out in front of the reporters and the lights, any of the uncertainty he'd shown over his dinner had fallen away. Cameron and Brecht stood over either shoulder. They had become the High General's guards of choice any time he made a public appearance, because Cameron was on the small side, making Sean Ellis appear taller, and Brecht's rough looks made the High General less fearsome. The speech went better than most. He answered the questions at the end with minimal sign of annoyance.

When the speech team had finished reviewing his performance, Brecht left, to be replaced by High Guard Benjamin Arora. Sean Ellis leapt to his feet with a fierce grin. "Do you know what I haven't done in a long time? I haven't sparred in ages." He looked from Cameron to Arora. "I bet you won't pull your blows too much, Kardell."

Cameron smiled. "I'm told I hit too hard, sir."

He clapped his hands together. "Good, let's go."

This addition to the schedule took a few minutes to work out, and the Master of the High Guard met them in the sparring room to oversee the practice. She frowned when Sean Ellis insisted on facing Cameron. Clemens always hand-picked the High General's sparring partners. Cameron had never made it into the rotation for good reason.

"For once, Kardell, pull. Your. Blows. The last thing we need is for the man to show up to peace talks with a broken wrist."

"That only happened once. And Vincent didn't roll out right. *And* I said I was sorry." Clemens glared. Cameron relented. "He won't be happy about it."

The Master of the High Guard smiled. "My job isn't to make him happy, it's to keep him safe."

Cameron took her place in the sparring circle. The High General set himself across from her. He returned her salute in full then raised a training blade in front of his torso. She kept her feet light, one foot forward slightly, her blade at her side in her left hand. He stayed still and watchful for a long time, waiting for her to lose her nerve and make a move, but she knew too well what she was doing. At last he grinned, tightened his grip, and rushed.

His feet moved fast across the floor, his face all hard lines. She could see the power he built behind that two-handed swing. His eyes were as dark as the bottom of a glacier.

She waited until just the right moment to sweep her blade out in a block that would either knock his training sword free, or throw him off balance out of the square. He read her well enough to change his grip and his stance. The lengths of wood clacked together, at a different angle than Cameron had anticipated, but it was still close enough to what she wanted. She moved through the block into a strike at his neck.

Sean Ellis was fast, his reaction time was good. His block was so strong both training blades creaked. Cameron and the High General moved apart, her feet light and low over the floor, his motions sharper, stronger. He jumped back in after a momentary evaluation of her position, every blow hard enough to crack bone if it landed.

She kept to defense for a few passes, taking more time to read him. He had years of experience over her, but his style was looser, relying more on his strength to overwhelm an opponent and provide him with an opening. A few rounds with him would tire her enough to put her in danger.

She ducked under a sweep aimed at her neck, slipped to his weaker right. He spun to meet her. She started a strike, but turned it just as he moved to block. Cameron brought her edge just to his armpit, so light he almost didn't feel it.

He saw the bout-winning blow, and his eyes narrowed as he stepped back. "Clemens! I am not in the mood for this!" Then he directed his gaze back to Cameron. "Pull another blow and I will show you what my anger really looks like."

The Master of the High Guard objected, but Cameron kept her attention on the High General. "Yes, sir."

He didn't reset, he just stepped back, giving himself enough distance to launch another attack. Cameron knew now how he fought. She met him more quickly, and began to work his weaknesses.

Sometimes the power of his blows took him just a little too far through a sweep. His focus on her was so strong he didn't always pay attention to what he did, except in the vaguest way. And she suspected that an old injury had made his left knee a little stiff, though he hid it well.

As their blades met, cracking together over and over, and their feet danced over the floor with smooth control, she watched his face. Her arms ached a little from meeting the strength of his strikes. But as she whirled around him, forcing him to move onto his left knee more to keep even with her, she saw him wince.

Then he went off balance for just a moment. She leapt forward, lashing out at his right knee as she made her way around the side of him. She drove the sword from his grip when he stumbled, then jabbed the rounded end of her weapon hard between two ribs in his back.

He caught himself before he hit the floor, his laugh a light counterpoint to the sound of Thea Clemens shouting. He waved away High Guard Brecht's attempt to help him up, and collected his fallen training blade. He swung his right leg back and forth a few times. He smiled at Cameron.

"You don't disappoint. It would have been nice to have someone like you with me in a few tight spots back when I was facing the raiders." He tested his left knee as well. "One more round."

This time he went to his side for a proper start. They exchanged salutes again. Then, as he took position, he said, "Did you know, this is the room where your father died?"

She knew he meant to throw her off, pull her mind away from his attacks and her responses. "No, sir."

He launched across the circle. She caught his blade, danced away from the next couple of blows. He grinned now as he swung. "I was there." His training sword cut the air beside her. She met his next blow, turned it, and struck. He blocked, then came at her from the left. "He was training my uncle and I. Armel V was still High General at the time, my uncle still the High General's son."

Cameron didn't speak. She kept her mind still, barely allowing the words he spoke to touch her. But storing them for later. The wood blades cracked together all around her head. Sean Ellis pushed her, a quiet fury in his eyes. He would do whatever it took to beat her.

"Your father was a confident man, just a little older than you are now. He decided my uncle was ready for an edged blade. He said it was important to train with the real thing."

Sean Ellis paused in his story, and concentrated on a complicated series of passes. *Do not make it easy for him*. She picked up her pace. They swept around each other, she precise, he fierce.

"My uncle cut him, just nicked his femoral artery. He told me to get help, but your father knew better. My uncle never forgave me for staying there, but I think *he* knew I'd do a better job remembering his last words." She'd worked Sean Ellis to the edge of the sparring ring. His focus wasn't entirely on the fight. He caught a blow, and leaned into it, wrapping his left hand around her hilt, trapping her hand against it. "It's funny, hardly anyone says anything very interesting before they die. 'Tell my wife I love her,' he said." The High General shoved, hard enough that Cameron stumbled, but she rolled, recovered better than he'd anticipated. She knocked aside the strike he'd hoped would end the match. She leapt up, drove past his defenses, and brought her blade down hard on his left shoulder.

He watched her with narrow eyes, breathing hard as she withdrew the training sword. She waited.

"That doesn't bother you?"

She shook her head. "I never knew him, sir."

The High General tossed his training blade to Clemens. "What does bother you?"

She could think of a few things. The way William alternated between seething rage and quiet stares. The way Tristan popped up without warning. The sacrifice of her freedom for this proximity to a dangerous man, with only shreds of hope that someday he'd reveal what he knew. What she said was, "Being made to wear a dress."

He laughed at that. Cameron pulled her scarlet jacket back on, smoothed her hair, and put away her training blade. Had Sean Ellis been trying to win by distracting her, or was his intent to annoy? Not for the first time, she wondered what he wanted by placing her in the High Guard. She doubted more than ever that he had given them their abilities. Most likely, he was just another experiment like the rest of them.

He wasn't as fast as Tristan; he didn't like to touch people much, suggesting he didn't read minds; he wasn't swayed by emotions like William; she wasn't sure he couldn't heal wounds, but she guessed that he was a Twenty-Four. Which would explain how he knew what she was.

But did he want to help? Or was he part of it?

Sean Ellis returned to his office to finish more paperwork before bed. Night had just crossed into morning when High Guard Lin replaced Cameron. She went to the Master of the High Guard's office, where she faced a lengthy and probably well-deserved verbal lashing. At last she was given a packet of information on those who would attend the peace talks. She walked home through the summer-warm city.

She slid into bed with Ethan. She didn't even dare put an arm around him. Let him sleep. She stared at the ceiling, and wondered what it felt like to have something that felt like home.

006

THE ROAD ROLLED out in front of them, passing further into the steep-sided foothills that made up the southern end of the Low Crescents. Deep, dark lakes punctuated the landscape, running in long lines at the bottoms of valleys. Here and there the blanket of an orchard lay across the hills, trees marching along in lines. Hawks wheeled overhead, gliding and sweeping. Tristan watched them tuck and bank and spread their wings to catch the air in different ways. He saw one fold up and fall out of the sky, looking like a dropped rag, with a wing flicking out occasionally. It all changed just before it hit the ground. The tail and the wings spread, the talons thrusting down. The bird landed on a snake. Tristan smiled as the hawk flapped away with the snake trailing from its claws.

It looked the same, really, whether you killed for food or stupidly large sums of money.

He pointed out the hawks to Niko. The boy wasn't sulking anymore, not since William had run his test and confirmed for certain that he was Altered. Melanie's theory that the boy had simply lacked nutrition over the course of his life made sense to William, so Tristan was going with it. Now the boy hung on his every word, as if he hoped to make up for breaking his leg, like it was his fault instead of Tristan's.

As they swept over the countryside, Tristan could see why the doctor would retire here. It was a quiet landscape, where it seemed nothing much happened. People sat at stands alongside the road, selling apples, or corn, or home-made jelly in glass jars. It was so quaint that it made Tristan shudder. Melanie would have loved it.

"So, how are we getting in the front door?" Tristan asked.

"You're a physician from a couple of towns over. You were curious about the paper he wrote on prenatal stress and how it related to his practice in Advon. I'm an undergrad interested in medicine, working for you over the summer. We thought, since we were driving through on our way to a medical conference, that we could stop by on our way."

Tristan had been working for days on memorizing the terminology, which hopefully he wouldn't need for much of the conversation.

"You have the cigars?"

"Yes. Really think that's going to work?"

Tristan smiled. "Doctor Shriver has a well-established weakness for them. It will work."

Niko frowned. "Never did gifts before. On the street, that was a good way to get kicked in the teeth, trying to give somebody something for free. It's suspicious."

Tristan raised his eyebrows. "This isn't the street, though. People like this, they aren't expecting someone who dresses like them to be dangerous. It's part of the social code. You look the right way, you act the right way, ergo you are trustworthy."

The boy shifted in his seat, like he wanted to escape. Hopefully he was ready for this. The deception was one of the most important parts of the job, gaining trust, getting people to talk, or to open this door, or sometimes pretend he wasn't there. Other methods were much messier.

Tristan turned down the road to the doctor's house. He'd timed the visit to coincide with Mrs. Shriver's weekly hair appointment, which always took a few hours. Timing, he'd told Niko, was critical.

The driveway was a long strip of crushed seashells, lined with old-growth trees and white fencing. A handsome brown horse gazed in the field to their right. It snorted at them as they drove by.

The house at the end was a decent size, not enormous, built of red brick, with white stone columns and arching windows. Tristan parked the car, grabbed the box of cigars, swung out, and sprang up the steps to the front porch. With his friendliest grin plastered on his face, he rang the doorbell. Niko trotted along behind him, trying to look like he belonged. He succeeded in looking like someone who was trying very hard.

Doctor Shriver answered the door. The doctor had tidy hair, mostly gray with a small vestige of chestnut brown. He looked at Tristan with a mild curiosity, and a willingness to return the smile, even to unexpected guests. "Good morning, can I help you?"

"I hope so, Doctor Shriver. I'm Doctor Henry Patton. I live over in Heston, and I recently read your article from a few years ago. My intern and I were driving through here on our way to the conference in Stilton. We thought you might not mind if we stopped by to chat a bit." Doctor Shriver's eyes had already lit up at the prospect of talking about his old work, and when Tristan offered the box of cigars, he knew it would ensure his invitation. "I spoke with Mrs. Patel at your old practice. She said you liked this variety. I thought since I was showing up unannounced—"

Doctor Shriver stepped back before he could finish speaking and spread his arm wide. "Come right in, Doctor Patton. And your name, young man?"

"S-Sam Holli," Niko said.

"You can call me Henry," Tristan said as he stepped inside.

Doctor Shriver asked about their drive, accepted the cigars, offered them something to drink. Niko hovered right beside Tristan, silent and wide-eyed.

Tristan admired the front room. It was a place with serious money behind it, rare hardwood for the floors, quarried stone around the fireplace, all the trimmings done just right. Niko stared at a statue of a young man with a water pitcher on his head, wearing nothing but an impractical piece of fabric draped around his hips. A pair of spindly hounds lay in a basket at the end of the couch, blinking their liquid brown eyes at the guests.

"If you want to come back to my office, I keep some better drinks there. And I can try one of these. I do try to keep the smoke confined."

Tristan agreed. Niko cast one last glance at the statue as the dogs unfolded their legs for the change in scenery. When they were seated in the office, which appeared to be storage for memorabilia and well-padded chairs, the retired doctor set out glasses for all three of them. He dropped a polite amount of whisky into each one. As he prepared his cigar, he said, "What were your questions about the article?"

"Your thoughts on the effects of a mother's stress levels on the unborn child seemed clear. I wondered, though, if you had suggestions for defraying the effects in cases where stress on the mother is extreme and unavoidable."

The doctor drew in the cigar fumes, then released them with a sigh. "I'm guessing you're dealing with a situation like this."

Tristan leaned forward, adopting an expression of concern. "A first-time mother, whose husband is up north, part of the fighting. It's been difficult."

Doctor Shriver nodded. "Encourage her to ask the people around her for help. But frankly, most of it is up to her. A young man like you, you still have time to learn that some things can't be controlled. You can give encouragement, but it's up to her to ask for help."

"Did you have many cases like this? I imagine in a big city like Advon . . . "

Niko exploded with coughs, overpowered by a sip of whiskey. Doctor Shriver laughed, Tristan thumped his back, and much to his dismay, Shriver got distracted into asking Niko why he was interested in medicine. The boy stumbled his way through his answer, covered at least by the last few coughs. They would definitely be practicing this more.

Finally, Doctor Shriver sat back in his chair, took another pull of the cigar. Puffs of smoke drifted from the corners of his mouth. He frowned, put the cigar down. "I haven't smoked in too long. Excuse me a moment." He turned in the chair, cracked open the window, and took a few breaths of fresh air.

When he turned back around, Tristan leaned forward. He didn't have long before the man's answers became unintelligible. "You were telling me about Mrs. Sitka, and the effect of her husband's death on her pregnancy."

The doctor shook his head, confused. "Were we? I doubt that, I never talk about that patient . . . " His brow furrowed. Tristan had a fighter on his hands. He pulled one of the copied pages out of his pocket to put in front of the old man. Giving him a focus, a way through the confusion, might pry out some answers.

Doctor Shriver looked at the paper. Instead of the tension easing out of his face, his eyes widened. The panic built slowly, impeded by the drug. "Where—where did you get this? Who are you?"

Tristan stood, walked around the desk. "This test you ran, right here. It wasn't a test, was it?"

Doctor Shriver shuddered. Not much time. Tristan knelt down, gripped the man's shirt, and looked him hard in the eye.

"I know the woman you ran that 'test' on. Do you have any clue what you did? Because I've *seen* it. I've watched her fight to understand and control the power you helped give her. I've watched people die when she failed. If you have even a fraction of her courage, then you will tell me who you were helping."

Doctor Shriver shuddered again, like a rotting windmill in a gale. "She said that it was a ground-breaking treatment, but the Physician's Board wouldn't approve the trials. I went to school with her. She swore no one would get hurt." His gaze grew hazier, his breath slower, more even.

Tristan tightened his grip. "Her name." The doctor shook his head. Tristan thought fast. "You read about it, didn't you? You knew as soon as you saw the articles. You calculated her age, and in your heart you knew why all those Sentinels died, why that village vanished. You were right. But you can still help. I need answers."

The doctor's eyes welled up, but no tears spilled over. It was just a mist in the old man's vision. "Violet Maikon. Doctor Maikon. I didn't mean any harm. She said it was for the good of all. She promised no one would get hurt."

Tristan lowered the man back into the chair, and smoothed his shirt. "Thank you very much, Doctor Shriver. You've been helpful. You'll be glad to know that when you wake up, you won't remember any of this. My friend and I will be far, far away, and you'll never see either of us ever again. You will have an atrocious headache, but consider it a moment of penance for doing such a stupid thing."

Tristan dumped the glasses of whiskey out the window, then handed them to Niko with instruction to wash them out. Then, while the two hounds slept on their pillow and their master snored, Tristan tidied up. He tucked the paper back into his pocket, and took the rest of the box of cigars. Outside in the field, the horse whickered. There on the middle of the desk lay a folder, and Tristan, never missing an opportunity, opened it. "High Guard on the Run Murders Fellow Sentinels, Leaving Two Survivors" shouted up from a newspaper clipping that lay on top. Tristan left it open for Shriver to see when he woke up. Let him remember.

From below came the clatter of shattering glass.

The boy was a mess. Worse, Tristan was no good as a teacher. He'd never really had to work at any of this.

Niko apologized while they picked up the glass. He apologized while he and Tristan placed the shards on the floor under the sleeping doctor's chair. He apologized for the first half-hour of the drive back to Advon.

"Look, kid, it's how you learn. That's why you don't just go off on your own." Niko, slightly appeased, pulled off his tie then dangled his hand out the window of the car. The boy nodded at every piece of advice dispensed. Finally, in a hesitant voice, Niko said, "That girl you asked him about, it wasn't Miss Stillwater, was it?"

"Nope. Not going to tell you who it is, either."

Niko cupped his hand over the air rushing by the window. "Are there a lot of people like us?"

"More every day."

"But no one ever talks about it? Seems like someone would."

"You knew better than to let anyone know. People don't like when someone is that different, we all learn that early on. And the more different you are, the more the lesson sticks."

Niko stayed quiet for a while. Finally, he said, "What's it all about?"

"I don't know. That's why we're following this trail of crumbs, to find out."

The boy nodded. He spread his fingers out to catch the wind, like a hawk's tail spread before it landed on a snake.

Tristan knew even before he opened his apartment door that someone was there who shouldn't be. He could smell it, and hear a slight shuffling, too. He pushed Niko behind him, grasped a throwing knife in one hand. He nudged the door open with his foot.

Red stood in his kitchen, eating a slice of pie his aunt had made. The assassin made faces as he chewed, but also returned for another bite. Tristan, familiar with his aunt's culinary skills, hadn't yet had the courage to try any.

"You shouldn't have broken into my apartment, Red," Tristan said, shutting the door. Then he remembered Niko, opened the door again to admit the much-annoyed boy, then closed it one last time.

His nemesis grinned, an expression that didn't rise up into his eyes. "You've done well for yourself recently. The Agency is happy you're finally making contributions equal to your ability." He bent down ever so slightly to bring his gaze level with Niko's. "Why hello there. Who might you be?" Niko, sensing the animosity hanging in the air between them, didn't answer.

Tristan glared at Red with all his might. "Do you have official business, or can I kick you out now?"

"Didn't you hear the news? I'm the new Inspector. I came by to make sure you're staying out of trouble."

A smile spread slowly across Tristan's face. "I can guess you've probably already completed your check of my records."

The assassin nodded. "Your personal research is a little odd, but not nearly as interesting as some of the data on your personal security system. Someone's been watching you."

Tristan shook his head. "No, I would know if someone was accessing my records." His system was as good as it got.

Red tossed the crumb-covered plate in the sink. "Yet someone has. Look closer. You have two months to sort it out. If you don't, then I'll take action." He went for the door, rubbing the top of Niko's head roughly as he went by. Red's smiling face appeared to be a carving, rather than anything flesh and blood.

"I told you, Tristan. You'll be your own undoing. And it's finally coming for you."

007

WILLIAM SAT DIRECTLY across from the High General for two days. Sean Ellis liked to face forward in the car, so William always rode backwards, often reading out of his notes or from reports while they travelled through low hills, high hills, then mountains. Even the car's smooth ride didn't stop his stomach from doing flips. He often stopped to look out the window and take steadying breaths.

The second day, Kardell sat beside him, her knee just an inch away, her shoulder even less. He ignored her presence. She could become just another High Guard, if he really tried. He didn't have to contemplate how her dark eyes had glinted in the firelight, one evening a long time ago when they'd been on the same side. If he really tried, he could dismiss the momentary impulse to discern if that gentle scent of cinnamon was her. It wasn't her bumping against him with every curve in the road. Just a body in a uniform.

William and the High General spoke for a long time about the number of wind turbines Cotarion had made since the war started, how many the north had lost, how many needed repairs, how much power Varcove might be taking for its own use. It was a game of estimates, but William felt confident that their supply of new turbines and replacement parts would be good leverage in the negotiations.

The food grown in the Bluestone River Valley was perhaps even more valuable. The mountains weren't rich with fertile fields. In years past even Varcove had imported significant amounts of food from Cotarion.

Finally, the High General turned to the scarlet uniform beside Will, as he often did when tired of talking about a problem. "You're holding up well, Kardell."

"I think I've finally sorted out the issue, sir."

There was a glint in Sean Ellis's eye. "Good. Stopping every half hour for you to be sick was getting old."

William expected silence. Instead, Sentinel Kardell said, "If I didn't have to ride backwards, it wouldn't be a problem, sir."

"Adversity is good for you."

She nodded. "Yes, sir." Then she lapsed into silence, the set of her shoulders stiffer than before. William sensed an increase in animosity, mostly on the High General's side. He remembered the hunger on Ellis's face when William told him what Cameron had done, the way she'd completed his ability.

On the third day of the drive, William switched to a car further back in the caravan while the High General consulted with a different set of advisors. He tried to carry on conversation with the others in the car, but he could only listen to Counciler Bo talk about her cats for so long.

To his surprise, Master Reese joined their party at the lunch stop. Apparently Sean Ellis had requested he come along for both defense and advice. The sword master negotiated a place in William's car for the last stretch of the journey.

"How are you doing?" he asked once he settled in. Just the way everyone started conversations with William. Of course, he'd last seen

Master Reese had been at Erika's funeral, when he probably wasn't at his best.

"I've been doing all right. Just busy, lots of travelling."

Master Reese gave William one of those long, hard stares. William had forgotten just how forceful the man's gaze could be. William cleared his throat. "I never did thank you for all those books you lent me. They were very helpful."

"I'm glad you were able to put them to use. There's nothing worse than a book languishing on a bookshelf. But I haven't seen any new articles from you recently."

"I've mostly been doing personal work for the High General. It hasn't left me much room for outside research, though I've tried to keep up." William really hadn't noticed how much the work for Sean Ellis had expanded, more than he'd realized or intended. "Did your summer class go well?"

The sword master smiled. "Yes, this group is promising, if malleable, but I've learned to appreciate that when I get it."

William liked the weapons master. He asked questions that led William down interesting paths. And he'd read enough to have some knowledge on almost every topic. The rest of the drive passed quickly.

By midafternoon they arrived at the Irion Valley where the meetings would take place the next day. It was a rolling land, flanked on one side by a high ridge, on the other by rounded mountains. Brown scrub rattled in the strong winds that rushed through it. Stands of twisted pine clustered here and there, creating pockets of deep shade. The shadows of fast-moving clouds flitted over the ground. William stepped out of the car, took a deep breath, and decided he liked the place.

A group of Sentinels, including some High Guards, had arrived the day before to establish their base on a rise at the western edge of the valley. Only a few miles away, the leaders of the secessionists and Varcove could be seen at their own encampment. Sheep grazed in clusters across the valley. In the middle, a canvas tent had been set up for the talks. Sean Ellis scowled at it.

"Kardell, Clemens, Master Reese, I want the three of you to comb that tent and the area around it until you know what every blade of grass looks like."

Master of the High Guard Clemens leaned close to the High General. They held a lengthy, whispered argument, during which Ellis's scowl only deepened. William, sensing that his presence was not required for this, walked around the hillock, avoiding all the people unpacking the incredible amount of stuff Sean Ellis seemed to require for his day-to-day operations.

Sheep grazed on one side of their hill. William watched them move slowly, their heads bent, the sound of grass being torn and chewed audible. They reeked of wet wool.

He knelt down in front of them. One raised its head. Under his breath, William said, "Baa."

The ewe took a couple of shuffling steps backwards. William leapt up and backed away. The sheep took a couple of stiff steps forward, lowered its head, and charged.

William ran. So many people began shouting advice and humorous comments that he couldn't hear any particular person. The sheep's head hit one leg, sending him stumbling and sprawling. It backed up again as he scrambled to his feet. He was only saved from the second charge by High Guard Brecht, who stepped in front of the sheep, gripped it by the horns, and twisted so that the animal's momentum carried it face-first into the ground.

Master Reese helped William to his feet, even as the sheep backed up for another charge, this time at High Guard Brecht, who was crouched and waiting. He repeated the dodge-and-twist, slinging epithets at the fuzzy combatant. This time the sheep hit the ground hard enough to be stunned. It clambered up, looking for a moment like it might give up the fight.

"Damned thing is the most determined ewe I've ever seen," High Guard Brecht muttered as the sheep backed up yet again.

Kardell and one of the younger High Guards had walked over to watch Brecht square off with the sheep. Cameron gave William a glancing smile of amusement. "Seen a lot of determined ewes, Brecht?"

In a bouncing curtain of wool, the sheep charged again. Brecht twisted it down before answering. "My parents are sheep ranchers, so yeah, a few." He grinned at Cameron. "I'm gonna bet this one is related to you. She's got that gleam in her eye."

Cameron smiled and turned away to go inspect the next day's meeting location. A couple more High Guards arrived to watch the showdown with the ewe. William returned to the encampment, where he was tormented for provoking the sheep. It was a relief when he finally found the tent he would be staying in, and could retreat to his books for a little while.

Their dinner was served in a long tent that was basically a mobile cafeteria. Ghosts of cafeterias from long ago lingered there. William could practically feel the cold ice cubes once dropped down the back of his shirt, hear the sound of his books hitting the ground when slapped from his hands. He struggled with instinct to keep his head down and vanish.

He stood in line for food, listening to the complaints of his fellow councilors and politicians at the accommodations. He fled such talk as soon as he had his food, even though the only available seats were at the Sentinel's table. He earned a few odd looks from them, although Master Reese welcomed him warmly enough to make up for it.

William ate and let the scarlet-uniformed High Guards return to the conversation they'd been having before he joined them. He'd expected them to be comparing notes on tomorrow's meeting place, or perhaps discussing fighting technique. What he hadn't counted on was that one of the High Guards was new, so they swapped stories on how they'd become Sentinels. The Master of the High Guard was just finishing her tale of hard work, with just a little bit of influence from her uncle, who was a general.

The new High Guard looked around and said, "Is that everyone?"

"No, Ki, you've missed the most interesting one of all," said High Guard Brecht, clearly in high spirits. "Sentinel Kardell hasn't regaled us with her origins yet."

Junior High Guard Kiara tried her best not to appear too interested as Cameron gave Brecht a dark look. The other High Guards exchanged increasingly noisy conversation. Even High Guard Lin called, "I don't think I've ever heard this."

Cameron, seeing no escape, swallowed and said, with as little inflection as possible, "It's not much of a story. My mother and father were both Sentinels, My Grandma Lee was a Sentinel. Her father was one, too. It's the family business."

Many of her fellow High Guards raised objections to a statement so brief. An older man down at the other end of the table said in a ringing voice, "You do a disservice to the man whose sword you carry, Kardell."

Cameron prickled. High Guard Brecht threw an apple at her head, by way of taunt. She caught it, earning a look of admiration from the new High Guard.

Holding the apple lightly, High Guard Kardell raised her eyebrows, and the corners of her mouth went up in an inscrutable smile. "Well, if you really want to know.

"My mother and father were both Sentinels. Not long after my mom got pregnant with me, my father was killed in a training accident. Mom left the Sentinels, swearing that she would keep me away from that life.

"For the first few years, she was successful. But, as previously mentioned, my grandmother had also been a Sentinel, and she helped take care of me when I was little. One day when I was about five, we were at a birthday party. There was another boy there about my age, who was a lot bigger than me."

High Guard Brecht laughed. "Some things haven't changed much, huh?"

Cameron smiled at a round of jokes at her small size, a line of teasing that only seemed accurate when she was compared to the rest of the High Guard. Once it had subsided, she continued, "So, this boy was a bully, and he shoved me a couple of times when we stood in line for cake. I didn't like it much, and so I waited for my chance to get back at him.

"It came when we played that game, where they keep taking seats away—"

"Musical chairs," William volunteered.

"Thank you, Doctor Harfield, I knew you'd have an answer. So, we were playing musical chairs, and we were down to just three seats. The boy and I were both in the game. The music stopped. I had just sat in a chair, when the boy ran in front of me. He'd already pushed a few kids down over the course of the game. He was about to do it again. So, I put my foot out as he passed me. He fell hard enough to break his arm.

"None of the adults believed I'd done it on purpose. Most of them hadn't even seen me do it. But my Grandma Lee knew that I'd meant to hurt him. She decided that I should train to become a Sentinel, hoping that it would keep me out of trouble. By the time I was ten, her teaching had more than prepared me for the Sentinel Early Training Program. She was relieved. My mother never forgave her."

She looked around at her fellow High Guards, who had apparently never heard the tale in its entirety before. They wore expressions ranging from confusion to disquiet. None of them, however, seemed able to comment.

"So," William said slowly, hoping that if he broke the quiet that the mood would lift. "Your grandmother decided to train you because she thought you were dangerous? That seems contradictory."

"I was five. In truth, I think it was what she wanted, and she was just looking for a reason to set me on the path. She considered it the greatest honor." Cameron didn't appear too surprised by the reactions of those around her, although she did look a little disappointed. "I've been too blunt."

High Guard Brecht cleared his throat. "You know what I was doing when I was five? Trying to ride my dad's best roping horse and stealing my sister's bow to shoot at my mom's begonias."

"I'm sure you didn't really mean to break his arm," Thea Clemens said. William heard the nudge in her voice, the suggestion that Cameron should take the opportunity to change her story.

Cameron sighed at last and said, "I was very young. It might have been an accident."

It was the first time William had ever seen her lie. At least he guessed that was the reason why she spoke with such self-consciousness, because her face showed nothing besides a sudden relaxation of the muscles which had been tight with various expressions as she engaged in the conversation. The spark of her interest faded. She tossed the apple at the new High Guard, say, "What about you, Kia?" After that, she sat in silence.

The Sentinels all ate quickly. Soon most of them had left. Cameron, when enough people had cleared away from the end of the table where Will and Reese sat, slid down to sit by them.

"I don't know what I expected, but it wasn't that." Her eyes were darker than usual, her eyebrows drawn down.

Master Reese waved a hand in reassurance. "You are compelled by justice, Cameron. It is a steadier landmark than honor and loyalty and accolades."

She looked over at William. Did he see there the weight of choices she had made, and more on her horizon?

"Maybe," she said. Then she left to return to her duties.

William walked the perimeter of their encampment as the sun dropped down over the ridgeline at one side of the valley. Evening crept in, misty and bluish-gray. His quarters, which he shared with several councilors, did not appeal to him.

He spotted the unmissable silhouette of Cameron at the edge of camp as she looked out across the valley. She stood alone. He remembered the looks the other High Guards had given her earlier. He walked up the rise to where she stood, formulating what he could say, but he stopped trying. She was easiest to talk with when he didn't try too hard.

Her head whipped around when she heard him. For a fraction of a second her face had the hard lines of focus with which she faced her enemies. Then her expression softened into a rare smile, one that drew a responding smile from him.

"Have I ever told you that you shouldn't approach me from behind? Especially when I'm armed." She patted her scabbard with her eyebrows raised.

William's face warmed. "I'm sorry, I don't mean to startle you."

"You don't have to apologize, just be careful." She looked at him askance. "The other advisors are going to notice that you're avoiding them."

He shrugged. "I spent the whole morning in the car with them. I'm going to spend all day tomorrow with them. A break was in order."

She made a noise something like a light laugh, but it was very dry. "So, what was it you wanted to tell me?"

The light faced fast from the landscape. The sound of a grouse calling in the distance made the quiet all the more poignant.

Eventually, he took a breath and managed, "About what you said earlier, that kid you hurt. Well, I wasn't much older than that when I killed my dog." He swallowed hard. Only his mother and Erika had known. His sister only because she'd lifted the memory out of his head. He had a feeling Cameron wouldn't think worse of him for it, so the words tumbled out.

"Did you mean to do it?" she asked, her voice almost blending into the susurrus of wind in the grass. A few strands of her hair escaped the knot at the back of her head. She brushed them out of her face.

"I meant to pull at the energy around him. I didn't mean to kill him."

She nodded. "Whoever did this to us is going to be very sorry when I find them."

From the head of the valley, a wail shivered in the air. It sounded very much like an agonized human voice, until the howl ended in a canine yipping. As the rest of the animals took up the cry, William realized it was a pack of coyotes. Their voices were piercing and discordant, even from a great distance. The hairs on his arms rose.

William said, "Sean Ellis knows who it is."

"I assumed he probably did. He's waiting for something before he tells us anything, though. What, I'm not sure."

Strange, to talk about these things openly. William remembered an evening when they'd talked like this, right before Erika died. He remembered thinking of Kardell as a friend for a few brief hours.

Cameron studied him for several long seconds. The coyote howls faded. The light of day, too, was almost gone. He stood, trying not to feel small under the force of her gaze. Why should he shiver, just because her eyes were dark and piercing?

"How long, William? How long will it take you to leave it behind?" Her lips made a line.

He looked away from her, his throat tight. Every time they seemed comfortable together, she said something that ran right through him, something that made the beat of his heart stutter and his breath stall. He wasn't sure what hurt the most, that the words were true, or that she'd seen him as he was, peered around the wall of his intellect.

She sighed. "Are you still listening?" He nodded, not trusting his voice. "Erika is gone, but you're still here, and there's a job to do. Not to mention a life you've hardly lived. You've got to stop waiting to feel better, because that's not how it works. It's a choice you make. It's something you fight for."

Finally she stopped. He heard her take in another slow breath, then let it out. He looked back over. She struggled with herself, or so he thought. Did it upset her as much as it upset him, that moment which stood between them, raw and difficult, that moment when Erika fell? He wanted to say that if he had any choice in the matter, he would most definitely have moved on by now, but he knew that was false. He was holding onto his anger and his sorrow, because that was all he had left of his sister.

"I'm on duty all day tomorrow, so I should get to bed. Thanks for trying to make me feel better, Doctor Harfield."

She left. The space where she'd stood felt empty. Not the normal type of emptiness, when nothing was there, but like a thing missing. As bad as he'd felt when she was standing there, he felt even worse when she was gone.

008

AT MIDAFTERNOON, THE talks paused for lunch. Sean Ellis, apparently relieved that Varcove wasn't asking for his head on a silver plate, relaxed a few notches. He even let Cameron have a break from guard duty to eat. She sat on the grassy hill, watching High Guard Brecht instruct Doctor Harfield in ewe evasion tactics. The scientist gained confidence with each pass, and soon he could drop the sheep to the ground every time it charged. He grinned freely as he did so, as if he'd forgotten that he was trying to redeem himself. As if the exercise was purely for fun.

He learned fast, when given clear direction. People underestimated him because of all that fumbling; even he didn't place his worth very high. The smallest error seemed to stick to him. But she watched him grasp the sheep's horns, step to the right, and twist, meanwhile leaping out of the way of the flailing legs. He was steady, when it mattered. She'd seen it before, but only when he stopped thinking so much.

She walked away, before any sharp-witted politician caught her looking at Harfield for too long. A circuit of their encampment was a good opportunity to stretch her legs and check in with her fellow High Guards. Grasshoppers leapt up in front of her feet as she went.

A bird sang nearby, a clear sound that rocked up and down, gaining speed as it went. The bird itself remained hidden in the tall grass. She paused in her rounds to look out at the Varcove/secessionist side. Clouds continued to sweep overhead, their shapes as round as the sheep that grazed below. The valley stretched wide, somehow appearing vaster than a flat plain, perhaps because of the way it curved up on either side to touch the sky.

For the first time in a long time, she felt the once-familiar urge to shed her uniform along with all that it meant. Just go. Wherever she wanted.

Master Reese stepped up beside her, his hands folded behind his back. He looked odd to her, all dressed up for the meetings. His eyes were as sharp as ever when he looked out over the valley.

"What do you see?"

He would always be testing her, in a different way than Sean Ellis, but it still chafed.

"I see a strange place for peace talks. Not exactly neutral ground, just secluded. But from a security perspective, this is probably easiest for all involved." She stayed very still, listened to the sheep bleat and run off at last out of frustration. People chatted behind her, their voices as careless as picnickers. They were all bubbling over with the hope that the war would come to an end. The wind tugged at her uniform.

Cameron said, "The High General is concerned that there's a personal grudge against him. I think it's strange that only the Prime Minister is here representing the government of Varcove. The rest are from the weapon's manufacturer. It was her brother Ellis killed." She crossed her arms. "It's like this a lot of the time, though. Every situation, I see opportunities and reasons for someone to attack him."

"That's why he relies on you so much. You've done very well, better than even I expected."

"Thank you, sir."

He opened his mouth to say more, but the Master of the High Guard called, "Kardell, we're moving!" Cameron went back to the High General's side.

They set off on the walk to the middle of the valley. Sean Ellis rolled his eyes as some of the advisors complained about the distance. Doctor Harfield fussed over a smudge of dirt on his pants, while trying not to show he was worried about it.

The tent rose up on the hill ahead of them. High Guard Arora, who'd completed the pre-inspection, signaled that they were cleared for approach.

As Thea Clemens crested the top of the hill, with Sean Ellis, Cameron, and High Guard Brecht just behind her, the tent flaps parted and a man stepped out. He walked with a polished cane, gripped by a hand netted with blue veins. His dark brown eyes locked on Ellis. The High General stopped. Even out of the corner of her eye Cameron saw his tension rise again.

They knew each other. Cameron drew in closer to Ellis. She forced herself to breathe evenly.

"Hayden Fold," the High General muttered under his breath. Cameron swallowed down a curse, but Brecht whispered enough for both of them.

The man stepped closer to them, helped along by his cane. He leaned on it heavily. It might be a weapon, he might be faking his weakness, genuine though it appeared. Cameron didn't see any other possible weapons on him, and he walked alone. Thea Clemens put out a hand to stop him before he could approach too close.

In slow, careful Cotari he said, "I have looked forward to . . . meeting you again for many years, Sean Ellis."

The High General gave him a long, cold look. "Can't really say the same, I'm afraid."

"You nearly cut my son in half."

Cameron heard, over the rushing of wind in grass, the whine of small engines. Their sound came from the other side of the hill, but they approached quickly. High Guard Arora peered around the tent to get a better look. When he turned back his face was several shades lighter.

The Prime Minister of Varcove crested the opposite side of the hill. She shouted in Varcove, "Papa, you promised!"

Ellis didn't lunge at Fold, but it appeared to take all his self-restraint to prevent it. Thea Clemens turned, and spun Ellis back towards their base. "Everybody move!" she shouted. The advisors, who up to that point had stood locked in confusion, turned and ran.

It was half a mile back to their encampment. Arora caught up to them as they started up the small rise. He said, "They're on terra-bikes! Ten to each side. We'll see them at the top, here."

Thea Clemens called their vehicles to meet them with her hand radio. Motion at their camp suggested the orders becoming action.

Engines buzzed ever louder from either side. Cameron looked behind, for just a moment when they reached the top of the next rise. Two clouds of dirt grew on either side, with the dark shapes of terra-bikes at the leading edge. Sheep scattered. In less than a minute they'd be cut off from escape.

"We need cover where we can hold for a few minutes," Sean Ellis shouted. His eyes lit up with the anticipation of combat as he pointed to a likely place. "Over there."

Clemens shook her head. "We don't want to get cut off!"

"We're about to be surrounded no matter what we do," Cameron said. The clusters of bikes appeared in her peripheral vision, both sides. One rider dismounted before readying a rifle. "Snipers."

The Master of the High Guard made a sound of pure frustration. "Everyone, form up in that ditch! Lin, pick off their rifles!"

The advisors scrambled into the creek bed with varying levels of grace, followed by the Sentinels. The sides were high, almost vertical, and deep enough that most of them could stand in it without their heads showing at the top. The section they stood in was a straight run, with deep bends to either side. They couldn't have made a better trench.

High Guard Lin readied her rifle. Since the Summer Solstice Feast, when a sniper had shot her in the leg, she had become an excellent mark. The best sort of vengeance.

Cameron remained beside High General Ellis as the roar of engines closed in. Master Reese stood at her other side. She looked to William, who crouched with the advisors. Before she could even make a motion, he crept up next to her.

"Can you do anything to their bikes?" She kept her voice low. The only sounds in the creek bed were the rustles of High Guards taking up position and exchanging information.

William closed his eyes, his face tight with concentration. Very slowly, he nodded. High Guard Lin swung herself up the side of the bank, helped by High Guard Vincent. Rifles fired, and earth burst at the edge of the banks. Dirt rained down. Some of the advisors crouched lower and whimpered. William's awareness had gone so far outside of his immediate surroundings that he didn't even flinch.

"Have at it, Doctor Harfield," Cameron whispered.

His eyes flashed open. To Cameron's horror, he peeked up over the side of the bank. She almost pulled him back down, but one engine stuttered and stalled. More gunfire punctuated loud cursing in Varcove.

High Guard Lin fell, landing on her back in the creek bed. A tidy hole marred the center of her forehead.

"Libra, you're on rifle!" Thea Clemens shouted. Two more engine roars ended in pops before Cameron grabbed William's elbow and pulled him back down. His mouth tightened in annoyance, until he noticed High Guard Lin at the bottom of the creek. First he blanched. Then he pulled her body out of the water, closer to the side where at least no one would trip.

Sean Ellis kept his back against one bank. He looked much the same as he did in his office, just angrier. He suggested tactics to Clemens as the bikes above halted. Clemens' radio crackled.

"We're still a couple of minutes out, and we'll have to fight through on the western side when we get there. The more you can take out, the easier the extraction will be."

"We need someone to go up there," the High General said.

The Master of the High Guard's gaze landed on Cameron. The request was clear enough, and there was no sense in forcing the woman to speak it aloud. Cameron nodded. Then Clemens looked to the High General as the gunfire intensified.

"One sniper down," called High Guard Libra.

Sean Ellis nodded at Thea Clemens before baring his teeth at Cameron. "It's a beautiful day, Kardell," he said.

Cameron gripped the hilt of her sword. Clemens shouted at Arora to take her place. "Perfect day."

Master Reese moved as Cameron did. "I'll take the other bank." Sean Ellis accepted this with another nod.

Cameron backed up against the bank, one shoulder brushing the High General, the other William Harfield. High Guard Brecht knelt at the opposite bank, and Master Reese stood beside him. Ellis himself knelt beside Cameron with his hands clasped for Reese to step into.

"When you can see the tops of their heads," Reese said to Cameron. She drew her sword, held in her left hand, her small Varcovian pistol in her right. She waited. Another Sentinel holding the bank fell, splashing into the water at their feet.

Cameron glimpsed a tuft of hair. She kicked off into a sprint. Master Reese mirrored her, and they crossed in the middle of the creek, gaining momentum. Cameron stepped up into Brecht's hands. He heaved her up over the edge of the bank.

She landed among heavily-armed mercenaries.

Several pairs of eyes tightened, the only sign of shock. Gun barrels swung at her. She sliced through the closest neck, then dropped low. Her arm burned. A grazing hit. Another mercenary fell, either to a Sentinel's bullet or a comrade's.

Cameron knocked the next closest rifle barrel up into the air, and cut its handler in both leg and arm. The other five danced out of her way, seeking better positions. A Sentinel fired. Four. She watched them, for just a moment, weighing their skill and experience.

She launched at the greatest threat, her feet sure over the grass. Her pistol fired, she hit his torso, but he returned with a shot that sent pain blossoming through her leg. She clenched her teeth, and then she was too close for guns. The mercenary had an edged weapon, a short, flat sword that he swung out to block her first strike. It bought him a few extra seconds.

As he fell, she cut his rifle free of his body. Three left. The escape vehicles burst over the rise. Cameron knelt, the rifle pushed tight against her shoulder. Her shot missed. Heat burst again, this time in her torso, making her gasp.

Keep the rifle up, keep it up or you're finished.

Cameron's second shot brought down the woman who'd hit her. The next time she squeezed the trigger, it clicked on nothing.

With sword in hand she spun around to the man approaching her from behind. She moved faster than should have been possible, through the fires radiating out from her leg and side, her breath coming in gasps. In a few more seconds her mind would catch up, and she would fall.

She knocked aside the gun aimed at her face, and took the holder's head off cleanly.

The last one had injuries of his own, so he was slow getting his gun up. If her leg didn't threaten to buckle under her at every step, she would have reached him before he managed that last shot, the one that struck her shoulder. The impact rippled out in waves, rattling muscle and bone. Cameron raised her sword, but a bullet took him in the chest before she could bring it down.

Scarlet uniforms rushed around her, past her. Sulphur bit at her nose, and the metallic smell of blood. But the guns were silent.

Her hands shook as she swept the red from her sword. It seemed a weight had been strapped to her chest, but she fought its drag. Her blade slid into its scabbard, scraping as her numb fingers let loose before it was seated.

Still the weight dragged, and the blood-soaked grass rose up. She threw her good leg out in time to stop the ground from striking her face. A roar filled her ears. Darkness threatened her vision.

The fire pulsed in her wounds. She couldn't get a full breath, one of her lungs wasn't working right, if at all. Her chest kept falling, no matter how she fought the pull.

Hands hooked under her arms, pulled up. A groan burst from her throat as her body unfolded, feeding the existing flames, kindling new ones. Darkness took her vision entirely for a moment, but she heard Ellis say, "Up, Kardell, you aren't done yet."

"Sir, there is no room in this vehicle for a dead woman!" Clemens shouted. But still Cameron was dragged across the ground. Bands around her chest tightened. She coughed, tasted blood. Someone cursed. Harfield, maybe.

Her sight cleared enough to see a door flung wide. Hands from inside drew her in, lowered her into a seat. She let her head fall against the headrest. The door shut, and the vehicle jolted into motion, a fast flight. Cameron almost slid off the seat, but several hands caught her, pushed her back up.

She raised her head. Sean Ellis smiled at her. "You did well, Kardell."

Another tightening in her chest, another cough. When her lungs stopped seizing, she mouthed, *Thank you, sir.* She closed her eyes.

Breath hissed against the back of her throat, in halting jerks. Was it going in or out? A hand enveloped hers. The fingers squeezed tight. A decent anchor, but hard to feel through the bursts of pain.

She fought back the darkness threatening to engulf her. If she fell in, there might not be a way out.

009

WILLIAM HAD NEVER heard breath sound so thin. He'd never seen anyone's face so white, either. The medic who'd been waiting in the vehicle ensured that Sean Ellis wasn't hurt, then the High General pushed him over to Cameron.

A High Guard and Master Reese kept her upright while she gasped. The medic cut away her shirt and the fabric around the wound on her leg. Within a few moments, red stained his hands.

William looked down at all the booted feet crammed together in the vehicle as the medic extracted the bullets one by one. The inside of the car held too many people, all sitting in complete silence. Did the others hold their breath, too, each time Cameron's paused just a little too long?

Master Reese kept a hand tight around Kardell's shoulder, his expression all fury. The High Guard at her other shoulder stared out the front window. The Master of the High Guard watched the medic work, perhaps considering how many High Guards she might need to replace by the end of the day.

And Sean Ellis sat with his shoulders hunched, looking much like a broody hawk. His hands were clasped, his elbows resting on his knees. His eyes were locked on Cameron's face. The turn of his lips suggested some emotion William had never seen before. He looked almost uncertain. But William wasn't great at reading faces.

The medic soon had a bag of blood hooked to the ceiling of the car, dripping into Kardell's arm. Color returned to her face, but it was purplish-blue.

"Brecht, your hands should be free," Thea Clemens said, her voice so loud. To William's horror, Brecht looked right at him. They switched places, colliding more than once as the car bumped. Then William found himself in the seat right beside Cameron, one of his hands gripping her shoulder to keep her from toppling, the other instinctively wrapping around her fingers. They were cold, and he received only the lightest squeeze of acknowledgement. Something lodged in his throat. He swallowed hard, but it wouldn't go away.

He remembered, more powerfully than he ever had, the way she'd knelt by him after Erika stabbed him. She'd hesitated there for a moment, her dark eyes steady on his, even after he answered her questions. He hadn't known how to read the expression on her face, and he still didn't. If only he'd been brave enough to ask why she'd paused there, when Erika was out in the world, getting further away by the moment. What he had known even then was that he believed in her as much as he believed in all his science.

The medic's hands moved around the hole in Cameron's chest. She gasped, her eyes flickering open for a moment. Plastic tubing whipped around, and medical tape unspooled, then the medic said, "All right, let's lie her down, now."

This involved a great deal of shuffling, made tricky by the cramped quarters in the car. In the end Cameron lay with her feet propped up on one door, her knees over Reese's legs, her head heavy in William's lap. The medic strapped a mask over her mouth and nose, and wrapped a blanket around her. Then he sat on the floor, his fingers pressed to her wrist. She still breathed in gasps, but it didn't sound so weak.

"How much longer to the base?" Sean Ellis asked the driver.

"About half an hour, Sir."

The High General looked at Cameron's face, his frown deep. "Give me a full summary of her injuries."

"Three solid bullet wounds, Sir, and a few grazes. One to the left thigh, damn lucky it didn't get any arteries. One to the left shoulder, significant bleeding there. And then there's the shot to the right lower chest. The lung collapsed, but I released the air in the chest cavity, so we're looking a little better. The blood loss is severe, though."

"Comforting," Cameron muttered.

Sean Ellis leaned forward and gripped her good shoulder. "I expect you to live, Kardell." He sounded like he meant it, which seemed strange considering he was the reason she'd been shot. He looked to William, his eyebrows raised. "She needs to stay warm."

William nodded. In spite of the blanket, Cameron was frigid. If he warmed the air around her, he might stave off shock for at least a few extra minutes. He closed his eyes, found whatever loose strands of energy he could, and translated them into the heat Cameron needed.

Sean Ellis leaned forward and said, "Drive faster."

Their car pulled up at the base in twenty minutes, tires screeching, a cloud of dust rising around the vehicle. A whole team of medics met the car when it stopped. Many hands reached in to pull Cameron out. The High General ignored the multitude speaking to him.

"Harfield, go with her. Tell Finch that I sent you along, and do whatever he tells you to do."

William ran to catch up with the medics who had carried Cameron off to one of the larger buildings, a field hospital that buzzed with activity. He followed through several doors and many halls, but hands pushed him back at the room where they took Cameron. William had to shout that the High General had ordered him to stay with Kardell before they let him in.

He blinked in the dim interior, a room completely in shadow except for the concentrated beam shining on Cameron, who was visible only in glimpses through the crowd of nurses and doctors bent over her. Once he was inside, everyone ignored William completely.

Finally he took a deep breath. "Is one of you Finch?"

A man with dark skin and hair touched with silver said, "Sure." He never looked up at William, just kept moving around Cameron.

"The High General sent me to help. I think."

Finch glanced up, just a flash. "Are you Harfield?"

William, glad for some sign that he was where he was supposed to be, said, "Yes."

"Go stand in the corner over there, I might need you later."

This was not what William had hoped for, but he took up position in the corner, anyway. He could see most of the monitors tracking Cameron's vital signs. He knew how to read more of the numbers and wavering lines than he liked. He tried to occupy himself calculating the number of floor and ceiling tiles, but he kept loosing track. Then he looked back to her heart rate and oxygen levels, helpless to stop himself.

He supposed this was all to be expected. A person could only throw herself into danger so many times without getting hurt. High

Guard Lin had fallen right in front of him, a bullet in her head, a clear statement of the dangers a High Guard faced. William had just grown so accustomed to Cameron getting it right, of her strength and speed conquering all enemies, that he'd never allowed mental space for the idea that she could be hurt. But of course, she was human. He just hadn't thought of her that way since the day he'd watched her remove Erika's ability.

If she died now, the rest of them would have to find out the source of their abilities on their own. William wouldn't even know where to start.

He should have been kinder to her. She'd always tried to lead them the right way, had always been honest even if it earned her anger. Usually from him.

"All right, I think she's as stable as she's going to get for now. Everybody, go about your business, I'll finish up."

The rest of the medics left, some taking a few seconds to finish a task. Then Finch and William were the only ones left in the room. Finch perched on a stool, his hands over the hole in Cameron's chest. He nodded William to his side.

"Ellis thinks you're Series Eight. Is that true?"

William nodded, and the man continued. "I'm Octavius Finch, the Five in Ellis's set. You know much about healing?"

"Not as much as I'd like." Melanie had never liked to talk about what she could do. On the rare occasions William did pry something out of her, it was so vague as to be useless.

"Fantastic. Well, what you need to know today is that I have to use her body's energy to make repairs, and the faster I can do that, the better her chances. The problem, of course, is that she's already spent."

William caught on at once. "So, you need me to supply the energy."

Finch smiled. "Thank goodness, you're the smart one. The catch is, the energy has to be in a form I can access, so it has to blend with what's in her cells. Do you think you can manage that?"

William knew very well how complicated and varied the energy coursing through a living being was. If only there were someone else to help. "I can try."

Finch shrugged. "You won't hurt the outcome, so might as well. She wouldn't even be breathing now if not for the respirator. That will only hold her for so long."

Not comforted much by this line of reasoning, William gathered up the ambient energy he needed. He pulled from the widest possible radius, trying not to drag too much from any particular place. When he had a manageable amount, he worked it, trying to change the quality and texture of it to match the gentle haze around Cameron. It was like being handed paints in only the primary colors, and being asked to reproduce an entire spectrum of hues.

Fortunately, William had some practice. When at last he was satisfied, he fed some of the energy he'd changed into the glow around Cameron. The intensity of the haze around her strengthened. Finch nodded.

They worked for a long time, until they were worn, and still on after that. Finch insisted that Cameron's lung had to be in perfect condition. Finally, shoulders slumping and voice gruff, the healer lifted his hands away from the ridges of Cameron's ribs. He looked at the displays and smiled slightly.

"Her oxygen levels are rising, look. The heart rhythm could be better, but we've put a hand on the scale, at least." He picked up a stethoscope and pressed it to various parts of Cameron's torso. His smile gained confidence. "The lung is perfect. There's nothing more we can do until we've both had some rest." He stood, his knees popping from sitting in one place for so long. William tottered to his feet. He couldn't remember ever feeling so tired. Finch said, "Do you know the healer in your set?"

"What is a set?"

"You're joking."

William shook his head. Finch let out a bitter laugh.

"Oh, to be innocent again. Doctor Harfield, we are made in groups, with one of each type of Altered, all of roughly the same age. Well, all the types we know of, I have no doubt there are many more. Then we are nudged together. So, do you know another Series Five?"

"Yes."

"Ask them to come here. More hands could make the difference." Then he nodded to Cameron. "It would do her good to have some encouragement from a friendly voice, before you go."

William didn't know if his voice would be friendly to her. Still, he stepped closer. All thoughts of encouragement fled when he looked down at her pale face and her mechanical breath. Finch watched him, though, so he took Cameron's hand.

"I know I can't figure all this out on my own, Kardell. We all need you." Weariness dragged at his mind and his words, but there was enough left in him to regret how hard he'd been on her over what happened to Erika. It was not her fault, it never had been. Yet he could not dredge the words up over the lump in his throat.

"Besides that, I know you love Ethan, and he loves you. If you fight for nothing else, fight for that." He squeezed her hand, then let it slide to the blanket.

"Good enough, I guess," Finch said. "Come on, let's find you a place to rest before you fall over."

Sean Ellis himself waited outside in the hushed hallway. He informed William that his sleeping quarters were ready, and a very young soldier guided him there. Outside the medical building, night had fallen. William stumbled through the dark behind his guide.

There was a phone in his room, so he called Tristan. He trusted that his garbled message would be translated into a request for Melanie's help. Then he hung up the phone, laid down on the bed, intending to rest for just a moment before removing his shoes, but he never got around to it before sleep rolled over him.

010

Tristan delivered Mel to Cam's side. He glanced at the Sentinel before he left. The hue of her skin told him well enough that she was no longer in a fight to live. There wasn't enough left for that. If she survived, it would be luck. A flip of the coin, a question of landing on heads or tails.

He wandered off, looking for something to do. He crept around for a while, dodging anyone who might ask him what he was doing up so early in the morning, until he found barracks. There, between sleeping bodies, he looked for a uniform his size.

A little while later he was outfitted, and every bit a soldier. He wasn't happy about it, but at least he could move around without having to dodge into the shadows every time someone else walked by.

This, it turned out, was only partially true. He could pass anyone of equal or lesser rank without incident, but every time he crossed paths with someone superior, they barked that his appearance was deficient. The first time, a Unibrow snapped that his headgear was not straight. Tristan remedied this, only to be told a moment later by a Sergeant that his salute was lazy. A Warrant Officer told him he needed a haircut. Then another Sergeant stopped, tucked his bootlaces in for him, straightened his collar, and studied his nametape, saying, "I'll be speaking with your commander about this, Specialist Harper. Running around in a sloppy uniform with the High General here, I've never seen anything like it."

Tristan escaped, unsettled. He stopped in an alcove between two buildings and watched a few soldiers go by, then tried to imitate every last detail of their uniforms. At last he stepped back out to march his way to the center of the compound. Surely if anything interesting was happening, it would be there.

And indeed, there in the middle of everything was a building surrounded by High Guards, all wearing grim expressions. Had any group of Guards ever seen more action than these? Sean Ellis seemed to be an unpopular man.

Tristan found a gap in the patrols, made possible by two Guards deep in conversation over Kardell's odds of recovery.

"Even if she lives, she was torn to shreds. How will she ever fight again at all?"

The other, a man with a hard-lined face, said, "It's a shame, it really is. She was born to do it. Made it look easy." The man sighed. "We all know that it could happen to us, but I didn't think it would happen to *her.*"

"Of course, Ellis did throw her out there. He could have given the order to anybody," the other Guard muttered.

There was a dry laugh. "We were all relieved not to be the best right that minute."

Tristan didn't tarry any longer. He crawled across the rooftop of the cinderblock building, listening for voices drifting out of windows. Eventually he caught the clipped tones of Sean Ellis.

The High General almost always demanded that his office have a window. Tristan wasn't supposed to know things like that (after all, Ellis was a client, not a target) but he liked to know things he wasn't supposed to. Just in case.

What had happened to Cameron was going to stir up trouble. Tristan wasn't sure yet what form it might take, but when it came, he would be ready.

Tristan rolled onto his back, tucked his hands under his head, and looked up at the stars.

So many more in the black night skies than in Advon. Then he concentrated, filtering out all the ambient noise around him, narrowing his world down to only the conversation in the room below him. It was one of his better skills, lifting out all the unnecessary sounds, but he didn't do it often. It left him vulnerable. But if they had a leader, it was Cameron, so he was willing to take the risk if it meant understanding why this had happened to her.

In the room below, a telephone slammed down. Sean Ellis sighed. Then another man spoke. "I did tell you, the government of Varcove had nothing to do with the attacks on you. This has always been about that boy you killed."

Master Reese. Few besides the weapon master dared speak to the High General that way.

"Except Fold convinced a quarter of Cotarion to secede! All this, for one man." The High General's voice was muffled, as if he had his face buried in his hands.

"There are few things a parent wouldn't do for his child, and we are talking about a man with power and resources."

Sean Ellis was quiet for a moment, but when he spoke his voice was taut with restrained rage. "She is not your daughter, old man."

"She is my pupil, and you meant for her to die today."

A chair moved back. Feet paced. "I did. I saw it all unfold, and I knew it was the moment I'd been waiting for. You were there to see it, which was even better. I regretted giving her the order as soon as she disappeared over the bank." The pacing stopped.

"All this because I stopped teaching you? Really, Sean, even you are better than that."

A snort of contempt. "The fact that you still think you can choose someone, and then cast them aside without consequence demonstrates just how blind you are." The pacing resumed.

"So now what will you do? Now that you don't want her dead?"

"Nothing that I'm going to share with you."

"What you plan has been tried before, you know," Reese said.

"I'm willing to wager my life that no one like her has ever given it a shot."

"You overrate her importance."

"I saw your face when you thought she was dying, old man."

Master Reese made a sound. Tristan imagined the two men standing across from each other, staring with venom. "So, it seems this is where we officially part ways."

"No, Reese, that happened a long time ago."

The door in the room below opened. One set of footsteps went out, and two entered. The High Guards had returned. The High General said, "It's time I get some rest."

Tristan listened to him organize his desk before leaving.

So, Sean Ellis had hoped Cameron would die in the fight, but seemed to have changed his mind about her fate. And Master Reese was angry about it all.

As the High Guards left in the wake of the High General, Tristan decided where to go next. He dropped down from the roof and slipped through shadows in search of Master Reese.

The weapon master had gone to see if he could speak with Cameron. Tristan arrived just in time to hear an administrator tell Reese that no one was to see Sentinel Kardell without the High General's permission, which he didn't have. Master Reese turned away without argument, but with a stony expression. Then his eyes flicked to where Tristan peeked around the turn of the hallway. Tristan strolled out as if he'd been summoned.

"Walk with me, Specialist Harper."

Tristan, always grateful for orders, fell into step beside Reese. The weapon's master glanced over the uniform, one corner of his mouth turned up. He waited until they were out of the building before he said, "So, I see you still follow Cameron. That uniform does not suit you, by the way."

"It's not the uniform, so much as the rules that come along with it."

Master Reese continued to smile. "I have a request for you."

"I don't do anything for free, you know."

Reese nodded. "What is your price for delivering a message to Sentinel Kardell?"

"Answers to some nagging questions."

"One question."

A firm answer, but Tristan had to try. "Three."

"One."

Tristan scowled. "Three, and permission to pass on any question you don't like. So long as you answer one in three."

"Two, then, same conditions."

They exchanged a handshake. Master Reese said, "When Cameron wakes up, tell her that I will always answer if she calls me for help."

"That all?"

The weapon master frowned. "I doubt she will listen to even that. So, what is it you want to know?"

Oh, so many, many things. Tristan wasn't the smartest, he knew that, but he also had an instinct for when someone knew a great deal more than they'd told. Reese reeked of secrets. The tricky part was having even the remotest idea which blanks were the most important to fill in. The right answer could lead to many more.

"What does Sean Ellis want Cameron to do?"

Reese should have shown some surprise that Tristan had overheard his conversation, but either he'd expected an eavesdropper, or didn't care. "He is hoping she will fight an entirely different sort of war on his behalf."

Tristan waited for more, but that was all Master Reese wanted to say on the subject. Stupid.

"Who is it Sean Ellis wants her to fight?"

Master Reese shook his head. "I've said all I intend to say on that subject."

Tristan refrained from growling, though he felt like it. "You know a lot more than you're saying. Kardell might not get into so much trouble if you told her more."

Reese curled his hands into fists for a moment before letting them go. "You have no idea what you are talking about, young man."

Ah, weakness there. "Who made us Altered? I know Doctor Maikon is part of it, but she's not at the top."

"Then you know more than I do. I have no idea who began this. But I have known Sean Ellis for a long time. If Cameron is your friend, if you feel anything at all for her, then you'll find a way to warn her. You'll make sure that she listens." The timbre of his voice rose as he spoke, his pulse quickening. Either he was a good liar, or didn't know anything about their creators. Tristan had met no one who could fool him. Reese certainly believed Cameron was in danger.

"Why is Cami so important in all of this?"

They were nearing the gate of the compound. It appeared Master Reese meant to leave quickly after the High General's dismissal. He halted, forcing Tristan to stop and face him. The sky was brightening, but it was mostly by the electric lights on the sides of buildings that Tristan saw Master Reese smile. He did indeed have the look of a proud parent as he said, "Cameron Kardell is at a critical point where she's choosing allies and the path her life will take. Soon all her potential is going to become something very real. Sean Ellis knows this. But he's not the only one."

Tristan nodded, then smirked. "You know nothing anyone says is going to influence her in any way, right?"

The weapon master shrugged. "Erika could have done it. But now, I only hope that the people still around her can save her if she chooses the wrong way. You understand, she could work for good, as well as terrible harm. Yesterday, she took the lives of four people based off a glance from her leader."

Tristan shifted. "I'm not the right person to steer her."

"No, probably not." Reese looked troubled. "Well, thank you for delivering the message. Know that Cameron is not the only person who I'm willing to help."

He shook hands with Tristan again, his ice-blue eyes taking on that hard, searching look, just before he turned away and strode into the night.

It was later that day before Tristan saw Cameron again. He returned to her room with Melanie, only because of reports that her condition had improved since that morning. He hoped to take care of delivering the message from Reese as soon as possible.

There were indeed fewer machines around her, no more tubing shoved down her trachea. William had left to get some rest, but Doctor Finch was still there, looking weary as he told Melanie about the progress they'd made during the day. Tristan approached the side of the bed, his arms crossed.

A mask was still strapped over her nose and mouth. Each exhalation misted the interior. The rhythm of her breath suggested weariness, struggle. Tristan could not help remembering watching his older sister Beth die so many years ago. Her face had drained of color, too, all her vitality seeped away.

Compelled by those dark memories, Tristan took Cameron's hand. Her fingers were cool, her skin dry.

Her eyes snapped open, the skin around them drawing tight as she looked at him. He answered her suspicion with his most charming smile. It had the usual effect.

"Had to . . . be *you*," she said. The words came painfully, but her eyes were sharp and clear. She would be fine. His smile broadened as Finch and Mel leaned over her.

"I don't know that it *had* to be, but aren't you glad that it is? This face was practically *made* to welcome fair maidens back to the land of the living."

She actually smiled a little. Tristan squeezed her hand. She rolled her eyes over at Melanie and said, "Don't . . . let him kill . . . me in . . . my sleep." Mel was too thrilled that Cameron could speak to catch her words. She just nodded, her pale blond ponytail bouncing.

Cami closed her eyes again.

Tristan and Melanie played card games through the night on a table at Cameron's bedside. Tristan was kinder to her than he'd meant to be. She asked for details on how Niko was doing. Tristan was glad to tell her that the boy seemed to be improving since he'd implemented her advice.

Cameron woke intermittently through the night. Each time she was more alert and irritable than the last. By daybreak she was fully aware, sitting up in bed, and demanding that Melanie let her get up and walk. Mel refused once, pointing out that Cameron could barely lift a glass of water without her hand trembling. All further requests were simply ignored.

Their watch was relieved by William. He arrived looking worn, but brightened as soon as he saw Cameron was awake. In fact, he grinned in a soppy way that Tristan hadn't seen since his cousin was a teenager with a crush on some mysterious and unattainable girl. Cameron, by contrast, gave him a quick greeting before returning to her argument with Mel.

Tristan now watched Will closely, even as Finch came in. His cousin occupied himself looking at the displays on some of the machines monitoring Cameron's condition, stealing glances at the patient, always with an expression torn between vulnerability and terror. Tristan rolled his eyes. Unfortunately, no one noticed him do it.

"Well," Finch said, clipboard in hand. "You'll be happy to know, Sentinel Kardell, that we'll be moving you back to Advon today. I'll be working with you on making a complete recovery."

Cameron's focus turned to this newcomer. And yes, there were the narrowed eyes, the long silence. "Who are you?"

"Octavius Finch," he said, extending a hand to Cameron, which she shook. "A friend of Sean Ellis."

"When can I get out of bed?"

The man's white teeth flashed. "If you continue to improve at your current rate, a few days at most."

"Good," Cameron said, relaxing back. "I have a wedding I need to be at."

011

Cameron unfolded the newspaper, her stomach tight with apprehension. The banner at the top was as bad as she'd feared.

PEACE TALKS END WITHOUT RESOLUTION

High General Sean Ellis admitted in a press conference last night that no agreement has been struck with Varcove or our northern brethren. With no end to the war in sight, Cotarion must prepare itself for continued conflict.

She threw the paper aside, too disgusted to read more. If only she'd paid more attention, she might have seen some sign of the impending attack. But it had happened. Sean Ellis had lost his temper. Not that it mattered. The whole thing had been a ruse.

Had it been mere days ago?

A noise behind her made her jump halfway out of her seat at the table, before she realized it was Ethan. He looked sheepish as she stared at him, her heart racing. She tried to master herself as he stepped closer. Ever since she'd returned home, he'd looked half afraid of her. It hadn't improved her mood. The knots of pain in her leg and shoulder were aggravation enough without her boyfriend behaving as if she might break or attack at any moment.

He leaned around her to pick up the paper, but he read no further than she had before he put it back down. He rested a hand on her right shoulder and kissed her forehead.

"Everything will turn out," he said. His tone lacked conviction.

She glanced up at him. Tight lines marked his face, weariness his eyes. "You didn't sleep well last night."

Rather than answering, Ethan sat in the chair beside her. "You were having nightmares." He squeezed her hand. She braced herself for what she knew was coming next. Not that it ever stopped the words from feeling like blows. "Do you want to talk about it?"

She tried for a reassuring smile, but it faltered. Easier to leave her face blank. Why relive it? And talk about it with Ethan? No. This was her refuge, the one place she didn't have to think about Sean Ellis, or the lives she'd taken, or how close she'd come to losing her own. She wasn't going to speak of those things here at the little square table where they ate together every chance they got.

"No, I don't."

He bit the inside of his lip to stop himself from saying what he wanted to. He'd been doing this a lot since her return. She ignored it, though it chafed like ill-fitting boots. "What are you doing today?"

"Training."

"You mean you aren't satisfied with the bruises you got yesterday?"

"I might as well keep going, a few more and I'll have one on every body part." She hadn't suffered so many solid hits during sparring since she was fifteen. She wasn't up to form.

Ethan kissed her knuckles. The muscles in her shoulder spasmed. Was it only days ago? "Maybe, sweetheart, it's time to stop?"

"This is what I do. It's my life, Ethan."

"There's more than one kind of life, you know. Someone like you has options, you can make your own way, you don't have to answer to someone like Sean Ellis if you don't want to."

He was right. If there'd ever been a time to get out, it was now. The struggle to overcome her injuries might exclude her from the High Guard, anyway. But she was certain, as much as she'd ever been, that staying close to Sean Ellis would get her the answers she needed.

"I'll think about it," she said. She knew what image he held in his mind. His band was more than just popular, they were getting plays on the radio, real money. Ethan had been able to cut back his hours at the printing shop. He wrote more songs, his confidence blossoming all the time. The chance of living like this opened before him. He wanted Cameron to be with him for more of it.

She stood, suppressing the wince as her thigh objected to the motion, and kissed him on the forehead.

"Have a good day," she said, "I'll be back this afternoon, I hope."

She didn't go directly to her destination. Instead, she strolled around Advon a while, hoping to work some of the tightness out of her leg before she had to face Tristan. It twinged with every step at first, but gradually her strides smoothed and lengthened, the slight limp dissipated.

Octavius Finch worked at the muscles torn by bullets, reassuring her that these things took time. She knew he'd worked on Sean Ellis's injuries for many years. But the pain in her shoulder hadn't budged at all. It might be time to resign herself to the idea that it might be permanently limited. With practice and experimentation, maybe she could work around it enough to fight again.

Eventually, she decided that her leg could get no better. She stopped by Three Sides coffee shop. It was, as ever, filled with a mix of scarlet uniforms, from formal to functional. Many eyes turned to her as she ordered coffee. How many had seen the full extent of her injuries? How much did they wonder, now that she was standing, walking?

She got her coffee and left.

As she walked up the hill to where Tristan lived, the buildings became in some cases sleeker, in others more ornate. Clean windows gleamed in the morning light. She passed a group of people in business suits.

"My firm is talking about moving everyone to the offices with windows, see if we can do without lights entirely. Hildegrad was in a state. He just got a corner office and he'll have to share it if they do that."

"The higher-ups at Adams are saying they want to move the factory out of Cotarion entirely."

"And just where are they going to go?" one older woman scoffed.

"East, I think. Young Adams' husband is from there, and they've been making contacts ever since Ellis came in; knew he'd make trouble."

Cameron passed them, and a moment later a hush fell over the group. In that silence came a whisper. "That was a High Guard."

"You sure?"

"Of course I'm sure!"

"What is wrong with all of you? I've never heard of anyone getting dragged off for talking about the High General. You know there's real trouble, if you see that."

Cameron pulled her jacket a little tighter as she neared an intersection where the cross-breezes battered. Had she only been gone days? Autumn seemed to have descended on her city in that time. Cameron clutched her coffee. Most of the well-dressed people on the sidewalks ignored her—the jacket Tristan had given her two years ago was fine enough to fit in here—but there were a few who glanced at her blade, and the scar on her face. A lot of these didn't seem to appreciate her presence.

It was not the first time she'd seen the citizens' annoyance with the High General's actions being reflected in their behavior towards Sentinels. High Guards in particular were barometers for the public's feelings.

The doorman at Tristan's apartment building smiled as he opened the door for her. He was apparently accustomed to unusual guests, because he'd never once glanced at her sword or tried to find out who she was, besides a guest of Mr. Rush. Did Tristan pay extra for his discretion, or was that merely one of the perks of living in such a place?

She skipped the stairs and took the elevator up to the top floor. When she stepped out, she saw a broad-shouldered man standing in front of Tristan's apartment. The door was open. In a deep voice that carried down the hall, the visitor said, "I'd like to have the information as soon as possible. I doubt I'll get a better time to use it."

Armel pulled the door shut, then, and his face paled as he saw Cameron. He rallied rapidly. By the time they met halfway between the elevator and the door he wore his usual grin.

"What are you doing here?" he asked.

"I could ask you the same thing," she said.

Armel's teeth flashed in the skylights. "You mean you can't figure it out? How very unlike you."

Cameron gave Armel her best glare, but he was unwavering. Anything that involved Tristan had to be treacherous. "You're getting married to my sister in two days. You'd better stay out of trouble between now and then."

"That's pretty interesting advice coming from the person who keeps jumping between my uncle and flying bullets." The tension in his voice as he mentioned his uncle said everything. Armel still blamed Sean Ellis for his father's death. Cameron had told him to find evidence before he accused the High General, hadn't she? Had she expected him to forget?

Would William have pointed Armel Tristan's way?

Armel continued to the elevator. Cameron shivered. What would Ellis do if he found out what his nephew was doing, or worse, if he was confronted? Hopefully Armel and Tristan wouldn't turn up anything.

She knocked on Tristan's door. He swung it open right away, and stood there smirking, pretending to be impervious to the same hard stare she'd just used on Armel.

"Have I mentioned," he said, stepping back so she could enter his spacious, sleekly-furnished apartment, "that you look really, really nice in that jacket? Because you do."

Cameron tossed the garment over the coat hook by the door. With a sound of protest, Tristan took it down and draped it over the back of a chair.

"Why was Armel here?"

"Can't answer that," Tristan said. "Do you want some water?"

"So it was business."

Tristan's silvery eyes flashed. "Can't answer that, either."

Cameron straightened up to her full height. "Come on, Tris. He's my only friend, and if he's doing what I think he is—"

The assassin looked genuinely saddened. "He's not your only friend."

She tried to think of a response to this that was both kind and honest. She didn't like being caught off guard by anyone, but least of all Tristan.

He sighed. "Well, there is at least William, isn't there?"

Cameron shrugged. Witnessing her close brush with death appeared to have finally shifted the scientists' opinion of her, but she was waiting for it to swing back the other way at any moment. "Maybe," she said at last.

She heard a soft curse from the next room, where Tristan's apprentice Niko was moving the last pieces of furniture out of the way for their practice. Footsteps out in the hall heralded the arrival of Finch. She dropped the subject of Armel, for now.

Tristan decided that, considering Cameron hadn't landed a hit on him the day before, she should practice with Niko. So she found herself in his living room, beside banks of windows through which much of Advon was visible, staring at the thin, dark-complected boy. He flushed when she corrected his grip on the training sword, muttering that assassins didn't often use a blade longer than a few inches.

"If you're going to work with a weapon, you should know how to hold it. Give me another excuse and I won't work with you."

Tristan, who had perched on some exposed scaffolding to watch, called down, "That's not harsh at all."

Cameron looked up, her eyes narrow. "He's training to steal things and kill people. That's not a game, whatever you think. If my methods are harsh, it's because I like him enough to prepare him." She looked back to Niko, who stood a little taller. He released and rewrapped his hands in the grip she'd shown him. Cameron made a few more corrections to his stance, which prompted Tris to drop, cat-like, to the ground so he could see better.

"I've been doing that wrong," Tristan said, frowning. "You didn't correct *me*."

Cameron shrugged. "I assumed it was a conscious choice."

She went to the opposite side of the room from Niko. Normally she would stand loose until her opponent moved, but for now she brought her sword up. She had to be competent with the simple things again before she could return to her own style.

She and Niko exchanged salutes. His was so messy she felt compelled to go across the room and walk him through it. When at last he'd completed the gesture, she went back to her position.

She let Niko attack first, and saw immediately that his reflexes and speed might match Tristan's, but his technique did not. At top form, she would have felt confident of winning. As it was, she didn't anticipate coming away with quite as many bruises today.

Cameron deflected a few sloppy blows. She ended the first round by sliding the edge of her training blade neatly up to Niko's wide open neck. "If there had been metal in my hands, that would have been the end for you," she said, her tone cool in spite of the vivid memory of slicing the edge of her blade through skin and tendon and bone. She held his eyes, hoped she was impressing on him the importance of this. "Don't lose your focus just because I blocked you. Your approach has to be fluid, responsive. You will not land every blow. Keep your weight forward. Again."

Niko's second round was worse than the first, but by the third he was focused. Cameron had a few close calls that tested the limits of her leg and shoulder. The fourth set she won easily, but it was on the fifth that she made the sweeping cut that sent pain lancing down her shoulder, through her arm. She failed to block Niko's strike at her ribs.

The boy apologized as she doubled over, her hands on her knees as she gasped for breath. She waved away his worried exclamations, even as Octavius Finch bent over her. The doctor's hands were clinical on the torn and re-knit flesh of her shoulder. He muttered, several seconds too late, "Excuse me, if you don't mind."

He poked and prodded while Cameron recovered her breath and fought down her frustration. Never before had she been physically limited in a way she couldn't work through. Never had she been gripped by cold fear that maybe the next ragged breath wouldn't come. And never had she woken in the middle of the night, weighed down by questions. Was she serving Cotarion, or was she a shield between a madman and the enemies he'd accumulated?

Was it a selfish need to know more that kept her in his service?

"Ah, there it is," Finch said at last. "There's a tendon here that's tight with scar tissue. Hmm." He was quiet for a moment, then said, "With time and some work it will get better. Or I can fix it now, but that's going to hurt."

"We'll do it now," Cameron said.

Finch sighed. "Of course. Damn Twenty-Fours. Mr. Rush, I'll need your assistance."

While Tristan swung down from his perch, Cameron said, "Are people of the same type really that much alike?"

The healer looked around for a good place to carry out the procedure. He asked Niko to drag a coffee table into the middle of the room before saying, "In some ways, yes. Certain personality traits are considered necessary to the use of the ability. My series, for example, tends to be practical and level-headed. There are variations depending on parentage and experience, so we aren't entirely without individual personality. Now, I need you to lie face-down on the table, with your left shoulder right at the edge."

Cameron did as he instructed. She pressed her cheek into the smooth, dark wood of the coffee table. Finch's face said trouble ahead.

"Mr. Rush, I need you to help keep her still."

Tristan stepped very lightly onto the table. He sat on the back of her thighs with his knees to either side of her hips, his hands splayed across her shoulders. She'd expected some lascivious comments from him, but he refrained.

Finch gripped her upper arm in one hand, her elbow in the other. The healer put his foot up on the edge of the table. Tristan's fingertips pressed harder. Cameron took a deep breath.

Finch yanked her arm hard. The same pain that had nearly made her drop her sword shot down her arm again. She gritted her teeth as the healer pulled back harder, twisted, and changed the angle. She looked up at his face, hoping for a clue of how long this might last. His eyes were closed. The expression on his face was familiar. William looked like that when he focused on the energy signatures only he could see.

The pain intensified, then shifted from the sparking of objecting nerves to the hot, concentrated fire she'd felt as the bullet struck. She couldn't help recoiling from the sensation, couldn't stop the flash of memory that accompanied it. She heard a small whimper, and wasn't sure if the sound had issued from her or from Tristan.

She took several gasping breaths. She knew she was struggling too hard against the pain and the memory of pain, that she couldn't hope to conquer. It was like trying to swim against a mighty current. Fighting would only lead to exhaustion.

Her next breath was deeper, smoother. The fire in her shoulder lessened slightly as the muscles in her arm relaxed. It still hurt, almost as much as it had when she'd been shot, but each even inhalation made it more bearable. Yet the intense concentration required was wavering.

Then Finch released her arm. The pain cooled. Tristan stood and leapt down off the table, freeing Cameron to sit. She wiped a sheen of sweat from her forehead with a shaking hand.

"You just had to do it the hard way," Finch said. "Go ahead, give it a try."

Cameron lifted her arm, rotated it, then got carefully off the coffee table. Her legs wobbled, an aftereffect of Finch's work she'd become familiar with over the last couple of days. She picked up her sword and ran through some practice drills. Her shoulder worked on each sweep, every part of the joint and muscle and tendon operating as it should from the start of each blow to the end. She went faster through the sequence again. Though she was worn by the end, she was sure that her shoulder was sound.

She sat down on the coffee table. Octavius said, "Well, I can see why Sean was so jealous of you."

"Hah!" Cameron said, but when she looked at Finch she realized he wasn't joking. "He's High General of Cotarion."

Finch rolled his eyes. "Sean wouldn't have gone for his current position if he hadn't failed so spectacularly at controlling his Alteration."

Cameron tried to keep her voice neutral and her question slow, but it was difficult when Octavius seemed so willing to talk. "It's unusual then, what I did?"

"You successfully completed two people's Alterations without harming them, without even knowing what you were doing. I don't think there's ever been a Twenty-Four who's done that."

Tristan handed Cameron a glass of water, then stepped back. She noticed that Niko had vanished entirely. She suspected that Tristan hoped Finch would keep talking if the two assassins stayed out of the way.

"Erika ended up dead, though," Cameron pointed out.

Finch settled into his chair, his stormy gray eyes glinting. "There's a reason Readers are completed under controlled conditions. It's not an easy process to cope with even under the best of circumstances. It takes time to build up the mental defenses necessary to tune out all the chatter." He canted his head to one side as if puzzled. "It's strange The Maker never stepped in. And usually a set is destroyed when things get so out of hand."

"Destroyed? You mean—"

Finch drew his finger across his neck in a swift motion, a mimed decapitation.

Cameron tightened her grip on her glass. "Why are the sets so important?"

Finch lifted his shoulders. "The Maker believes that when a set is complete, there's stability. The loss of even one leads to catastrophic imbalance that makes the entire set dangerous. That's the theory, anyway. Personally, I think it's just chaos no matter how you do it."

"We're still alive, though. And so are you, and it sounds like your group wasn't successful. Whatever that means."

Octavius nodded, a sardonic smile tugging his lips. "Trust me, The Maker tried to kill us, but Sean put himself into positions that made it nearly impossible. I was smart enough to stay close to him. The rest of our set wasn't so lucky. As for your group, well, you must have something The Maker's waited for too long to throw you all away." Finch looked at her closely, his head to one side again.

"You aren't going to tell me who it is, are you?" All of his teeth flashed as he shook his head. "Why not, if this person is already after you?"

"You know Sean pretty well. I am neither crazy nor stupid. Consider that I allied myself with him to stay safe from The Maker." His eyes went distant. "My sister was the Twenty-Two in our set. We hid together for a while. She made sure to scream before she died so I had time to get away. I ran to Sean, even though his plan of living in the open seemed crazy. It was better than waiting to be found. And it's worked. But if I make too much trouble—"

"Why, though? What's the point of all this?"

"Hell if I know. When you meet The Maker, you should ask. *You* might get an answer." Octavius seemed to realize that he'd said more than he intended. "Well, I'd better report to Sean on your progress. No more practice today, and no more than an hour tomorrow. The wedding is the day after, correct?"

Cameron swallowed. "Yes."

"Maybe we can get the leg worked out on Monday. Then after that we'll focus on fine-tuning. You'll be back by Sean's side before you know it, which I'm sure is your sole ambition in life." He favored her with an arched eyebrow. She felt it necessary to smile in return. This, for some reason, made him laugh as he left. "Twenty-Fours!" Then the door closed.

Tristan reappeared from whatever corner he'd been lurking in during this exchange. "Nice to finally meet one who likes to talk, isn't it?"

"If only he'd tell us who this mysterious Maker person is. Even Sean Ellis is so scared of them that he avoids gender pronouns." The idea of someone who had the High General terrified was disconcerting, particularly in light of the fact that their set was already a member short.

Building the sets must require significant planning. It seemed that they had all been placed so that their paths would cross. Tristan, Erika, and William were family, Erika and Cameron peers, Tristan and Melanie lovers. Sean Ellis had been gathering them closer to him before Erika died, which still didn't make much sense to Cameron if he wasn't The Maker.

Master Reese was a candidate. He'd known about the Alterations even before Erika went to him for help. And Melanie had lived right under his nose all her life. Yet Cameron knew he was observant, well-travelled, and well-read. It was possible he'd cobbled together enough to learn what an Altered person looked like.

If he was The Maker, wouldn't he have said something by now? Wouldn't he have tried harder to save Erika?

Tristan cleared his throat, dragging Cameron up out of her thoughts. Her attention back on the assassin, she asked, "Have you found this other doctor yet?"

Niko was back, returning the living room furniture to its usual arrangement with the occasional thud accompanied by curses.

"Getting close."

"Have William or Melanie given you anything recently?" As Tristan shook his head, Cameron decided. "We've all been operating in the dark for too long. I think that after you've tracked down this other doctor, we should have a meeting, and see what we can come up with together." She might not consider Tristan or Melanie trustworthy, and even William had stood in opposition to her at times, but they didn't know who their enemies might be. When they'd worked together two years before, they'd accomplished what Cameron had not been able to do by herself.

She exchanged her practice blade for her father's sword, then Tristan cleared his throat. "Before you go, Cami, I have a favor to ask."

"Okay." He leaned closer, his shoulders hunched before he continued.

"Someone's been spying on me using my own surveillance equipment. I'd like you to take a look, and tell me what you think."

Cameron nodded. Tristan led her out of the living area, down a hallway and into a room that looked like it had once been a large closet, but now housed a desk, above which monitors glowed. Cameron stared at the ones currently running video, most of which showed images from inside people's homes. She averted her eyes. Tristan tapped a few buttons and the images vanished. The assassin at least had the good sense to look embarrassed at his intrusion on other peoples' private lives. A few more taps lit up a different set of screens, all of which displayed paused images of the inside and outside of Tristan's apartment. Cameron noticed that the dates and times on all of them were for an evening eight months ago.

"This is the first video with an obvious glitch. I don't suspect Niko, he wasn't assigned to me yet." Tristan hit a button, and the time stamps moved forward, faster than normal. Seconds blurred. Cameron watched for a few minutes, seeing nothing. Then she drew in a sharp breath.

"Stop, take it back."

Tristan rolled the tape backwards, then played it again at normal speed.

One of the cameras showed the hall outside Tristan's door, and another was on the door from inside the apartment. The video from inside showed a shadow pass the front door, as if someone had walked down the hallway outside, but the hall remained empty.

"Someone patched in video from two different times," Cameron said.

"That's what I thought, too," Tristan said, stopping the video again. "There are a few more discrepancies like this. The time stamps are perfectly replicated on all of them. It's good work, the best I've ever seen. And whoever did it has left no physical evidence." Cameron saw genuine worry in his silvery eyes. "I don't even know how this is possible."

Cameron folded her arms, and considered. "Do you think Melanie could have done this?"

The suggestion was met with the reaction she'd expected. Tristan smirked and said, "Be serious, Cam. Do you really think Mel could sneak around my apartment without me noticing? Besides, this didn't start until months after she moved out."

Cameron persisted. "We don't know that much about her. I wouldn't be too quick to rule her out."

Tristan considered for a minute, then shook his head. "I mean, I love her, but she's not exactly much of a plotter, or even a deep thinker for that matter. I just don't see it. Besides, why would she? And where would she have gotten all the necessary tech?"

Cameron looked over at him. She wondered how much time he'd spent practicing that pathetic, beseeching expression.

She said, "I think we must be getting close to who did this. That lab, the historical archive, had advanced tech that could probably do something like this. When we find The Maker, we'll find out who did this, too. I assume you disconnected your cameras for now?"

He rolled his eyes. "Of course. Not that being blinded is much better."

"Whoever did it will start to get frustrated, and this might draw them out sooner." She cuffed him on the shoulder. This time he let her leave. "Keep working on your form, Niko," she called before she shut the door behind her.

As she walked home, she wondered if she called Master Reese and asked him outright whether he was The Maker, what her odds were of getting an honest answer. The more she turned it over, the less likely it seemed. Erika had been one of his prized pupils, as much, perhaps more, than Cameron. If he had possessed the knowledge to save her or help her in any way, he would have.

Ethan was there when she returned to their apartment, sitting on the floor of the living room surrounded by hand-written sheet music. His guitar was settled into the padded corner of the couch, cradled by pillows.

She sat next to him. She looped her arm through his, rested her head on his shoulder, and closed her eyes. He wrapped an arm around her to draw her nearer.

"Oh sweetheart," he whispered into the top of her head. "I wish you didn't have to go through all of this."

The corner of her mouth pulled tight, her forehead furrowed. "I'm alive, Ethan, when I could easily have died. This is really not so bad." She raised her head, and he kissed her, but she was sure he only did so he didn't have to say anything.

012

THE HIGH GENERAL was in full roar, and William realized he'd never really heard Sean Ellis angry before. Even High Guard Brecht winced, but snapped when the brand new High Guard at the other side of the door shifted his position. William imagined that the Guard was probably in some turmoil after the loss of Lin and Cameron.

Apparently thinking in the same vein, Brecht asked in a low voice, "Seen Kardell recently?"

Will nodded. "Just last night, she was at the rehearsal."

"Oh yeah, Armie is getting married today. I joined the High Guard when he was fifteen. Now *he* can yell when he's mad. Is K feeling all right?"

"As far as I know. It's sort of hard to tell, isn't it?" She'd laughed with Armel and Owena, but there'd also been times when she'd shrunk back out of the way, silent, her eyes dark. He'd noticed the limp as the evening wore on, and she'd left early enough to disappoint Armel. William had been the one who'd finally sent the groom home, with a firm reminder that the wedding would happen the next afternoon, no matter how tired or hungover Armel might be.

Brecht grinned. "Damn, she's got you scared, doesn't she?"

William was saved the task of responding when the door opened, and a blank-faced general hurried out. Sean Ellis was behind him, his face still flushed. The High General gestured William into the office. The scientist gathered his courage and went in. The door snapped shut.

William's orb from the desert sat on the High General's desk, cradled in what looked like a thick copper ring engraved with geometric symbols. He'd forgotten about the thing so thoroughly that the sight of it brought his mind to a standstill for a moment.

"I did not forget. It took a couple of days to acquire the necessary supplies. Some of the information isn't accessible this way, but . . . sit, Young Harfield."

William moved into the chair across from the High General, who appeared both smug and apprehensive. William put his bag down on the floor. Between the High General's hands lay another copper ring, or rather two copper rings stacked on top of one another, both of them much smaller than the one holding the orb. Wires wove back and forth between the large ring and the small rings. The whole setup looked finicky, delicate, and improbable.

"Watch," the High General said.

He reached out to the smaller rings. When he rotated the top one, marks on both rings glinted in the light, aligned in brief flashes like bursts of lightning.

Light coalesced into a hazy shape above the rings. Ellis kept twisting. The shape cleared, softened, and cleared again. A ghost city hovered above the desk between them, but it was not like any city William had ever seen. The tall buildings rose up like narrow, twisting blades of grass. Clouds moved in the windows' reflections. Miniscule figures walked along the streets. It could not be real. And yet, the details were too perfect. Birds smaller than gnats fluttered up from a street corner. Tiny doors opened.

A small but very clear voice spoke, the sound seeming to vibrate up out of the rings. It made William's teeth ache.

"The Skylark Program suffered its greatest setback after the fall of Orion, when the International Coalition determined that the Altered were beyond the control of their makers."

A ripple ran through the image. One of the towers shuddered. William saw that the streets around it rocked like the ocean in a storm. He remembered sending energy through fissures in the earth and bringing down the walls of a canyon. His breath stalled in his throat. He willed the building to stop swaying. People in the streets ran. Figures poured out of the swaying building. They stumbled over deepening cracks in the sidewalk.

Then the tower swayed too far. It torqued and twisted. Parts of the structure popped, throwing glass, jabbing metal struts out into the sky.

William watched the tower fall, as gently as grass bending in the wind. Then as tensions within snapped, it crumbled.

The image jumped, and became a wasteland of broken pieces. It looked like a pile of plates shattered on a kitchen floor, except William still saw the outlines of some of the tower walls that had, a moment before, been whole. No more streets for people to run down.

"The Skylark Program was ordered to shut down. Elmond and Lang had prepared for the possibility, and established a network of laboratories and repositories which allowed them to carry on the project in secret. They began intense work on a new series that they hoped would end the Geno Wars."

William looked up at the High General through the smoke and dust rising over the image of the ruined city. Ellis's eyes were bright.

"What is all this? Did this really happen?"

"As far as I can tell, yes. This is our history. This is where the Altered came from." He spun the copper rings, and the ruins vanished.

"That city. How many people died?"

"More than live in all of Cotarion right now, even factoring in the secessionists."

William swallowed. "Why are you showing me this?"

"There are reports of a band of soldiers coming down from the north. Sporadic sightings, not enough to be in the papers, but word reaches me. Fold is still coming for me. And if the worst should happen, I don't mean to leave this world without ensuring certain people pay."

"I don't understand."

The High General bared his teeth. "I am giving you information, Harfield, because if I die, I hope that you and Kardell and the rest of your sorry set will have the courage and the knowledge to end the Skylark Program and all the people who have taken part in making us into monsters. The people who took away our choices."

He picked up the orb, the rings, the wire, and put it into a box. "This will be delivered to your home office, Doctor Harfield. Make good use of it. Everything you see will be enough. Now, go enjoy my cousin's wedding."

William left, and felt the set of knots he always associated with the High General's office unwind. Brecht whispered as he went by, "Tell Armel I said congratulations." William nodded.

He was soon out in the open air again, strolling from the High General's Residence to the building Owena had chosen as the wedding venue. It was a 200-year-old manor on the eastern side of the Arts Block, surrounded by a garden which was currently bright with autumn foliage. The inside was airy, with curved Remnant glass for skylights, and an extraordinary number of benches along the walls. Today the décor was heightened by frothy floral arrangements in white, ivory, and blush.

William bounded up a flight of carpeted stairs to the second floor, where he found Armel avoiding his preparations with a few friends. They sat around a table, playing Rocks and Rivers, a small pile of money in the middle of the table. They all greeted William and invited him to join, but he declined. Card games had been far too serious in his family.

Flowers for pinning to lapels burdened another table, as well as a tray of cheese and fruit. William, who hadn't eaten since breakfast, made amends to the neglected spread at once. Then, plate in hand, he pulled up a seat at Armel's side.

The broad-shouldered man glanced at William. "I knew we could count on you to eat. Owena's parents put it together, and none of these uncultured fools would touch it." A chuckle went around the table. Armel dropped his game pieces on the table and said, "Well, my friends, I better start getting ready. Gordon, I'm counting on you to keep Leo on schedule. Drink lots of water, Leonard, Owena will have my head if you faint during the ceremony." William saw that Leo the groomsman did indeed look like he'd had too much to drink the night before, and was suffering for it now. "Come on, Will."

William followed Armel to the adjoining room, where all the suits hung in garment bags on a rack. Armel sighed as he threw himself into a squishy chair. "They're good guys, and Palmroy is as reliable as they come, but if I had to go another round of that game, I think I'd have punched one of them. So, how's my uncle?"

"About as well as could be expected, under the circumstances," William answered in as neutral a tone as possible.

This seemed to cheer Armel. "Hah, good. It's about time he suffered."

A knock at the door cleared away Armel's glee. Owena's father entered. As always he carried with him an aura of calm which seemed to radiate out from him like light from a lamp. He was already dressed, in ivory shirt and gray jacket. He smiled at his future son-in-law, and said, "My daughter is convinced that if the groom isn't dressed soon, then all hope of running on time is lost. I told her that you didn't need so much time, but she insisted it would be best if everything was ready early."

"So we've been defeated at last. We'll be dressed right away."

Mr. Kardell nodded, then settled his gaze on William. "I heard that you're at least partly responsible for saving Cam's life." He stretched out a hand, which William took while his face got hot. "I can't possibly thank you enough for getting her home safely. No, no objections. Now, I'll leave you to your extensive preparations."

William was straightening his tie before the back of his neck had cooled.

By then, Armel stood resplendent in his scarlet jacket, though he seemed to be having some difficulty with his tie. He squinted at William's, and. "What the hell kind of knot is that?"

"Ah, it's a Torema, I think the one you're doing is too small a knot for a tie like this." Armel looked at him, one eyebrow lifted as if Will spoke a foreign language. "My father has an encyclopedic knowledge of tie knots. I can show you a Mills if you like."

After a few false starts, Armel managed his tie and was happy with the result. William was then tasked with knotting Leo's and Oliver's ties, although Sentinel Gordon Palmroy, whom William sensed was competent at just about everything, did his own without trouble. Owena's cousin Oliver declared the final result, "Bad." When William looked disappointed, Oliver assured him that "bad" in this case meant "extremely good."

Even with the extra time spent on the ties, and then making sure all the medals and pins on the Sentinel uniforms were straight, they still only spent twenty minutes getting ready. Then they all stood around smoothing jackets, afraid to sit.

William spent the next forty-five minutes spinning his cufflinks and speaking reassurances to Armel, who looked nervous now that he was dressed. It was then, in the absence of instruction and unable to stand around waiting anymore, that they wandered out into the hall. They had drifted all the way downstairs and stood in the entryway when they heard a clamor. It sounded as though many people had begun shouting all at once. A door slammed, followed by hurried footsteps. A tall woman with pale blond hair ran past the staircase. Seren Kardell, Cameron and Owena's mother. Armel went to the bottom of the staircase and said, "We're here, Mrs. Kardell!"

The footsteps returned, even as the voices above dropped away, until just one was left shouting above all the others. Seren stopped at the top of the stairs and said, "Armel, I think you should come up—"

Owena's voice cried out, even as Armel started up the stairs, "Mom, no! He can't see me until the ceremony!"

Seren rolled her eyes, then hurried down the stairs and straight to William. In a low voice she said, "Come with me, Doctor Harfield. We need a neutral party just now." Before he could ask what was happening, she had gripped him by the arm and was pulling him up the stairs.

The scene in the bride's room was difficult to make sense of at first. For one thing, there were clothes and little bottles and jars of makeup strewn over every surface. For another, five young women seemed to be making a lot more noise and taking up a lot more space than seemed possible.

Cameron, at least, was easy enough to spot. She stood well out of the way, her arms crossed, her expression drawn, her eyes hard on two of the bridesmaids, one of whom was yelling at her. The other was bent over, her hands cupped around her face, blood dripping from between her fingers. Her raging companion took a hiatus from the torrent of abuse flung at Cameron to peel away her hands, revealing that the source of blood was her nose.

Another bridesmaid knelt in front of Owena, scrubbing red spots out of her gown with soda water. Even distressed and splashed with blood, Owena looked the loveliest she ever had. Seren elbowed William in the ribs, to which he whispered, "What am I supposed to do?"

"Get Cam out of here, Owena will get the rest settled down."

That seemed simple enough. "Kardell, Armel would like to talk to you," he called across the room. Cameron separated from the wall, passing right by the young woman trying to stop her bleeding nose and her friend, who was still glaring.

Once they had gained the hall with the door was shut behind them, Cameron walked away, to a window at the end of the corridor.

Was cheering up the Maid of Honor part of William's sworn duties? He followed her.

He stood next to her. They stared out the window at the shrubbery below for a few moments. Then he said, "So, um, what happened in there?"

The Sentinel sighed. It was odd to see her in makeup and a dress. Less odd to see her looking pensive.

"Dana came up behind me while I was helping Owena with her shoes. She says she was just trying to straighten the strap on my dress. I felt her touch my shoulder, and I elbowed her in the nose." Her dark eyes found his. "I didn't mean to hurt her. Everything is on edge right now. And she's trying to get into med school, and she's been suspicious all morning, kept saying how amazing it is I'm doing so well after the kinds of injuries I had. I'd bet decent money that she was trying to see under my bandage." Cam put a hand to her forehead.

"I shouldn't have hit her."

She'd never looked so weary, so low. He considered, then asked, "Are you all right?"

She shook her head. "Not really. I almost broke her nose. That should never, ever happen." It was a whole lot more than that, though, wasn't it? That day in Irion Valley was written all over her face.

The door behind them opened. Owena drifted out into the hallway, still rubbing at some of the spots on her dress. She came over to the window, and smiled enough for both herself and her sister.

"I had no idea Nikki was so good at getting stains out. Of course, I also didn't know Dana would be so jealous that I didn't make her the Maid of Honor. I'm really sorry, Cami, she's been a nightmare."

Owena hugged Cameron, and William saw the Sentinel's face take on that blank expression she wore when she didn't want anyone to know what she was thinking.

"It's okay, Owena."

"No, it's really not. I've had a stern talk with them, and they're going to be friendly. The only thing is, you might need to apologize to Dana, just to smooth things over." Owena said this last part as quickly and quietly as possible, as if hoping the words would slip straight through Cameron's brain to her subconscious.

Kardell nodded. "I can't say no to my sister on her wedding day, can I?" She gave William an odd look, and then followed her sister back to the room where the rest of the bridesmaids were waiting, now quiet. The Sentinel set her shoulders before she went in, and William was reminded of the way she'd stood, cool and confident, when the High General asked her to defend him. Except, of course, today she was swathed in yards of delicate fabric, with her dark hair falling over one shoulder in glossy curls.

William realized that he probably should have told her how nice she looked. He filed it away as the door shut, for later.

Armel and the groomsmen still waited in the entryway. William's return was met with an onslaught of questions, and when at last it was quiet enough for him to speak, he said, "The Maid of Honor hit one of the bridesmaids in the nose. It seems Owena smoothed things over, and Nikki got the blood out of the dress—"

"Cameron hit one of the girls?" Instead of looking reassured, Armel's concern increased significantly. "Which one? Is Cam okay?"

The other groomsmen clearly thought it strange to ask if the attacker, rather than the victim, was all right. "It was Dana. And I think Cam is fine." Liar. But best for now to reassure the groom.

"Never liked Dana," Armel muttered. Then his face brightened. "Did Owena convince Cam to wear a dress?"

"Ah, yes."

"Hah! Cam owes me at least twenty—"

"Boys! The photographer needed you in the garden ten minutes ago!"

Someone William had never met herded them all outside, and they spent the next half hour standing where they were told and smiling until their faces hurt. The photographer seemed to have an excess of cheerful energy, which made them all nervous. They were then herded back inside and up a side stair to avoid any risk that Armel might glimpse Owena.

When they arrived back at their room, the clock informed them that the ceremony would begin in forty-five minutes. This seemed to come as a blow to Armel, who took his jacket off, sank into a chair, and put his head between his knees. Leo, whose condition had not improved after the half-hour in the garden, did the same.

"Gordon, go get a beer for Armel, and Henry, go see if you can find some tea for Leo," William ordered. To his great surprise, the other two men rushed away to fulfill his command. He leaned over Armel. "Is there anything else you need?"

There was a head shake. Then Armel's voice. "How did this happen?" Or at least, that's how William interpreted the rumble that came through Armel's crossed arms.

How could William answer a question like that?

"Well. You met Owena, and you though she was very pretty, and you went out with her. And you kept going out with her until you decided you liked her enough to marry her, and she liked you enough to agree it was a good idea. And, um, here we are."

Armel raised his head, his eyes wide, his skin a shade lighter than normal. "One person for the rest of your life. How do you do that? It seemed like a good idea, but now it just sounds crazy. What if we fight? Sometimes we already do!"

William rubbed the back of his neck. His own parents were separating after thirty years together. His cousin skipped from one woman to the next, or fell madly in love with women who wanted nothing to do with him. He himself hardly knew the scope of madness that seemed to take hold of people in love. He'd skirted the edges, perhaps, but hadn't learned what it was that made anyone decide they wished to be together for as long as they lived.

Nothing to do but dive in and hope for the best.

"Armel, you love Owena, and she loves you. Anyone can see that. And nobody knows what might happen tomorrow, but you're both making a promise to stick together, no matter what happens next. That's a really nice thing. You just go one day at a time—"

Armel stared at him, and then began to laugh. Even Leo looked up. It took a while for Armel to settle down, and when he did, looking a little fragile and wiping his eyes, "Oh, Will, you idiot. 'One day at a time'. That's what you say to people when someone dies!"

The groom was still laughing at William's horrified expression when Gordon returned with his arms full of beers. Armel didn't lapse back into his panic, though his nerves weren't entirely assuaged. Anytime he started to get dour, he would mutter to himself, "One day at a time." Then he chuckled and cheered up.

Ten minutes before the ceremony was to start, Armel polished off his second beer, and then plunged his hand into his pocket. He produced an small golden ring, which he handed to William. "My dad told me once that the original purpose of a Best Man was to marry the bride if the groom decided to take off, or died, or anything like that. That's why you hold onto the ring."

"I guess that gives the Best Man pretty good motivation to make sure the groom gets to the ceremony."

"Or perhaps it motivates the groom not to run off or die."

A few minutes later, Owena's father came to the door to lead them down to the atrium. Armel took on a look of nervous excitement. Leo just looked ashy. There was a quick straightening of coats and ties, and some smoothing of hair, then they filed out.

After that, everything happened very quickly. Violins took up a rhythmic song in the Atrium, and the groom with his retinue marched through a crowd of expectant-looking people to an archway at the front of a light-filled room. William shifted under the force of so many unwavering gazes. Fortunately the bridesmaids filed in soon after, and they stole all the attention. William noticed that Dana still looked very sour, and red around the eyes and nose. Armel laughed again when Cameron appeared at the top of the aisle. She smiled when she saw his amusement. She took up her station across from William, and her presence at the head of the aisle seemed to make Armel much more confident. A little girl, another cousin of Owena's, carried a basket of flower petals down the aisle, two of which she dropped, and they lay very lonely right at the front of the atrium.

The music changed, then, and Owena appeared in veil and gown. She and Armel were at once suffused with some energy that William could sense even if he didn't understand it. She made the trip down the aisle rather hastily.

The vows and the rings took very little time. William stared when he was asked for the one he carried, having not expected the request so soon. Cameron, of course, handed Armel's ring to Owena right away.

An enthusiastic kiss was exchanged, the guests laughed and cheered, and then it was over. William found himself smiling a little soppily as Kardell hooked her arm through his and led him back up the aisle.

Armel and Owena then stood together, brilliant, while guests filed by. The wedding party retreated to the background. Leo sat while Dana and the bridesmaid William didn't know fussed over how adorable Henry looked. Nikki attempted to flirt with Gordon, but gave it up when she found out he had a girlfriend. Cameron stood off to one side with Ethan. Before William could attach himself to any group of people, Nikki turned her attentions on him.

Her alarmingly overt advances were brought to an end by the photographer, who rushed them all back into the Atrium for the last few photos. When the bridal party was freed, Cameron caught William and pulled him off to the side.

"Is your toast written down? I'd like to see how long yours is." He handed over a much-creased piece of paper, the result of several hours of labor, in spite of the fact that he'd produced little more than a page. "Damn, this is really good, Harfield. Maybe I'll go first. You know Owena wants us to start the dancing, right?"

"Um. Well, I guess I do now?"

"I'm about as enthused as you are," she said, handing back the paper. She cast a glance at Nikki, who was taking a long time to study a floral arrangement nearby. Cam grinned at William, then left with a whispered, "I'd say 'good luck,' but I don't think you need it."

When they were seated in the hall where the reception was to take place, and Nikki could no longer distract him, William kept unfolding his toast, reading it, and refolding it, trying to decide if he knew it well enough to recite it by heart.

Armel, now in buoyant good humor, clapped a hand on William's shoulder. "Stop worrying about it, and you'll do fine. Trust me, if my dad could get up in front of the whole country and speak, you can talk to this room." Then he turned back to his bride.

Cameron went first. She stood, glanced once at the guests, then read dutifully from her notes. When she handed the microphone to William while the guests applauded, she whispered, "I warmed them up for you."

William did manage his toast without any notes. People laughed at the parts he'd meant to be funny. A few even dabbed their eyes at the end. After they'd raised glasses, Armel enveloped William in a hug, saying, "I knew you had it in you!"

The rest of the evening passed in a haze. The dinner was superb, and everyone at the head table was in a cheerful mood now that all the preparations and ceremony were complete. The champagne was an excellent vintage. William soon found himself deep in conversation with Gordon Palmroy about the changing responsibilities of Sentinels in a time of war. As they turned to public opinion on the High General's actions, William felt someone tap his shoulder. Cameron stood over him. "We're on duty again, Harfield."

She exchanged jests with Gordon while William stood, then she took him by the elbow while Armel and Owena started their dance. The lights had dimmed. The bride and groom wheeled around, impossibly happy and elegant. Cameron glanced at William. She whispered, "Harfield, if I'm not mistaken, you're a romantic."

"I don't see how you can watch them together and be unmoved. This moment is good. What else matters?" Perhaps he'd had one glass of champagne too many.

Cameron didn't say anything, but he saw her looking over at Ethan, who sat at a table nearby. Even in the dim light he made out her expression of sorrow.

Oh.

As Armel and Owena's dance ended, he took her arm in his own. She walked out into the spotlight with him. He said, as he put a hand on her waist, "Don't be sad, Cam. A lowcountry waltz is just ridiculous if you look sad while you're doing it."

She smiled. He squeezed her hand. The violins took up a bright and measured song. For about two minutes they danced. It was not the first time they'd done this. William found it much easier this time from the first step. Cameron was a good partner, in that she did not ask too much. She knew all the steps. She did not crowd him, nor keep him too distant. She maintained a light stream of conversation. They were going around in smooth circles, when she winced and her face paled. The next step she took clearly caused her pain.

William drew her a little closer. She whispered, "Sorry," as he took some of her weight. Just a couple more circuits of the floor before the song ended. Then the floor opened to everyone, giving Cameron and William cover to escape. He helped her to the head table, where she sank into her chair.

Both Ethan and Seren Kardell were by her side at once, Seren carrying a heating pack. Cameron could not hide her annoyance. She snapped at William as he hovered, "Harfield, get out of here, go dance."

He retreated, leaving the Sentinel to the overabundance of concern, which only grew as Armel and Owena arrived. He spotted Nikki's brilliant red hair, still at the bridesmaid end of the table. She smiled when she saw him approaching. "Your toast was really good! And you can dance!"

"Oh. Thank you," he responded. Paused. Considered. She looked at him. "Um. Would you like to dance?"

She grinned and grabbed his hand. Apparently there was nothing more to say in the matter.

It was much later when Nikki was finally ready for a break. She and William sat together at the head table, sipping cool champagne. She slipped off her shoes and wiggled her toes. Armel and Owena were still in the middle of the dance floor. They looked as if they might go on all night. Cameron and Ethan sat over at his table, close together, looking at least content. Kardell met his eyes. She lifted her glass. He returned the salute.

"Are you friends with Owena's sister?" Nikki asked.

William didn't pause for a second. "Yes, actually, I am."

013

Mist rose in curls over the streets of Advon as Tristan pulled up in front of his cousin's apartment. He found the spare key on top of the doorframe where William always left it, in spite of persistent warnings not to. Tristan let himself in. He smelled fresh-baked goods. Surely it was too early for William to be awake and cooking, particularly on a Sunday morning following a late night.

When he went into the kitchen, he found it was his aunt cooking, which made the tantalizing smells more warning than invitation. Tristan crept in behind her as quietly as possible, so that when she turned abruptly she shrieked and dropped her mixing bowl. Tristan caught it before it hit the ground. She whacked his shoulder.

"You scared me half to death! What in the world are you doing here, Tris? Oh, never mind. Come give me a hug."

She wrapped him up in the embrace that only mothers knew, and which he hadn't experienced in years. For just a moment he could imagine that he might be a decent person.

When she'd gone back to checking whatever was in the oven, Tristan said, "I'm here to see Will."

Teague now somehow managed to look both worried and satisfied. "He's still asleep. Or in bed at least. With a girl, I think."

Tristan nearly dropped the glass bowl still in his hands. "He what?" William had never made a move like that with a girl he didn't know, and Tristan could only think of one woman at the wedding who William knew well. "Did you see what she looked like?"

"Red hair, but that's all I know. I didn't introduce myself, just kept out of the way. I think he forgot I was staying here." She pulled a pan of lumpy mounds out of the oven, frowning when she saw how brown they were. "I was actually planning on getting out of here before they woke up, I just wanted to leave them something for breakfast. So, what did you want to tell Will?"

"Just that I'm going out of town for a few days. I was hoping he'd be able to pass it along to Sentinel Kardell, too."

His aunt's eyes went distant. "I hope you're staying out of trouble, Tris."

"Now, auntie, who would I be if I weren't in some kind of trouble?"

"I don't know what you boys are up to, but I know I don't like it. I've seen some of that stuff in Will's office, you know. And I haven't missed that this Sentinel Kardell you all keep talking about was involved in what happened to Erika."

Tristan cocked an eyebrow. "We're just looking for answers, that's all."

She sighed and reached up to ruffle Tristan's hair like she used to when he was small. She nodded. "I understand. You kids and your strange abilities, I'm sure there are so many questions. Be careful, though." She pulled a few muffin-things out of the pan and put them on a plate. They clanked like bricks. Then she handed one to Tristan, and nudged him to the door.

She walked with him out onto the sidewalk. As he unlocked his car, she said, "This Sentinel. Who is she?"

"She's like us, auntie. It's why she was involved in everything with Erika. She was trying to help." True enough, in its way.

Teague nodded. Tristan recognized in her eyes that look William had when pieces fell into place. But she kept it within. "Well, take care of yourself, Tris." After one last hug, she walked off into the city. Tristan swung into his car, and drove through the streets out of Advon, leaving curls of mist in his wake.

By midafternoon he reached the border crossing between Advon and Gestos to the east. The checkpoint stood at the entrance to a tunnel that cut through the Crescent Mountains. Tristan left his car for the inspection, during which a guard examined every part of his vehicle. He himself endured a pat down, although this was not entirely unpleasant. He flirted a little with the older woman inspecting him, carefully and with light humor.

The tunnel was long and the traffic flowed steadily in both directions, as the border crossings were few. The lights were not enough to keep the tunnel very bright, so Tristan drove with his lights on. The glow from the walls and the other vehicles flashed across his face rhythmically.

Eventually a pinpoint of daylight appeared ahead. It grew. A minute later the tunnel opened up onto a landscape unlike anything in Cotarion.

Mile after mile of grassland stretched out in every direction, impossibly flat beyond the foothills Tristan now descended. Cotarion looked like a sodden piece of paper by comparison. Pale brown feathers of grass met a pile of blue expanse, on into infinity.

Sheep and cattle grazed everywhere, interspersed with herds of horses. Even as the landscape flashed by, Tristan felt that he wasn't going anywhere at all.

After a couple of hours drifting through the unvarying fields, he exited the highway and turned down a smaller road. He couldn't read the sign, but the symbols were what he'd memorized. The next hour or so he turned onto ever narrowing roads, until at last he pulled up to what he could only describe as a diner. The metal plating on the outside was a little rusty. Tristan divested himself of his leather jacket.

He stomped up the steps in the work boots he'd worn that morning, knowing he would be in farmlands. He grunted at the waitress who greeted him with words he couldn't understand. His contact sat at a table positioned under an array of photos of prizewinning sheep. He sat across from the stout woman with a sun weathered face. Her gray hair was tightly curled, and there was dirt under her fingernails. She did not regard Tristan with anything resembling friendliness. He was just the lesser of two evils.

"You found the place," she grunted in Cotari.

"Yeah. I'm pretty good at finding stuff."

Her wrinkled face pinched together at his levity. A waiter stopped at the table. The woman gave him a brisk order. Ah. Rude to everyone, not just Tristan.

"I'm having lunch," she said. She waited for Tristan to object, but he kept his mouth shut. "After that, I'll take you where you want to go."

He sat across from the woman named Susan while she ate her way through a plate of cured beef and something that looked like flatbread. She never offered to order anything for him, and as he could not read the menu, he had little choice but to watch while his stomach rumbled. His aunt's muffin had been as inedible as it appeared.

At last Susan cleaned her plate. She drank a cup of something that neither looked nor smelled like coffee. She squinted at Tristan. He refrained from showing any of the impatience that he felt. Was she having second thoughts now that he was here?

Finally she made a sound halfway between grunt and sigh. "I know a place where you can put your car. You can't drive that thing up to the house."

"All right." Tristan stood as she did. He wanted to ask a thousand questions, but it wasn't worth risking attention by speaking in Cotari.

Outside, the gardener climbed up into a battered truck with a bed full of tools and sacks of—well, probably dirt. Tristan had to hurry to keep up when she pulled out with her tires spinning over the gravel in the parking lot.

His contact drove down the roads at dangerous speeds. His car bounced and jostled over rough patches as he fought to keep up. The most terrifying moments were when they encountered a vehicle coming the opposite direction, and neither party slowed nor moved to the side. Each time it was a surprise that Tristan's side mirror wasn't knocked off.

At last she jerked her truck into a crescent of packed dirt on the side of an especially lonely stretch of road. She did not move from her seat, so Tristan parked behind her and got out. When he climbed up next to her, moving aside piles of what appeared to be gardening magazines and catalogs, she huffed.

"How would I explain you up here with me? There's a guard at the gate. You have to ride in the truck bed."

Tristan arched an eyebrow. "They won't check the bed, but they'd be suspicious if I rode in with you?"

"I don't bring people onto the property. Ever. But they trust me, so they never check the truck."

Tristan frowned. "Never?"

Susan grumbled. "Look, boy, this is your only way in. You want to get to Maikon, it's gotta be in the back of the truck. Security everywhere else on the place is too tight."

This only increased Tristan's suspicions. There seemed little point in building a wall and installing security cameras if the gardener could drive in and out unchecked. She was missing something.

As Tristan considered this, she snapped, "Look, I'm not going to get you into any trouble if I can help it. You're my only chance at getting back home. This will work."

Well. Even if he did get caught, he could wriggle out of trouble. Crouching in the back of a truck just wasn't his usual style. "Fine."

He jumped down from the front seat and leapt into the back, where he found a tarp among the shovels, rakes, and bags of soil. He weighted down three of the corners with stones, then shuffled under the fourth corner. When he was satisfied his shape would be indistinguishable from the bags he shared spaced with, he weighed down the last corner with a fourth rock.

"The smell is never going to come out of this coat," he muttered, just before the truck jolted back onto the road.

Susan's driving was as uncomfortable as he had guessed from following her. The truck tires dove into every rut and pothole with reckless abandon. Tristan's head often banged into the hard plastic of the bed. The tarp flapped, and he had no escape from the frigid air streaming through. He unzipped his jacket and tucked his hands close to his chest to keep his fingers warm. He couldn't afford stiff hands if this shoddy plan fell apart.

After a long time, during which Tristan was much battered, the truck rolled onto smoother roads. A minute later it turned to the right, hard enough that one of the rocks rolled off the tarp. Tristan, sensing by a sudden decrease in speed that their destination was near, scrambled to replace the stone over the flapping corner. Seconds after he stopped moving, the truck halted. Tristan held his breath.

A man's voice to the left called what must have been a greeting. Sue grunted a response while the man's footsteps started to move around the truck. He walked slowly. Tristan remained as unmoving as the bags of fertilizer beside him. Waiting. The worst. But the guard went back to Sue's window. This time he spoke in thick, halting Cotari.

"Your mother. Sorry. The lady, she should let you go. Can do without gardener for a few days."

Susan responded, her voice still gruff, "It's a security risk for us to go back there. We knew how it would be when we took the jobs."

The guard spoke again, in a more business-like way. Then the truck jerked forward. Tristan slid a few inches against the grimy plastic before he got a good grip. He cursed under the sound of the shovels rattling. Hopefully, the guard had turned away.

At last, the truck stopped for good. Susan jumped down, her door slammed. "Okay, you can come out now."

Tristan threw off the tarp and emerged into a garage. It was dim, lit by a couple of high windows. Spiderwebs infested the corners by the ceiling. More gardening tools lined the walls.

Tristan jumped up on a shelf to peek out one of the dusty windows. He could see the landscaped grounds through the brown grime. Tall grass clumps with feathery seed-heads bobbed in the wind. A low, flat-roofed house sat, pretty damn far away. The little gardener's shed in which he stood would not be visible from much of the main house.

"Doc must've done good work to retire in a place like this."

Susan responded with her signature noncommittal grunt. Tristan considered his options. There wasn't any kind of cover between the garage and the house.

"So, besides the gate guard, Maikon only has one personal bodyguard?"

"And the cook. *She* lives in the house."

"Well. Not much for it but to give it a go." Tristan jumped down. After a quick check to ensure all his weapons were in place, he went out the door onto the grounds.

He crept from one clump of shrubs to the next. Halfway to the house he ran out of cover. He crouched behind a tall ornamental grass, which sighed each time the wind blew. He studied the windows for a long time. All was still. But cameras lurked in the architecture.

If anyone was monitoring the cameras, Tristan had already been seen. He picked a likely-looking window and sprinted across the lawn to the house. He spent longer than he liked getting the window open, but finally it swung out enough for him to slip inside.

He found himself in a small dining room. The round table could seat four. A casual space, probably near the kitchens. The floorboards out in the hall creaked. Tristan leapt out to intercept the person passing by.

The woman in the hall wore a neat black jacket. She carried a tray burdened with a tea pot and cups. Tristan's appearance in the hall did not seem to surprise her. Her lips, painted a fetching ruby color, turned up in a smirk. He smirked back, and cocked an eyebrow at the tray in her hands.

"It looks like I'm just in time for tea."

She moved then, flinging the entire tray in Tristan's face. The hall was too narrow for him to entirely avoid the scalding water, but he caught it on his arm. The iron teapot hit the wall, cracking the wood paneling.

Tristan crouched and lunged forward. His adversary now held a kitchen knife in one hand and the wood tray in her other, apparently as a shield. Tristan bit back a laugh.

He lunged, sliding two daggers from concealment as he did. His first sank into the tray with a delicious thud. He twisted the handle of his dagger, wrenching the makeshift shield out of the chef's hands. He tossed aside both dagger and tray.

The woman lunged, sweeping her knife at his face. She attacked without fear, and her form was good, but she wasn't fast. Tristan dodged her blow and pulled her arm, throwing her off balance. He twisted her wrist until the knife dropped from her fingers. She tried stomping on his foot, but he danced away, laughing.

"If you would tell me where the doctor is, I'll gladly get out of your hair."

The woman growled in response. Tristan sighed. He brought his dagger up to her throat. "I don't like to make threats, but I can come up with a few good ones if that's what you prefer."

The chef went stiff at the touch of the cold metal. "Down the hall and up the stairs on the left. You go after her, though, and Addler will kill you."

Tristan pushed the woman into the dining room. With a length of cord from his coat pocket, he tied her to one of the chairs before moving on. He scooped up iron tea kettle where it had rolled to the floor. Normally he didn't like a blunt weapon, but if any other denizens in this house were willing to fight like the cook, it might be the quickest way to end things without doing serious damage.

A dagger in one hand, the kettle heavy in the other, Tristan went up the stairs as indicated. He listened as he moved through the house, but heard nothing besides the prairie winds prying at the windows.

The ceilings in the upstairs hall were high, and skylights gave it the illusion of stretching even higher. Tristan should have heard sounds of human activity, but nothing reached him. Perhaps the thud of the pot had warned Doctor Maikon to his presence. He crept along faster, his dagger higher.

The first door on the right stood ajar. Tristan saw evidence the room beyond was an office through the crack. He heard the gentle rustle of fabric moving. This was the place.

Tristan kicked the door fully open and stepped into the room, pausing a moment to scan for threats. He saw no one besides a woman in her sixties who had pressed herself into a corner, her back against bookshelves. She twisted her silk scarf in her hands, but her narrow chin was lifted.

Tristan tucked his dagger out of sight. "Doctor Maikon?" She nodded. "My name is Tristan Rush. I understand that I'm trespassing, but I'm not here to hurt you. All I want is to ask a few questions."

She glanced at the tea pot in his hand. "You broke into my house. You—you hurt Arlene . . . "

Tristan allowed himself a small smile. "I just borrowed this, Arlene is fine. And you've hid yourself away so well I had no way of reaching you. I only did this because what I need to know is very important. You see, twenty-eight years ago you joined an experiment. And I, for better or worse, was one of your subjects."

This was the right thing to say. Doctor Maikon's hands stilled and her eyes lit up. She could not help smiling even as she said, "How did you find me? You were never supposed to know."

Tristan was listening for the guard, but his only warning of the approach was a flicker in the doctor's eyes. He spun, his dagger in his hand again, but this opponent was much more adept than the cook. Motion flashed in Tristan's vision before pain flared in his arm. It took a second for him to realize his dagger wasn't in his hand anymore.

A man, at least ten years older than him, stood in front of Doctor Maikon. He was broader than Tristan, with bulldog jowls and small eyes. Tristan's dagger spun in the man's hands. He almost had to be another Twenty-Two, to move so fast.

Never before had Tristan faced someone of equal skill. As a new dagger settled into his palm, he pushed aside strange feelings. Uncertainty.

The man dove at Tristan, who blocked the incoming stab with a jab from the teapot. The beady-eyed man danced to the side for a lunge at Tristan's ribcage. Tristan dropped low to swipe at his opponent's legs.

He tried to remember the things Kardell had been teaching Niko, most of which he'd ignored because he thought he did not need them. *Every person you face will have a weakness. Learn to see them. Some are physical, some mental, some emotional. Learn to see weakness, learn to vanquish your own, and you live.* He remembered that much, but he felt like the details were important and those he hadn't heeded.

Beady-eyes was good on his feet, and avoided Tristan's swipe. He forced Tristan back with a flurry of strikes, which left a burning, dripping slice on his arm.

The surprise of the pain unnerved him. He dropped the pot behind him and brought a second dagger from concealment.

For a moment he had an advantage. With a familiar weapon in both hands he moved with confidence. He managed some solid jabs. His self-assured smirk returned.

Tristan must have moved too close. All he could remember later was that one moment he was driving a dagger in at Beady-eye's chest, hoping to at least nick the aorta, when a hand closed on his upper arm. He was spun on his own momentum. His attempts to twist out of the grip were futile. When a dagger punched between two ribs in Tristan's back, his gasp was more from surprise than pain.

He tried to determine where, exactly, the knife had hit, even as he stumbled away from his opponent. Ice crept across his back.

He wheeled and backed away, his daggers up. Beady-eyes came at him now with a dagger and the teapot. Tristan managed to avoid the dagger, but the hard edge of the teapot struck him in the gut, the arm, and the head in rapid succession. The last hit was the one that sent him to the ground.

Light lanced through his head and burst in front of his eyes. He knew that one last blow was coming, but he could not rise.

He heard Doctor Maikon cry, "No! Don't kill him!"

The doctor's defender objected. "Because of him, now you have to run!"

Tristan felt hands on his face and neck. Doctor Maikon's amber eyes peered into his. "He's one of mine. It's worth running." She stood. Tristan struggled to sit up, but his head was still convinced the room had tipped forty-five degrees.

A moment later he felt a pinch in his neck. Maikon had jabbed him with a needle. "This will accelerate the healing process. As a bonus, it will certainly prevent you from following us."

"You're . . . The Maker," Tristan managed.

She laughed and kissed his forehead. "Oh dear, no. Just a coordinator for The Maker's work. You were never going to learn much from me. I have little to offer besides medical jargon."

Tristan looked up at her. "Why?"

"Because, the box was opened, all that was good and bad escaped. Putting it back in isn't possible. The only choice now is to make it work. Besides," he heard a smile in her voice, "look at you. You're *magnificent.*"

Her guard scoffed. "Doc, it's time to go."

Tristan watched them leave. Their footsteps faded down the hall. He tried to stand, but he only managed a wobbling step before he collapsed onto the carpet. He lay there waiting for his skull to stop throbbing, marinating in embarrassment.

Susan found him lying there a long time later. She frowned at him and said, "I told you her guard was dangerous."

Tristan had to rest for a day before he was ready for the drive back. As promised, he smuggled Susan over the border into Cotarion. She smiled with a glint of tears in her eyes when they pulled up in front of her family's home. "You don't know how much family means until you can never see them again," she said.

Brothers and sisters, his cousin Erika rose in his mind. "Trust me, I know."

Susan patted his hand. "Thank you." She climbed out of his car, threw her bag over her shoulder. Tristan waited for the front door to open, and then pulled away. For once, returning to his city was little comfort. He dreaded telling William or Kardell that Doctor Maikon was lost, that he'd learned nothing.

When he opened his apartment door, he groaned. Niko sat in the living room, his spine straight. He glared at the man lounging across from him, whose red hair was all at odds with Tristan's steely apartment.

"God, Red. Don't you have anything better to do?"

"Red gave him a cheeky grin. "I wish I did. Your work, though, keeps getting stranger. Where have you been?"

"In Gestos, which you should know from my paperwork."

"Your paperwork is hardly worth glancing at. You only put down the least information required. The Agency is starting to wonder what you're doing with company resources."

Tristan spread his arms. "*Everything* is company resources. I might as well submit a form every time I go take a piss."

Red's lips twitched. He stood, smoothing his coat. "I expect you to make more progress on your security problem soon. And since I'm here, I might as well tell you that The Agency will not condone any action on the recent request."

Tristan knew from the glint in the bastard's eyes that this was something important. "What request?"

"The enormous price on members of the High General's person guard, of course. Some of the other agencies have been pushing it, but we will not undermine our own government." Red slammed the door behind him.

Niko jumped up at once. "I wanted to tell you, sir, but he waited here all this time—"

Tristan was already out the door and dashing down the stairwell before Niko finished the sentence. He took a side door out of the building to avoid Red in the lobby, and sprinted across the city. Hopefully, Cameron hadn't returned to duty yet. Hopefully she was still at her apartment.

He turned down Slinger Street, and leapt up a fire escape in the alley. He stopped just below one of the windows of Kardell's apartment. When he heard the sound of Ethan's voice, strained and angry, he winced.

"I've been here for you this whole time, Cam! But the only person who can count on you is Sean Ellis! What I'm asking is not unreasonable."

"You want me to give up everything I've worked for. This isn't about Ellis, this is about my job. I swore to protect Cotarion, and I'm not going to give that up because you're bothered by some new scars." Cameron's voice was cool, detached.

"I don't want to stand here and watch you get hurt! Sean Ellis's enemies are coming for him, and you're the one standing in front of him, over and over again."

Cameron was quiet. When she spoke again, there was danger in her voice. "Don't lie, Ethan. That's a lovely sentiment, but we both know that's not the problem."

"But it's true!"

"I'm going on a walk. I'm a Sentinel, and you've always known that. So you need to finally figure out whether or not you're okay with it." Tristan heard Cameron zip up her jacket. He rushed down the fire escape. They met on the staircase between the first and second floors.

Her eyes narrowed as they always did when he appeared unexpectedly.

"It's important," he said before she could reverse direction. "Let me walk with you and I'll explain."

She considered, longer than was flattering, then nodded. "You were outside my apartment listening, weren't you?"

Tristan fell into step beside her. "Might've been, for a minute. You want to talk about it?"

She pushed the front door open, with more force than was necessary. "No. I want to know why you're here."

"I think that guy who is after Sean Ellis must still have a plan for taking him out. There's a price out on all the High Guards. Lucky you, my agency is discouraging participation, and the rest of the agencies aren't nearly as good, but I figured you should probably be careful."

Cameron let out a string of impressive curses. Then she growled, "How long ago did this happen?" She scanned all the rooftops, subtly. Good.

"Yesterday. More than likely some of the newest Sentinels, the ones considered easy targets, will be watched a few days before anyone makes a move. But once there's been a kill and the reward is collected, things will move fast."

She cursed again, and wheeled around to go back to her apartment. Suspecting her intent, Tristan rushed to catch up and said, "You can't warn the others."

"Why the hell not?"

"How are you going to explain your source? 'Hey guys, I'm buddies with an assassin and he says that we're all being hunted by other assassins'?"

"I won't have to explain. They trust me."

Tristan shoved his hands in his coat pockets as a bitterly cold wind swept the street. "Just be careful, Cam. And don't mention me."

She paused before opening the door to her building. "I won't. Thank you, for telling me."

He gave her his very best smile. "That's what friends are for, right? Letting you know when a city of bloodthirsty killers are out to get you."

014

THE UNIFORM DID not feel strange, not even after the eight weeks she'd spent getting well enough to wear it again. Cameron twisted her hair into a knot in front of the mirror. And that looked right, too.

A Sentinel was the only thing she'd known how to be, once. It had become a way to find out why her friend had died in the Crescent Mountains. She had always known this path would cost her.

She knew the price was going to be high. Paying it just hadn't been a question since the day Erika died.

Ethan looked up from making coffee when she entered the kitchen. He frowned, but passed her a cup, anyway.

"I made some eggs, if you want some."

"Thank you, but I'm meeting Armel for breakfast. What are those?"

Ethan's hands shuffled the papers on the countertop. Even when he wasn't playing, his fingers were quick, light. She liked his hands. She liked *him*. He smiled, but there was something bitter in the upcurve of his lips.

"It's the paperwork for renewing our lease. It isn't due until next week, but it's time to think about it."

Cameron swallowed hot coffee. "If you have to think about it, then you already have your answer."

He sighed and clutched his own mug. "I knew you would say that. I just didn't think you would say it that way."

"I don't want to drag this out. If we're done, then there's nothing to discuss."

Ethan put down his mug. He stepped closer to Cameron, wrapped his arms around her, and drew her into a fierce kiss. She yielded easily, could not stop herself from kissing him back.

At last his grip loosened. A moment before all she'd wanted was to pull him closer, and now it took all her self-control to stop from pushing him away. What was the point, if they were about to say goodbye? But she stayed, balanced between that glimpse of normalcy and what was right.

"Isn't this worth at least a little fight?" he said.

"We've been fighting for weeks now. Have you changed your mind?"

"No."

"I haven't, either." She stepped back from him. His grip loosened. "No matter what we feel, we can't get past this."

He turned away and smoothed out the papers. "I love you."

Cameron swallowed again and bit her tongue. Anything else she said would hurt him. Finally, he brought his fist down hard on the counter.

"Damn it, Cam, just say it!"

"I can't."

"Go, then. If that's it, then leave."

It was easy, now that it was happening. She walked to the door and put on her boots. She didn't look at him, but she felt his eyes on her.

"I've never really known what you were thinking, have I?" he said.

"Probably not."

"Did you ever love me?"

Cameron's stomach clenched. A little tendril of anger grew, coiled in her chest. "What the hell kind of question is that?"

"It would be nice to know, before you go, if this ever meant anything to you or if I was just a place to be when you were in town."

"Do you want me to hurt you, Ethan? Would that make this easier?"

He looked like he wanted to slam his fist into the counter again. But through the anger, his eyes were wide open. He'd take her back right then if she just took off the uniform for good.

"I would like to see you show anything at all, really. I'm feeling a little used right now."

Cameron smoothed out her jacket and tied her sword to her belt. "Yes, I love you. I just don't want to talk about it, because it doesn't matter. It won't change the facts. Even if I quit being a Sentinel, I wouldn't be what you need." She stopped. Reason would make no difference. This was going to hurt no matter what she said. "When I come back this evening, we'll work out the details."

She left before he could respond. It was better not to drag it out.

She pretended she couldn't hear the thump of a coffee mug hitting the door after she closed it. Maybe he had a right to be angry. She hadn't seen the harm in escaping the uniform, in escaping the loneliness that had lingered over her since that day in the mountains, when she'd lost her friend and lost her humanity. She was not a person. She was a made thing, planned in a lab.

With Ethan, it had been a little easier not to think like that.

She walked to her meeting with Armel. Her blade brushed her leg with every step, reminding her that this was her choice. It soothed her annoyance. With Ethan, with the ache in her thigh, with herself.

The last leaves of autumn swirled around her feet. If the weather continued to cool the next few weeks, then she would need to switch to her winter uniform.

People packed into Three Sides Coffee Shop, seeking refuge from the winds outside. Cameron found Armel at a table near the back, with breakfast pastries and coffee for both of them. She had expected him to be buoyant, but instead his greeting was grim.

"Well, you look the same as I feel."

"At least I have an excuse, I just broke up with Ethan. You, on the other hand, just got married. You should be happy."

Armel made a face. "I'm sorry, Cam. I knew it didn't look good at the wedding, but I hoped it would get better. Here, drown your sorrows in this coffee and the chocolate-sugar-bread-thing."

"So why are you so down?"

"You know what, let's not talk about it. Let's concentrate on finding your next boyfriend. First candidate is the barista. He's got potential if you don't mind whatever that dead critter is on his chin."

"I think that's a goatee."

"Sure, I just don't think the matted hair is his best look."

Armel spent the next twenty minutes pointing out potential new mates, occasionally detailing what their children would look like. The exercise cheered him up as much as it did Cameron. The coffee was nutty, the pastries crispy, and laughter flowed more easily than it had in a long time.

They finished their breakfast and walked to the Military Quarter. Cameron noticed that any scarlet uniforms they passed on the sidewalks moved hastily. She and Armel were by far the moist boisterous on the street. She supposed it was unwise to draw attention to herself when there was a price on the heads of all High Guards, but she found she did not care so much.

Armel did not return to the grim state in which Cameron had found him. She did not bring it up. It could hardly be anything serious. What could a newlywed have to bother him? Disagreements with Owena about pillow cases?

They went in different directions in front of the High General's Quarters. Cameron's thigh only twinged on one of the steps up to Thea Clemens's office.

The Master of the High Guard did not look as happy to see Cameron as she should have, all things considered.

"The High General seems to believe you're fit for duty, Kardell. What do you think?"

"Probably better than anyone else you have, ma'am." Cameron spoke with bravado. It was true, but better if it sounded like a joke.

Clemens laughed, but Cameron heard too much tension in it. Like a rattling bridge girder about to snap. "Go on, then."

"I have one question, ma'am. Are there quarters available for High Guards nearby?"

"Some in this building, in fact. You aren't scared of the assassins, are you?"

"I'm moving out of my current apartment, actually." She hadn't mentioned Ethan, but still there was a rush of memory, of concerts and breakfasts and sleep-tinged smiles.

Clemens stared at her as if she could see some vestige of what Cameron felt. Damn. She needed to be more careful.

"You won't be distracted?"

"No, ma'am. Like they say, heart's made of ice. Or is it stone?"

That elicited a sigh. "Go do your duty, Kardell. And I hope Sean Ellis is grateful to have you."

Was that bitterness directed at the High General, or at Cameron? Or just the universe at large? The High Guard did seem to be standing in an ever contracting ring of enemies. The walls of safety shrank and the monsters outside grew.

Cameron heard the High General shouting as soon as she entered the hall to his office. High Guard (was his name Sloan or Sleat?) stood right outside the office door. He fled as soon as Cameron took his place. She'd been put on second ring, rather than personal guard. That stung a little.

The shouting ended, and the office door slammed back. Ellis stood there, his face flushed and his eyes glinting. He saw Cameron and bared his teeth, more grimace than smile.

"Kardell, you're with me, now. Tao, you're on second ring. And we're going outside."

High Guard Brecht said, "Sir, we need time to go out and clear the area. And Tao has never been on second—"

"Do you think I care? Kardell, move!"

Cameron and Tao switched positions while Ellis stormed down the hall. An advisor tried to deliver some papers, but the High General didn't break his stride. Brecht trotted fast to get far enough ahead to open doors.

Once out in the open air, Ellis turned right and kept walking. He passed through two courtyards and finally stopped in a walled garden. Some plants still held onto their autumn reds, but most of them were brown. They rattled together.

"Brecht, take the archway. Tao, go back to the garden entrance. Kardell, stay right where you are."

No one hesitated or argued this time. The High General trembled and his voice snapped. It might have been rage, but Cameron suspected he was frightened, too. She waited.

"You can't completely hide that limp," he said.

"It's improving, Sir."

He smirked. "Do you blame me for it? You should. I sent you into that fight hoping to finally be rid of you. But as soon as I'd done it, I knew I'd made a mistake." His smile broadened. "You're very good at hiding it. Better than I ever was. But it shows in that moment right before you become aware of it. You hate me more than almost anyone. The good news is, I hate you, too, so we're on even ground.

"This is what I realized when you fell. I can have revenge, or I can have freedom. I saved you because together we can fight The Maker. If anyone can put an end to all this, it's you."

"You tried to kill me, and now you want me to help you?"

"It seems better than waiting for whatever The Maker has planned. Besides, I made sure Finch saved you, didn't I?"

He couldn't be serious. But the look on his face suggested the offer was genuine. She knew that if The Maker decided she was expendable, then she would be hunted just like him.

"Who is it?"

He shook his head. "Nothing until you're on my side. I might be indulging false hope, but I'm not stupid."

Cameron bit back her frustration. Ellis wasn't someone she could twist into telling her more. He was at least as good at maneuvering as she was, possibly better. If he could read her as well as he claimed, she wasn't going to get anything from him until he was ready.

Nothing wrong with trying to crack his resolve a bit, though.

"You're afraid. The negotiations failed, didn't they? Now Hayden Fold is coming for you."

His scowl etched deep lines on his face. A chill wind rattled the trees above them. A few skeletal leaves scurried around their boots.

"Damn you, girl."

"I wouldn't curse the people who stand between you and death, if I were you."

He stood straighter. "Don't imagine that you have some kind of power over me. Someday The Maker will come for you. When it comes, you'll want me on your side. Let's go, I have work to do."

Brecht sprinted across the garden to take up his position as Ellis made for the garden entrance. Tao didn't see the High General in time, and followed in his wake as Ellis went through the gate.

They rushed in disarray up the sidewalk, Brecht using whatever breath he had to berate Tao for lacking focus. Cameron and Ellis saw the broad-shouldered figure approaching at the same time, and they both stopped. Tao bumped into the High General's shoulder, but he might as well have struck a rock.

"Sean!" Armel roared. His black hair, always too long for a Sentinel, fluttered in the winds blowing across the Military Quarter. At least his hands were empty, because his posture was all danger. Fury glinted in his eyes.

Don't make me choose, Armel. The thought rose up before Cameron could stop it. There would be no choice.

"Cousin. What has you so worked up?" Ellis tried to look distant, but his cold veneer was under too much strain. The cracks showed.

"Admit it. You killed him as much as the assassin with the knife."

"Damn it, Armel, are we still on about that?"

"Of course we are! He was my father!"

Cameron took a step forward, put her hand between Armel and Ellis. Her friend seemed not to see her. "Stop, Armel. You need to leave." If he had been anyone else, he'd already be on the ground. He was too close, too angry.

Apparently, he couldn't hear Cameron, either. She opened her mouth, but Ellis spoke before she could.

He'd had a long day. He always said the worst things when his world was fraying.

"Let it go. Nobody cares but you. Most of Cotarion has forgotten the weak old man, and it's better off without him."

For just a breath, Cameron thought that Armel might control himself. His eyes flickered over to her. *Think of Owena. Think of your life.* But then the rage came roaring back. Instead of hitting Ellis, he plunged his hand into his pocket.

Cameron moved, already dreading the rift this would cause. Even Armel wouldn't forgive her for wrestling him to the ground and restraining him. Hopefully Ellis wasn't in the mood to convict him of treason.

Out of the corner of her eye she saw Tao lift his arm.

The shot was loud. It reverberated between the stone buildings. It echoed inside Cameron's head and chest. That near, it was impossible to miss.

Red blossomed on Armel's chest. He sank to the ground. One hand continued to clutch at whatever was in his pocket, but the other rose, weakly, to the bottom of his ribs, and he pushed in. Blood soaked his shirt and his hand as he slid to the ground.

Brecht shouted at Tao, tore the weapon from his hands. He cursed like Cameron had never heard him curse before.

Ellis knelt beside his cousin. That startled her most of all. Everything else had made sense. The High General reaching out to cradle the head of his dying cousin was the only thing that she never could have predicted.

And no one, no one was keeping guard but her. She had to stand and scan the buildings while her friend lay on the ground, life slipping out of him. Cameron hoped he wasn't looking for her, then, as she watched for danger.

Brecht spent his rage on Tao. Brecht, who had been in the High Guard since Armel was a boy, who had watched him grow up, knelt beside Armel, too. And all the while, Cameron stood guard. Brecht reached into the pocket. He brought out not a weapon, but a piece of paper. He read it, then handed it to Ellis in silence.

Cameron gripped hard the hilt of her sword. As Ellis reached out a hand to draw Armel's eyes shut. As he stuffed the paper into his pocket. As he shuddered. With grief? Not possible.

"Sir," Cameron said. "We need to go back to your office. We aren't secure here."

Why wasn't anyone listening to her, couldn't they hear? People were coming out of buildings all around. Still Brecht and Ellis stood and stared at Armel's body.

"Tao, stay here with Armel," she snapped. "Don't let anyone touch him." She grabbed The High General by the elbow, pulled him up to his feet, and pushed him back towards his office. "Brecht, come on."

Once she had Ellis moving, his mind seemed to start functioning again. At least he walked quickly and kept his mouth shut. His hand kept smoothing the pocket where he'd put Armels' piece of paper. The paper her friend had died for.

Don't think. Don't feel. Just do the job. Stay sharp.

Clemens met them at the door of the office building. She led the way down the halls to the High General's office. When the door was shut behind them, she said, "What happened?"

"Armel confronted me," Ellis said. His voice was heavy, tired. Cameron had never heard him sound like that before.

"He's dead?"

"Yes. Tao shot him. Send over an investigation team."

"I already did, Sir. Kardell, take the rest of the day. Go to your sister."

Cameron shook her head. "Tao is out, and Brecht is compromised, ma'am."

"And you aren't? Stop being a damn hero, and go."

"I am not compromised," Brecht said, though his eyes were rimmed red.

"Kardell, you should go," Ellis said.

"Not until there's someone here to take my place. Now is not the time to loosen security, Sir."

"Cameron," Clemens spoke like someone trying to reason with a child. "You've proven yourself. You don't need to impress any of us."

"It's done, ma'am. Armel is gone. It's done, and I have a job to do, and there's nobody else to do it."

What kind of person talked like that? She felt something cold spreading through her bones. As if everything human had leached away.

Clemens relented. There wasn't anyone to take Cameron's place, anyway.

Ellis spent the rest of Cameron's shift dealing with the day's two events: his failure to halt the progress of Hayden Fold's soldiers as they closed on Advon brought most of Cotarion's top leaders into the office. Last-ditch strategies were proposed, but hope ran low, especially as the day wore on and news of Armel spread.

And that was what everyone really wanted to talk about. That was easy. A tragedy. The more Cameron heard it, the more annoyed she became. Armel had been so stupid. His own anger had killed him. It was just a waste.

Finally her replacement arrived. Sean Ellis, beyond the point of hiding anything from any of the Guard, stopped her and handed over the paper Brecht had taken from Armel's pocket.

It was a notice Ellis had received before the Summer Soltice Feast, over two years before. Stating that the possibility of an attack that night was high. The Intelligence Corps had picked up "suspicious talk." The paper was taken from a Top Secret file.

Damn you, Tristan.

"You didn't know he had this?"

Cameron shook her head. "No, sir. If I had, today would have been different."

"Of course. Go home, Kardell."

Cameron left. Every damn person she passed as she left the Military Quarter tried to talk to her. She ignored them all.

Ethan was at their apartment. She'd hoped he wouldn't be, but he stood there, all warmth and sorrow. A better person, might have caved, and accepted the comfort he offered.

Cameron wrote him a check for the last month's rent. She gathered up her most essential items into a bag. That was it. One bag. Her whole life fit in it. With empty spaces.

"I'm so sorry," Ethan said. If everybody kept crying, she was going to have to start yelling at them.

"Me too. I'll see you around."

She closed the door, this time in peace. He didn't hate her, but that hardly seemed to matter.

A cold walk took her to a new room in the Military Quarter. It was barren, even when she unpacked. That suited her, though, didn't it?

She thought about Owena. Everyone expected her to go to her sister, but what good would it do? She couldn't share in Owena's grief when she didn't feel any. Better if she stayed away.

Cameron changed out of her uniform, and went to bed.

015

WILLIAM STARED AT Cameron the entire funeral. It was impossible for him to look anywhere else. Her face was blank. Even High General Ellis shed a tear. But not her.

She'd been Armel's best friend. Hadn't she? He deserved better than cold eyes and stiff shoulders. Was she even human?

She could have at least spared a glance or a flicker of sorrow for Owena. But no, even her sister's sorrow didn't penetrate. He swore he would never forget that, Owena's tear-streaked face on one side of the flower-swathed casket as grief bowed her shoulders, Cameron's visage on the other (because of course the High General would put her on duty that day) chill and remote.

How often had Armel turned to Cameron, how long had their friendship been simply assumed amongst the Sentinels? How often had Armel run when Cameron called? His faith had been unwavering.

The least she could do was remember him.

William thought going to his office and getting some work done might help take his mind off it. He flipped through notes, seeing nothing but her chilly gaze. He pulled books off shelves, thumbed through the indexes, and put them back.

Had she ever cared? She couldn't have. Why had she bothered to pretend, though? Armel hadn't held any power for years. It would have gained her nothing.

William had a feeling that he was being irrational. But the anger felt right, and it was simple.

He went out after dinner. He cut through the city, straight to Armel's favorite bar. The bartender had a glass of William's preferred ale on the counter before he'd ordered. William hadn't realized he'd been there so often.

He took his beer to a corner, and there he contemplated all the appropriate things: the brevity of life, the shock of loss, the spinning wheels of blame.

His mug was half empty when the door opened and a loud group tromped in. They weren't wearing their scarlet coats, but their postures and their haircuts gave them away as Sentinels.

One wore a dark leather jacket. In the midst of such a boisterous group, she should have been easy to overlook. But William knew that cutting stare too well.

The anger rose again, hot in his throat. He pretended not to see them. Gordon Palmroy ordered drinks and carried a tray back to the table where the rest had settled in.

Palmroy whispered to Kardell when he handed her a small glass. She frowned but stepped up on a chair in the midst of her fellow Sentinels. She lifted her glass.

"The world is a darker, less hopeful place today. I don't like many people, and he was one of them. Here's to Armel."

Cameron tossed back the drink while the others shouted, "Armel!" She leapt down off the table, her eyes glistening. Another glass was pressed into her hand. She downed that one, too. Palmroy laid a hand on her shoulder.

They settled into chairs and told stories, laughing a great deal. Sentinel Kardell was occasionally passed a drink. It was never in front of her for long.

The conversation quieted, grew more somber. Cameron left the table. To William's horror, she walked straight to his corner. She dropped into the chair across from him.

"Are you hiding over here? I saw you, pretending not to see me."

"I didn't want to intrude. Nice speech, though."

"Doctor Harfield! Are you *mad* at me?"

William clenched his beer. "I am not."

She laughed. "You're an awful liar, you know. It's okay, everybody else is mad at me, so you might as well join in."

"Who's mad at you?"

She waved a hand, narrowly missing his drink. "Everybody. Owena is mad enough to make up for anybody who isn't."

"Maybe if you even pretended to be sad—"

"I don't do sad, Doctor Harfield. It goes against my nature. Do you know what Armel would say if he were here?"

"No. And he's not. That's sort of the point."

Cameron raised the glass in her hand and carried on as if she hadn't heard. "He would say, 'Will, cheer the hell up. There is a girl sitting in front of you who is interested in your welfare. You have a half-full glass of beer. Life is—"

Her glass shattered. A splinter flew up from the table. Her forehead wrinkled. She poked her finger into a divot in the table.

"You're going to cut your hand," William said, trying to clear the glass away.

"I think that's a bullet. Look, there's a hole in the window." Cameron's voice was more bemused than concerned.

"Someone just shot at you?"

"They might have been shooting at you."

"Don't you think we should move?"

"Well, yes."

She still hadn't stood, so he grabbed her arm and dragged her to her feet. She stumbled, but it was enough. A second bullet cracked the window and sank into the bench where she'd been a moment before.

Cameron cursed, spitting out words and phrases that William had never heard before. In there he heard, "The bastards, they knew we'd be distracted tonight. Stupid, stupid, stupid."

William pulled her towards the rear entrance. As they emerged into the alley, she cried out, "I didn't pay! I didn't warn any of the others!" She twisted out of his grip and rushed back, barely hindered when she bumped into the wall.

William ran after her.

Tristan dropped down beside him from somewhere overhead. There was no sign of laughter or sneer. He dashed after Cameron and pulled her out of the bar, even as she struggled against him.

"Sweetheart, I will carry you if I have to. They've started picking off High Guards."

Cameron stopped fighting. William followed as they strode away.

"Who did they get?"

"Tao."

"Bastards. Damn it all to Hell, why did I drink? Stupid."

Tristan's head jerked around, then he pulled Cameron down to the ground. An arrow hit the pavement at William's feet. The wood shaft skittered into the shadows.

Tristan leapt up. "Get her to your house, I'll cover you. And hurry!" Then he was gone, up onto the rooftops.

William swallowed a lump in his throat, and held out his hand to Cameron. Their eyes met. Was that fear he saw in her face? She needed help getting up. She swayed as they walked towards William's house, sending them both on a sinuous path down the sidewalk. William was but a tugboat in a stormy sea.

"So, why are people firing arrows at you?"

"Hit out on High Guards."

"All of you?"

"Yep. Having that kind of week, Harfield."

He cringed. She'd used the same nickname she'd always used for his sister. If he'd felt sorry for her, it evaporated. He kept his mouth shut and tugged her along dark streets until they reached his house.

She stumbled going up the stairs. It was like watching a cat fall. How much had she had to drink? He remembered at least five glasses pass through her hands, which was a lot for someone he'd rarely seen drink at all.

Abruptly she pushed off his arm, leaned over the railing of his front landing, and was very sick. William reached out, then stopped. He had as much chance of frightening her as giving comfort. He stepped to her side, where she could see him, and from there put a hand on her shoulder.

"Do you remember what I said about getting inside quickly?" Tristan's voice drifted out of the dark over their heads.

"Working on it," William said.

When Cameron stood, William guided her through the front door.

His mom looked up from the book she was reading. Cameron froze and swayed in place.

"Hi Mom. This is Sentinel Kardell. Um. She's not feeling very good right now." Cam elbowed him in the ribs, hard. "The bathroom is down the hall on the right."

When she was gone, his mother raised her eyebrows. "Will, I don't want to intrude in your personal affairs, but aren't you dating Nikki?"

"This isn't like that. She's in danger."

His mom put her book down. "Will, what have you gotten into?"

"Nothing that he could help, Auntie," Tristan trotted down the stairs, his silver eyes sharp. "We were born into this trouble. I recommend everybody stay inside. How much did she drink?"

"Too much, apparently."

Kardell stumbled back up the hall, bleary-eyed. She threw herself into an armchair, peeled off her boots, and drew her knees up to her chest.

"I thought drinking was supposed to make you feel better."

"It never helped me much," Teague responded, draping a blanket over the Sentinel.

"Why the Hell do people do it, then."

"It always seems like a good idea at the time," Tristan said. "I called Mel, she'll be here soon to sort you out."

Kardell shook her head. "Don't trust her."

Tristan arched an eyebrow. "Would you rather be completely helpless when some second-rate assassin comes after you? I'll bet you didn't even get a glass of water when you finished guard duty.

Now is not the time for you to be dehydrated with your head in the toilet. I'm going up on the roof to watch for her."

Kardell grumbled under the blanket. She did look pathetic. Every now and then her limbs shook. Her face was pale, strands of hair plastered to her forehead by sweat.

William might not like her, but she was human, and she was miserable. Besides, his mother gave him the sort of look which suggested he was being remiss. William sighed, and went to the kitchen for a glass of water and a damp towel.

Kardell refused the water, and stared at the towel. "What am I supposed to do with that?"

William shrugged. "Put it on your face? I don't know."

She took it, draped it on her face, completely covering her features from forehead to chin. Then she lifted a corner. Her lip quirked up. "Like that? Come on, Doctor Harfield, lighten up. Besides, if you're mad at me, you might as well be mad at yourself, too." Then her face blanched even more. She stumbled up, then bumped down the hall.

William's mother shot him another meaningful look. He sighed and followed Kardell.

He pulled up a stool and sat beside her. She coughed and gagged, her whole body curling up without any result. He reached out and put a hand on her shoulder again, and rubbed, his mind far away.

Eventually she leaned back against the wall. Her head thunked against the tile.

"What did you mean, I should be mad at myself?"

She cracked one eye open. "Stupid. Nevermind."

"Everything about these past few days has been stupid."

She sighed. "You pushed him, William. You told him about Tristan. A few more steps down the path that led him to the confrontation." She closed her eyes again. "You weren't the only one, though."

William sat back, as far from her as he could get in the tight space. "I didn't think he would find anything."

"It wasn't much. Not enough to bring Ellis down publicly. But enough to make Armel sure that his father's death was planned. Or at least avoidable."

William rubbed his hands together. He didn't realize that the anger was there until he saw the tendrils of fire licking around his fingers. He balled up his hands, focused on the muscles in his jaw and shoulders, forced himself to breathe deeply. The lines of energy stilled, the fire went out.

He looked up. Cameron watched him. In spite of her rather sorry state, he felt her measuring his resolve. Why did it matter to her so much, even now?

The door opened, and Melanie's head popped through the crack. "So it's true. The mighty Sentinel is struck down by her own hand."

"I'm sure I deserve that."

"And then some. But I think you've had enough for now." Melanie knelt on the floor in front of Cameron. "Here, give me your hands." The Sentinel didn't move. William didn't need to see her face to know Melanie rolled her eyes.

"I don't trust you."

"That's fine. Because now is absolutely the time to waste valuable minutes sitting in here."

The muscles in Cameron's face tightened, and her skin blanched again. She held up her hands and growled, "Can you do it before I try to puke up my stomach lining again?"

Melanie took Cameron's hands. She bobbed her head in time to the rollicking tune she hummed. The ends of her ponytail, tipped in pink dye, swished back and forth.

The Sentinel's eyes fluttered shut, and she grimaced. Melanie continued to hum cheerfully, as if she hadn't a care in the world. Maybe she was more capable than William gave her credit for.

Abruptly, Melanie stood and stretched. "Drink lots of water, try to eat something. I'm going home." She spun around and looked at William, her expression inscrutable. "You're a better friend than she deserves."

William paused a moment, and Cameron looked up at him. He reached out and helped her up to her feet. "How do you feel?"

"Like a cow kicked me. But my stomach seems fine, at least."

She trudged out of the bathroom and back into the living room. She drank the glass of water William had brought her earlier in just a few gulps. He was lost in thought about Armel, so he was only vaguely aware of her conversation with his mother and Tristan.

He had pushed, hadn't he? If he hadn't encouraged Armel, would the issue have dropped? If he hadn't given Armel Tristan's contact information, would he still be alive? He'd even had the option of encouraging Armel to let it go. Of distracting him. Of doing anything, anything at all, other than what he did.

It was only when he felt a touch on his arm that the stream of thoughts broke. He looked into Cameron's face. Her dark eyes pulled words from him he would have rather not spoken.

"You're right. I wanted him to fight."

"Will—"

"I told him about Tristan. I told him he needed to look for answers."

"William."

"I'm responsible. It's my fault he's dead. I wanted him to take Ellis down, I never thought—"

"It's not your fault!" she said, so sharply that William froze at once. "I killed him! It's my fault." William stared, disbelieving, as a tear slipped down her face. It reached her scar and traced the shape. "I killed Armel."

She covered her mouth with her hand, and dropped to the couch. Her body shook, tremors running through her, radiating out from her chest.

Cameron Kardell sat on William's couch and cried.

He sat beside her, reached out, and then her head was buried in his chest. He felt each wracking sob, but she never made a sound. She seemed about to come apart at any moment. William closed his eyes, and a few of his own tears fell. For a few rare moments, they were joined in grief.

How long it lasted he didn't know, but eventually Cameron pushed back from him, and wiped her face. His fingers curled around the memory of her hair, her back. He felt bad about that, and tried to swallow it down.

"Did you, did you shoot him?"

"No. But if I'd done my job, he would be alive. If anyone else had come up to Ellis like that, I would have restrained them right away. But it was Armel. If anyone else had shouted like that, I would have had them on the ground. But I knew how angry Armel would be if I did that, so I let it go. I didn't do my job. So he's dead."

He wanted to reach out and touch her, but what had seemed natural a moment ago was now impossible.

"I'm sorry."

Cameron pressed her lips together. "He was my friend. And because I cared about him, he's dead." She looked at William. She stared for long enough that he felt the urge to crawl out of his skin. "Don't look at me like that, Will."

"Like what, exactly?"

"Like suddenly you think I'm an okay person. I cried. So what? It doesn't change a thing."

His face, for some reason, was very warm. "It's just nice to know you care."

She sighed. "Oh, Will. You fool." She stood. "Do you happen to have anything to eat? I'm starving, and then I need to sleep."

Her expression had gone all distant. Because of course it had.

He helped her find food in the kitchen. His mother kept up a steady conversation with Cameron while they were there, sparing him the task of coming up with something to say to her. It was somehow more difficult than ever. He had to swallow several times before he could even manage to tell her he had found a box of crackers.

Somewhere in there, under layers of stony determination and icy expression was a person. Someone who had loved Armel and mourned him, who blamed herself for his death.

Did he know anything about her at all? All day he had thought she had no heart, and all day she had been carrying the weight of her best friend's death.

"You're on first watch, William. Tristan says he has the outside covered, but he wants someone inside awake just in case."

William shook himself. Cameron arranged a borrowed pillow and blanket on the longest couch in the living room.

"I'm not very confident in my skills as a lookout. Do I need to patrol the house at regular intervals?"

Her smile was dilute, but it was there. "Just stay awake. There's a lot more, but that's the essence of it right now." She looked at him again, hard. "We aren't going to be friends, all right?"

"I don't know what you're talking about."

She took off her jacket and folded it before setting it on the coffee table. "You look like someone who found a lost puppy."

The sound he made was derisive, but she didn't argue. She threw herself down on the couch, pulled the blanket up to her chin, and closed her eyes.

William picked a book off the shelf, settled into the chair across from her, and read. Occasionally, he stopped and looked around the house, which seemed to grow quieter by the hour. Even more occasionally, he glanced over at Cameron, who seemed to be asleep, though there was a furrow between her eyebrows.

Who was this woman Sean Ellis relied on, who his sister had regarded so highly, who Armel had trusted? She had warned him once, had teased him often, and her tears still stained his shirt. He'd watched her fight off death, cut down enemies, make impossible choices. She had even strengthened his abilities.

Still, he didn't know her. He couldn't make all the pieces fit together. For the first time he wanted to figure out how they might.

William woke abruptly, aware at once that he hadn't meant to fall asleep. He threw off a blanket that had been draped over him. Sunlight glowed gently in the windows.

A clatter and shriek burst out of the kitchen. William leapt up, jumped over the couch, and stumbled in, expecting blood.

Cameron stood by the stove, stirring something in a pan, while his mother picked a pot lid off the floor. They were both laughing when William burst in, but as soon as they saw him they stopped. His mother screamed and dropped the pan lid again.

"Will. You're on fire," Cameron said, her voice as tight and even as a guitar string.

He looked down. Flames flickered in his hands, ran up his arms. He balled up his fingers and the fire flicked out. "Sorry, it just sounded like you might be in trouble. It's okay, Mom, really."

"Well, I don't think many mothers have to deal with seeing their sons on fire," she said, her voice peevish as she retrieved the pan lid again.

"The room isn't even cold," Cameron said brightly.

"I can pull energy from pretty far away, now. Not just one place, obviously, that would be dangerous, it's more like a really big net, a little here, a little there. I was looking at an equation for producing relatively random numbers one day, and I thought if I applied the basic principle that I could get a broader and safer method of drawing in power. It took some tweaking, but—"

"You're babbling, Billy." Tristan had slipped in and perched on a stool. "Good to see no one's hurt."

"Anyway," Cameron said, "you want to take the eggs off before they turn brown." She flipped the contents of the skillet out onto a plate. "See, that's just right. And that's the extent of my cooking knowledge."

Teague observed the finished product, then tried a bite. Her eyes went wide with delight. "Wow. Those are perfect. So, did you ever get Armel back to his room?"

Cameron hopped on a stool beside Tristan as both he and Teague filled their plates with eggs. William occupied himself with making coffee and avoided looking at his mother.

"Let's see, so after we lost the bodyguards, Erika and Armel got spectacularly drunk, even though Erika had promised to keep her wits about her. As the only sober member of the group, it became my responsibility to return everyone safely home, and of course it was well after curfew. But I wasn't going to let them off easy.

"So, I found part of the wall around the Military Quarter that wasn't heavily guarded, and I made them climb it. After they'd both fallen over the other side, I made sure to warn them that an irritable instructor was approaching every time we were near some thorny shrub. By the time we got back to the dorms, they were covered in scratches and seriously regretting relying on me to return them home.

"We came to Armel's room, and I was feeling all self-righteous, when I saw the bodyguards standing there in front of his door. The way they were watching, I knew we weren't going to sneak in that way. I started telling them we needed to climb in through the window. Thank you, William." She smiled as he handed her a cup of coffee.

"Armel looked at me, as well as he could, and he said, 'I'm in trouble no matter what I do. So I'll just face this head on.' He walked right up to his bodyguards and turned himself in.

"I was going to just walk away and leave him to his fate. He wasn't going to get in too much trouble. But the next thing I know, Erika is going up to the bodyguards, too."

"Wow, she must have been drunk," William said.

"No kidding. Because she was for sure going to be in serious trouble. She was a Senior Cadet, leading the High General's son astray. I did the only thing I could think of." Cameron rolled up her shirt sleeve, showing a small scar on her arm.

"You stabbed yourself?" Tristan said. "That seems extreme."

"I wasn't going to let Erika get herself kicked out of the Sentinels. I yelled, the guards pushed Armel into his room, and by the time one of them came back to investigate, Erika had come to her senses and vanished. I got stitches and some lectures, Armel had to organize some files, Erika didn't lose her chance at donning the Sentinel's Eye."

"You did not really stab yourself so my sister could get away," William said.

"Erika watched out for me, too," she said lightly. "Trust me, there were plenty of times when she got Armel and I out of trouble. He was brilliant at pranks, but awful at dealing with the repercussions."

"Pranks? Such as?"

"We wrapped the covers of every single book in the library with red paper."

"You did not."

"We did. In one night. Along with all the other cadets in our year, of course. Plus a lot from the lower years, too."

"That's not possible. I've seen that library. It's almost as big as the one at Gates."

Cameron wore a sly smile, unlike anything William had seen before. She grabbed a piece of paper and a book—objects that were always close at hand in his house. "Observe." Her fingers flicked, the paper creased, the book flipped once, and was wrapped. William opened the covers, and found the simple procedure almost impossible to reverse without tearing the paper off.

"Did you get banned from the library for life? I would have banned you for life. That's devious."

"The books bit back. Look, that's from a papercut." She held out her hand to display a thin scar. It certainly wasn't the only one on that hand. William frowned and leaned closer.

"That is not from a papercut."

"Yes, it is."

He put down his coffee and held his own hand up next to hers. "I got this doing research for my dissertation. *That* is a papercut. Look at how much thinner it is."

"Okay, so maybe I picked it up during training. The point is, it took the librarians three weeks to unwrap all the books. It was epic." She sat back and sighed. "I need to leave. Thank you, Mrs. Harfield, for tolerating my terrible behavior last night. William, Tristan, I appreciate your efforts at keeping me safe."

"Anytime." William and Tristan walked with Cameron to the front door. "If you need anything else, just let me know."

"I'm walking with you to the Military Quarter," Tristan said.

William expected Cameron to object, but she didn't. She just carried on tying her boots. As he often did when the Sentinel was on the verge of leaving, William felt a thousand words gather on the tip of his tongue. None of them had anything to do with how he felt or what he thought, so he was rendered mute as he tried to find whatever it was he needed to say.

Finally, as she opened the door to go, he managed, "Just be careful, Cameron. Okay?"

Her dark eyes were hard on his face. Did she enjoy challenging him? He didn't look away, though. If she was testing him, then he would pass.

"Don't worry about me, Will. Just try not to let him see when you're angry with him."

Before William could ask what she was talking about, she and Tristan were gone. They walked down the sidewalk, looking relaxed, like a couple out for a morning stroll rather than a pair of warriors on the lookout.

Had she just warned him about Ellis again? It was the only reasonable conclusion. Who else would she be afraid of referring to by name?

"She didn't eat any of the eggs," his mother said. "That was a lot of trouble to go to and then not eat any."

"She doesn't usually eat breakfast, unless it's some pastry."

"You're worried about her?"

He turned away from the window, and sighed. "She's the center of everything." It all swirled around her. Had she placed herself there, or had it formed around her?

"She's worried about you too, William."

"I don't know about that."

His mother smiled. "I was married to your father. I know how to read people who would rather not be read."

William ran his hand through his hair. "I'm not sure I can control it, Mom. I'll be doing okay, and then I get scared or angry—" He swallowed. "All the work I do can be undone in a second."

She hugged him, the top of her head barely brushing his chin. Only his mom had ever squeezed him like that. As if the last twenty years meant nothing, and he was still a little boy.

"I know it's not the best situation for you, but I'm glad you're here," he said.

"Me, too. Now, go get ready for work."

It was only when William was knotting his tie that he realized Cameron had touched his hand to get a better look at his scar. He hadn't felt the pressure of her fingers then, but now it was there. A tingling, connecting that moment to the other rare times she'd touched him.

Every time they'd both been in grave danger.

016

Somehow, Cameron kept showing up at Tristan's house on her days off. Octavius Finch missed one session, then another, but not her. What had started as testing the effects of her injuries had progressed into training for Tristan and Niko.

She was hardly slowed by her leg anymore, and improved every time he saw her. Tristan, on the other hand, worsened.

"Do you see?" he cried out after she beat him soundly for the fourth time. "I'm not *supposed* to use all this fancy technique. It just gets in the way."

"You've never thought about it before. And you don't practice."

Tristan scowled. "Why do you care so much, anyway?"

The blank expression she adopted was worth every stinging slap of the blade that he'd endured. Ah. Something personal, then.

"Niko, you're up. Tristan, try to figure out the difference between the ball of your foot and the heel."

Tristan should have snapped back, but he refrained. Her expression had returned to the same impenetrable mask she wore all the time now. Even he found it hard to tease an expression like that.

"So. You have someone you want me to take care of? Someone you don't think I could beat without some training?"

Cameron finished giving Niko directions, then silently watched him drill. Just when Tristan was sure she meant to ignore him, she looked to where he perched on the back of the couch. "Something like that."

"You might have a lot of money saved up, Cami, but not nearly enough for that job. Besides, my agency has a very strict policy on unsettling the upper tiers of the government."

Her frown deepened. "That's not what I'm talking about. Niko, watch the elbows. You're getting too loose." She gave Tristan one of her stares. It lacked the usual bite. "You remember what Finch said about how the group is important. In The Maker's eyes, we each have some vital importance."

"So we're taking that bullshit seriously?"

"I assume we each have more than one role to play. That's how I'd do it, anyway. I think you're meant to both protect us, and contain us."

"By 'contain,' I'm guessing you mean that it was my job to stop Erika."

"I've seen the way you act around William when he gets angry. You've reined him in before."

Tristan smirked and pulled out a dagger to toss. He couldn't discourage this conversation, but he could muddle it.

"You spend one night at his house, and now it's 'William,' eh? I thought you'd be calling him 'Doctor Harfield' forever."

Niko yelped as he smacked his own shin with the training blade. His face was red, and he pretended to ignore both of them looking at him.

"Watch your stance, Niko. Tristan, I remember what I was when my ability was activated. Two weeks ago I let Armel die right in front of me, and that's even when I had some scrap of humanity. The next time that my powers have to be turned on, I need to know you're ready."

Tristan stopped tossing the dagger. He looked at her. "Are you training me so that I can kill you? You know I won't do that, right?"

"You will. If the circumstances are right."

Tristan hopped down and stood in front of her, leaning down slightly to meet her eyes. She stared back. He suppressed a shudder. He'd seen grief strip people down to the core before, and he'd always known Cameron was single-minded, but, with all the excess scrubbed away, the woman looking at him was so cold that he wondered if perhaps he was on the wrong side of things.

"Look, Cami, you're going through hell right now, but it will pass."

"Tristan, your whole life is an unending series of escapes."

"I've been doing better recently," he said. "Two months since the last time I went drinking. More than I can say for you."

She stood still for a few more moments, then looked at her watch. She didn't look angry. No more than usual, anyway. But she did pull on her jacket. The one Tristan had ordered for her, and which had broken in nicely. For all her gruffness, she was taking care of it.

"About your security issue. I'd hoped we could talk to Dr. Finch about the capabilities of a Five, but it seems he's left Advon . . . "

Tristan scowled. "You want me to find him."

She shrugged in the open doorway. "That's up to you. You could just try talking to Melanie. She can tell you better than Dr. Finch what she can do. Niko, your form is improving. I recommend you read Donning's Strategies. Tristan, maybe practice."

And she was gone. Tristan refrained from flinging epithets at her back. She got enough of that, already.

She could *try* to be nice though. Just a little.

It hurt, though, that she was right. He'd been beaten at Doctor Maikon's. He'd lived all his life many times faster and stronger than anyone else, but now he wasn't the only one.

"Niko, can you show me that Raven's offensive thingy again?"

"I'll do my best. But it's the Ravenna Offense."

"Just show me how it goes. Then we have a job to do. As usual."

It took a few days for them to turn up any sign of Octavious Finch. In the end it was a coworker who gave him away. The young man had noticed a bead on Finch's bracelet. He'd bought something similar while vacationing on the southern coast, and Finch had mentioned it was his home town. He'd hoped to return there, soon.

The next morning, Tristan and Niko drove towards Esanad. At first, Tristan blamed Niko's silence on sleepiness, but after a couple hours he figured the young man had something on his mind.

"What's going on, buddy?"

Niko started up from staring out the window, shrugged. "I don't know, sir . . . "

"Stop calling me 'sir'."

"It's just. It seems like it would be better sometimes if we pretended to be normal. I mean, your cousin died looking for answers, and you and Miss Kardell and Mr. Harfield have all been hurt. And if you don't mind me saying so, you've all hurt a lot of people, too."

Tristan sighed. "Trust me, I've thought about all that. A lot."

"But?"

"If it was just us who were like this it wouldn't be so bad, but it's not. There's you. There are more kids like you. I think we have to know. I think that maybe we have to try to stop it."

Niko looked hard at him. Tristan felt for a moment like what he'd just said might be true. He wanted it to be. He wanted, so badly, to believe.

In Essanad a few hours later, scarlet, indigo, and golden flowers spilled over balconies like streamers. Every house was stucco over brick, with the brick peeking out in enough places to suggest that the town wasn't the most popular vacation spot. Still, the town had a resilient cheer to it, in brightly painted shutters at every window and humble courtyards bursting with greenery and blooms. Crushed shells paved the walkways to either side of the road.

Most of the people strolling the sidewalks wore jackets. Tristan expected the air to be chill when he stepped out of his car, but compared to Advon it was warm.

"Do you think it ever snows here?" Niko asked.

Tristan shrugged. "Probably not."

"Someday I'll live here," the boy said fervently.

Tristan sniffed. "It's so . . . quaint. But if that's what you're into. Let's take thirty minutes to get an address, and then we'll meet at that food stand." He squinted. What the hell was a 'Sea Cake'?

Niko grinned. "I'll have it done in twenty."

"Fifteen?"

"Is it a race?"

"It is now."

Niko scurried off without another word. Tristan strolled over to a large merchant's shop on the main road. He went in, and watched the owner's face. The look was slightly guarded, but there was hope.

"Hello there. Visiting from Advon?"

Tristan flashed his best smile. "Is it that obvious?"

The woman's lip twitched. "Well, there are a few clues. And this place is always the first stop for most people. I don't see many tourists this time of year, though."

"I wanted to spend a few days not suffering from frostbite. Seeing the sun is nice, too." Tristan browsed the shelves and picked a few familiar-looking packages. Spiced almonds, Raven Street Chips, and the freeze-dried cheese that he always got for Niko.

"So what brings you to Essanad in particular? Out of all the warm, sunny places?"

Too easy. "A friend of mine grew up here, and he suggested I visit when I had a chance. Octavius Finch."

The woman laughed. "Octavius Finch! Yeah, he grew up here. Surprised he said good things about this place, when he was so quick to get out of here. How's he been, I haven't seen him in almost ten years."

Damn. No good. "Sarcastic."

She laughed again and Tristan paid for his snacks. When he stepped out of the store, Niko stood on the sidewalk, grinning. When Tristan tossed him his food, he tore the bag open at once.

"Impossible," Tristan said.

"Maybe for a nice-looking penthouse dweller like you, but not for a street urchin."

Tristan followed Niko back to his car, equal parts annoyed and impressed. "I'm guessing Octavius is holed up somewhere."

"Oh yeah, he's gone underground. But he can't help trying to make people better. Like you said, maybe we really just can't hide what we are. I mean, his life depends on staying hidden, right? But anyone in this town who's really down knows how to find him if they have a broken bone, or a fever that just keeps getting worse."

Niko destroyed the bag of almonds while directing Tristan to Finch's hiding place. They drove a mile to the south-western edge of town, parked beside the road, and then walked along a sandy path through a patch of scrub.

Ten minutes and several turns later, they came upon a tiny house. The trees grew right up to the sides of the building. It looked forlorn.

A boy and a girl played with marbles in front of the door. They wore clothing a little better than rags. When they saw Tristan, their eyes went wide, and they crouched, poised to spring away at any moment.

"He's all right," Niko said. "Friend of Doc's. Is he around?"

Finch stepped out the front door, which slammed shut being him on squeaky springs. The bowl of food in his hands steamed. He frowned at Tristan, but went ahead and knelt in front of the urchins. They held a brief conversation before Finch gave them the food.

"Did Kardell send you, or are you on your own business? Nevermind, I already know. I'm not going back to Advon, so if she wants her leg worked on more, she'll need to come here. And soon."

"I'm not here about that. I need to know more about what you and other Fives can do."

"Melanie is a lot closer to you than I am."

"But Mel doesn't like to talk much."

"Maybe I don't, either."

Tristan arched an eyebrow and Finch sighed, stepped closer, and dropped his voice. "I can't help it, you know. I've learned a lot after all the shit I've seen, and you kids know nothing. Someone has to tell you."

"That's the spirit."

"Besides, Sean is finally going to get taken out by one of his enemies any day now. Then The Maker is going to come for me, and I'll be dead, anyway."

"That's less the spirit."

Finch shrugged. "We lasted longer than most do. So what do you want to know? Consider me an open book."

If only he'd brought William. Tristan kept ending up in a position to ask questions, without any idea what they needed to know.

"So, what are the limits of what a Five can do?"

"I, personally, can heal wounds, help the body combat some diseased, change the rhythm of body systems. Slow or increase heart rate, respiration—"

Niko looked up. "Could you stop someone's heart entirely?"

Finch got that haunted look. Tristan didn't need to hear his "yes" to know the answer.

"Damn," Niko said. "So, we're all just killing machines, basically."

"There's good and bad that comes with it. But for there to be much good, you have to learn control. I've saved more lives than I've taken."

"That's what you can do. What about Mel?"

"Ah. Melanie is very gifted at regulating systems, much better than I am. The work I did with Cameron, eliminating any sign that the wound had happened at all, I don't think Melanie could do. But she can fine-tune biological rhythms on a level I've never dreamed."

Tristan narrowed his eyes. "What does that mean, though?"

"How much time do you have? Practically, it means a lot of things. She could calm someone who was very angry with a touch. She could probably cause the heart to race. Any kind of physical reaction like that, I imagine."

"She could make someone sleep, maybe? More deeply than usual?"

Finch regarded Tristan. "I haven't seen her do that, necessarily, but theoretically it's not that different from what I have seen her do. When I reviewed Cameron's vitals the night after her injuries, I was convinced that she would have died if not for Melanie's interventions. And it was damn subtle work she did, too. Balancing respiration, temperature, heart rate, brain activity in a body that was horrifically damaged." He paused. "What do you suspect?"

Tristan couldn't answer. What did he think? That she'd dulled his senses so that she could circumvent his security system? That she'd made him fall in love with her by mucking with his body chemistry?

If Finch was impressed, she was more skilled than Tristan had given her credit for. But she'd always taken a passive role, hadn't she? She skirted conversations about what they could do and kept to the background when anything important happened.

Except when they'd been in that lab. That day she'd been the most willing to follow Cameron in. It should have been Will, who wanted answers above all else. But Melanie had taken Tristan's hand and pulled him forward.

"You think she did something to you?" Finch said. Tristan shook off the prickles that had swept over his flesh.

"Just a little creepy to know someone who used to live with you could have killed you anytime with a touch."

The older man snorted. "It changes your perspective, doesn't it, knowing you might not be the most dangerous one. So what else do you want to know?"

"No idea. Billy is the one with a notebook full of questions."

"I've got one," Niko said, quietly.

"All right."

"How much of our lives has been planned out? How much of where we're born and who we meet is intentional?"

Finch had ghosts of long-carried pain on his face again. Years of watching people around him suffer, fall away, as his life carried him in directions he'd never intended.

"What do you think? Our parents are carefully selected. And after that, the number of our siblings controlled for. Teachers who might encourage our thinking in the wrong direction are swept away. Whatever The Maker can control, is controlled. Do you remember, Tristan, the epidemic that swept through western Advon about fifteen years ago?"

He saw it, of course. His oldest sister, lying in bed, her eyes glassy. When the day before, they'd thought the worst was over. He'd held her hand so tight. Her nail polish glittered even as her skin grew waxy. She'd taken care of them all, even when she'd caught the cold from the baby.

Tristan could only nod.

"We all had genetic immunity. That was no accident."

Tristan had no words. But something very pure and very terrible had wrapped around his heart. A pulsing and horrible thing that meant someone, somewhere, would die at his hands, if he ever found them.

"What is this about?" Niko said, his voice all fury.

Finch shrugged. "Like I said to Kardell, I don't know. But I sure do want to know. I think your set has an actual shot at finding out. The Maker is treating you very cautiously. I don't know if it's because you have the potential to put a stop to all this, the way Sean believes, but I'm watching with interest. And hopefully from a distance." He looked at their somber faces, and sighed. "Let's take a break. There's a nice beach just through those trees, and I have some lunch. Stretching your legs will be good after that drive. You ever swim in the ocean, Niko?"

Niko had not, so they carried some sandwiches along the path through the trees until they came out onto a long stretch of sand swept by waves. The water was turquoise, the sand pale gold. Niko pulled off his shoes. The boy walked right up to where the last edges of the waves could brush his feet.

Tristan sighed. Niko was not so thin as he'd been a few months before, but still awkward, with that cobbled-together look of someone in between one form and another. Not child, not man.

Certainly too young for all this.

Within minutes Niko splashed in the waves, joined by the urchins who'd sat in front of Finch's house. They laughed and yelled for nearly half an hour, children playing.

At last Tristan's apprentice took a break to eat, flopped on the sand, even though the grains stuck all over his arms and legs.

"You really do like it here," Tristan said.

"Yeah. Don't you?"

Tristan shrugged. "It kind of smells like fish. And it's all open. Too messy, I guess. Advon is my natural habitat."

"Advon is too damn cold. I nearly froze to death there a couple of winters." A shudder swept over him with the memory. "I knew some kids who did. And my buddy Blaze lost some fingers to frostbite." He looked out over the brilliant blue waves, catching sunlight. "Yeah, this is better."

"Lots of things are better than freezing to death."

"Which is how I ended up in the Agency. I wonder where the rest of my set is. I keep trying to think where I would be if my parents hadn't died. It's impossible."

"Melanie told me not to worry about what might happen. Enjoy what you have. Something like that."

Niko stood and brushed the sand off his arms and legs. "It's going to be time to go back to the city soon?"

"I don't have any further questions about the terrible things some unknown Maker has done to us. Unless you're going to give us a name, Finch."

"I don't know who it is," Finch said. "They only talked to Ellis directly, and he's never told me who it was."

"Bloody hell," Tristan muttered.

Finch shrugged and gave a half smile. "I can't help that there's so much you don't know."

The sun was high as they walked back to Finch's hiding place. The healer said goodbye to them both, as if he suspected he would not be seeing them again.

Tristan and Niko strolled back to the car, both of them quiet. Tristan tossed the keys at Niko, who grinned as he snatched them out of the air. This cheered the boy right up.

While Niko drove, Tristan thought. How many games was he a player in? He was twisted by his uncle, the agency, The Maker, Cameron, and Melanie. None of them trusted him, but they would all use him. Even though he was the one with the most power. Who was safe from him, besides other Twenty-Twos?

It was time he made use of his strengths.

017

The High Guard could have been in shambles, but it wasn't. Clemens somehow used what few resources were available to keep their schedule going without overworking anyone. She'd recruited extra members from odd corners of the Armed Forces. People who'd been overlooked for political reasons, who had skills but lacked training, who were bereft in some areas but exceptional enough in others to compensate.

All of them approached the job now with a sense of hard resolve. The odds of death had grown high. Every day one of them came to training with a story of an attempted assassination. They had started to laugh at the especially poor traps.

Sometimes one of them missed training, and Clemens would send someone to check on them. The news was always bad.

They had all moved into the Military Quarter, where at least when they slept they knew they were near other High Guards.

"We're all in one sinking boat, now," Brecht said when he showed up to take the room across from Cameron's.

The weather turned cold in November. At least half the nights power in Advon went out. The best possible place to be when this happened was pulling a shift as Ellis's personal guard. The hearths in his rooms blazed. At least half the time Cameron was so lucky. The other half she shivered under a pile of blankets.

The worst part was listening to Ellis struggle in the negotiations with the North. In spite of all advice, he refused to make any concessions. "They need us more than we need them," he growled. "If anything, they should be begging us to take them back into the fold. All the good people I've lost in this stupid charade, I'm not letting them die for no reason."

Cameron watched him stand, a stubborn rock in a poisonous sea. She would never be so short-sighted. She hoped. If the High General never revealed what he knew, then her years spent in his service would be hard to reconcile. She began to feel every minute she stood at his side, waiting for something that might launch her down the path to real answers.

Seat Member Harfield had finally achieved his greatest ambition of rising to become the most trusted politician in the High General's retinue. Cameron stood in the meetings and marveled at his attempts to rein in Ellis's temper without obviously doing so.

"Sir, will you allow me to be honest with you?" he said one morning as an advisory meeting huddled around a table, shivering while pretending not to be cold. The seat members to either side of Conrad Harfield scooted away. They seemed to know how thin the line was that William's father walked as he tried to coax Ellis into reason.

"I imagine you will be, whether I like it or not. Go ahead."

"We've discussed at great length your moral stance on the frozen negotiations. And I applaud how firmly you believe in the value of the lives lost in the conflict. I agree that such a sacrifice should not be wasted—"

"This isn't honesty, Harfield the Elder, this is pandering."

"Advon is freezing. The blanket manufacturers might be praising your name, but no one else is. And while we are freezing, the North is starving. People might not be dying in combat, but they are dying."

"I already know all this."

Cameron didn't see even a flicker of irritation on Conrad's face. In fact, he smiled. Would Sean Ellis, plagued by frustration and doubt, finally begin to let the words sway him? Cam had little love for politicians, but Seat Member Harfield wasn't wrong, even if he was only trying to make things right again so he could gain more power.

"I know you do, sir. I point all this out because I know that these problems run counter to your hopes for Cotarion. When you took this position, it was with the desire to make this nation more powerful. Instead, we find our borders crumbling and our people suffering. We are facing the very real possibility that Cotarion will soon collapse."

He stopped speaking, leaving a deep vacuum behind his words. The High General stood tall, his face going ruddy and then pale in turns. He turned to look out a window at his city, cold and still.

"You have a plan to prevent this impending doom."

"Every person in this room believes he or she knows how to do a better job than you are, sir."

A shuffle ran around the advisors as Sean looked back to them. He scowled. Their faces were furious and frightened. What the hell was Conrad up to? It must be a big move if he was willing to betray so many of his fellow politicians at once.

"Conrad. Really, now, you're exaggerating," said a woman seated next to William Harfield. She tugged at her silk scarf, and her voice wasn't steady.

"And what about you, Seat Member Harfield? Can you do a better job than me?"

"None of us can do anything without you. All of our fates are tied to yours. But I think I can help you keep Cotarion intact."

Ellis had to know that he was being used. But Seat Member Harfield had timed his speech well. The High General was desperate for solutions. But was it even possible at this point to salvage Cotarion's government?

The High General scowled deeply, then snapped, "Harfield the Younger."

William couldn't sit up any straighter than he already did, but he managed to look as if he had. "Yes, sir?"

"Any thoughts on what your father's trying to do?"

"I'm sorry, sir, this is not . . . I'm not comfortable even guessing at political machinations." William stared down the table at his father, who showed not the slightest sign of annoyance that Ellis was needling his own son about his plans.

"You must have some idea. One theory."

It was a test of loyalty, Even William could see that. He kept looking at his father, as if hoping for some sign of what he should do. It never came, but the woman with the scarf nudged William's elbow.

Finally, Will drew in a breath and said, "I don't know exactly, sir, but my father will exchange his help now for a higher position later. Of course, under the current circumstances, if he has an idea for making things better—"

"That's enough. This meeting is not a call to discuss the direness of current events. So, does anybody have anything to contribute besides vague promises of miraculous assistance? No? Then you're all dismissed."

The meeting broke and the advisors left. Cameron wondered if William's father had Tristan watching over him. If not, there was a good chance he wouldn't see the end of the day. Not after throwing all his comrades under the sword.

"Kardell, I want to speak to you before your shift ends. Kao, wait outside."

When it was just them, Ellis sank into a chair. His fingers drummed the table. "What would you do, Cameron? He wants to use me."

He'd never before addressed her by her first name. She almost felt sorry for him.

"I wouldn't accept his help. He will turn on you. But I would have negotiated with the North a long time ago."

The sneer returned abruptly. "Helpful. Well, for both our sakes,' I hope you keep dodging the assassins. When you go, I recommend you speak to Doctor Harfield about reining in his temper. I was moments from taking him down in a meeting yesterday. He's an explosion waiting to happen, and your set can't afford to lose someone else. Dismissed."

Cameron left. Her salute with Brecht as he took her place was automatic. Was there anything she did, now, that wasn't automatic? Everything seemed to consist of a cold, gray-toned series of edges. *Stand guard, train, remember to laugh at jokes, try to sleep even though it was freezing and all the other High Guards were bunking up out of desperation, and no one's ever asked or even hinted at you, because your humanity is suspect, and besides, you jumped at High Guard Stacy last week when he came up behind you while you were making coffee.*

She arrived at the door to Harfield's office. She took a couple of moments to clear her mind of bitter thoughts. She had a task. She knocked.

William whipped the door open, his face an open book of betrayal and anger. He must have been expecting his father. It all fell away in half a heartbeat to be replaced by a weary smile.

"Cameron. Come on in. I see you all the time but we never talk. How have you been?"

"I'm fine. Sean Ellis sent me to talk to you."

William groaned. "Did he tell you that he was goading me? He wanted me to get angry."

"It doesn't matter. He's the High General, and he can do what he wants. If you lose control and throw fire at him, you'll be dead." She swallowed hard. Her throat had tightened, her chest, too, and they did not want to loosen. William, thankfully, was looking at his feet, so he didn't notice her struggling. The last thing she needed was for him to think she cared.

"I'll try harder," he said. Then he looked up at her. "Since you're here, I just want to say, I think you should go and talk to Owena. She's had a rough time."

"She doesn't want to talk to me."

"I think she will."

Cameron sighed. "Look, it's probably best if I give her some more time. Besides, I'm so busy right now, I'm mentoring two of the new High Guards—"

"Do you know what Armel would say to you right now? He'd tell you not to spew so much bullshit. And as far as I'm concerned, this should be your top priority. I didn't value Erika at all, you know. I was always so annoyed she made me go out and talk to people. I fought with her about it all the time. Family is important. You don't know how much until they aren't there."

Cameron would have liked to point out that William's own father had just yanked the rug out from under a whole room full of people that included William, but the reaction wasn't something she felt like dealing with.

"Fine. I'll go see what I can do. But I better damn well have something to give her when I go."

William smiled. "Good. I think you'll be glad you did. I know she will."

"Don't forget what I said about keeping your temper in check in front of the High General."

He gave her perhaps the sloppiest salute she'd ever seen. He must have been hoping to get a laugh, but she didn't have the energy to fake one.

Cameron left the Military Quarter later that afternoon. She moved quickly and avoided the main streets. The wind was bitter cold, but her jacket rebuffed most of it. She definitely would have liked to wear a hat, but she couldn't do anything that might muffle sound. Better to have frozen ears than to miss the shuffle of an assassin's step. The creak of a bowstring.

Owena and Armel had bought a house in one of the quieter neighborhoods close to Gates. It was little shabby, but they'd given it fresh paint and had begun patching it up. Cameron had laughed at Armel when he'd first shown her the place. "But Armel, you've never lifted a hammer. Who's going to do all the work?"

She went up the steps onto the porch. The handrail didn't wobble, so someone must have done something about it. Cameron clutched the bag of things she'd brought, feeling now that it wasn't enough, that it would never be enough. She rang the doorbell.

Her sister answered. When Owena saw it was Cameron, she went utterly still. She did not even appear to breathe.

"Hi. I know I should have been here. I didn't want to feel it. I knew it would hurt, and I knew that if I was with the people I loved, the people who loved him, I wouldn't be able to keep it at a distance. But I hurt you, and I'm sorry. And I brought some stuff. Please don't cry like that." This last was in response to the huge sobs that now shook Owena.

"Come in, stupid! Cam, you're such a complete ass." Owena pulled her through the door and hugged her, still sobbing. She remembered to let go before Cameron started to feel claustrophobic. Then she stood there wiping her eyes. "Are you hungry? I have all these frozen things that people gave me, and I don't feel like eating any of them these days."

Cameron agreed to the food. She sat in the breakfast nook while Owena popped something in the oven. She watched her sister as she moved around the kitchen. There was something strange about her. She walked like she carried something heavy.

"Harfield talked to me this morning."

Owena smiled. "He's a bit meddlesome, isn't he?"

"He does think he knows what's best for everything. Besides himself."

Owena sat at the table across from Cameron. She looked tired. Strange. "I need your help, Cam."

"Okay . . . "

"I'm pregnant, and I need to know what you think."

Cameron's already oft-mocked verbal skills fled her entirely. She felt some small blossom of something that wasn't gray or bleak. But she kept it to herself. Owena had tears in her eyes again, and her fingers were knotted together. Cameron reached out and took her sister's hands in hers.

"It's okay to be scared," Cameron said. Owena clasped her fingers hard, her hands shaking. "It's okay to be angry, for now."

Owena's eyes lit up. "He should be here. He knew when he left that day that he might not come back. He was in such a weird mood. I can't ever understand why he'd throw all this away. Me. Our life."

"I wish I could tell you. He never talked to me about it." She and Armel had both taken the idea of justice seriously. It was why they'd gotten along so well, why she'd trusted him when it was time to find Erika. She knew she could count on him to do what was right, even if it was hard, even if it meant sacrifice.

Maybe he'd seen the mess his uncle had made of running Cotarion. Had he hoped to force his uncle to step down with the scrap of evidence he had? Had he hoped to make things right?

The timer for the food went off. Cameron jumped up to pull it from the oven while Owena pulled out a plate and a fork.

"Listen, Owena. I'm really happy for you. And I think you'll be happy, too, when you're ready."

Owena smiled weakly. "I am happy. At least a little, I think. Ugh, that really does not look appealing. I told Mom she needs to tell people to send boxes of crackers."

"I've been eating in the mess hall the past few weeks, so this is practically gourmet. I'll come over and take care of clearing them out of your freezer anytime. As a matter of fact, all the High Guards might. So, how long have you been pregnant?"

"I'll be twelve weeks on Monday."

Cameron did some quick math. "Owena! That was before the wedding."

"Oh, don't act so shocked. You and Ethan lived together for a year."

Cameron cleared her plate and scooped up some more casserole. It was the cheese. She never got real cheese in the mess hall. Just flavorless yellow goop.

"Anything I didn't know before, I certainly do now. When the High Guard barracks are cold, no one sleeps alone. And it's been cold a lot recently."

Owena raised her eyebrows. "Oh? And who's your bed-warmer?"

"Nobody. I've got too much of a reputation. Besides, I really don't need to get attached to anyone right now." She looked up from her plate to find Owena staring at her, mouth agape. "What is it? Do I have something on my face?"

"You just confessed attachment to fellow humans." Her brow creased. "I guess you've been having a rough time, too."

"Nothing I can't handle. How about you open this thing I bought you, and we'll never speak of it again. I don't need the whole world thinking I'm anything less than solid ice."

Cameron received another hug over the gift she'd brought, which was a book of short stories and some candles for when the power went out. "Armel read this collection a few years ago. He kept bugging me to read it, too, and I never did, not until last week. They really are good."

She stayed a little longer while she and Owena tried to figure out why the bathtub faucet leaked. Then Cameron insisted on reattaching a piece of trim that had fallen off a doorframe. They talked about baby-proofing, and baby names, and strange pregnancy symptoms. Cameron fluctuated between being appalled and strangely giddy by proxy. At last, after looking at the absurdly small hat Owena had knitted, she declared it was time she left. And Owena looked sad to see her leave.

The bubble of warmth which had surrounded Cameron at her sister's house was stripped away within a block. The wind felt colder than ever, and the sky was black. All the good things had become so fragile with bitterness streaked through. Armel would never know his child, he had left his family bereft. Did it matter if he'd been trying to make things right, when the result was this?

I could have stopped it. So many times, I could have told him to stop.

By the time she got back to the Military Quarter her face felt frozen. She exchanged perfunctory salutations with the High Guards in the hallway. Someone said her name several times before she realized it.

She looked up. Clemens stood in the hallway with the newest High Guard recruit.

"Palmroy? Did they tell you there was free bacon? I'm sorry to say there is no bacon here. We even buy our own coffee. Clemens always says she's going to get us free coffee, but it never happens."

Thea Clemens said, "Do you mind showing him around, Kardell? I've got to work him into the schedule."

Gordon grinned at Cameron. She sighed, and showed him around the training room, the common room, and their mess hall, making introductions as she went.

Finally, she stopped in front of his room.

"There you go. I hope you can run while you're still falling, because the job starts now. Rely on what you're good at. You put people at ease. You have good focus. The rest you'll learn as—"

The lights overhead flickered and then went out. Cameron's sigh was drowned out by cursing from the other High Guards. Cameron clicked on a small flashlight, which she kept in her pocket at all times.

"It's going to get cold. Don't be shy about asking to share a bed with someone else. Everyone does it."

He looked around, and indeed, the other High Guards were in the process of negotiating who would sleep where. Then he looked back at Cameron. "Can I stay with you, then?"

"Everyone but me."

She turned away. When she reached the door to her own room, and stared at the blackness within, she paused.

"Palmroy."

"Yep."

"You can, but you have to promise not to touch me while I'm sleeping. I keep a dagger under my pillow, and I'd hate to stab you."

He laughed, but stopped when she didn't join him. "You're serious?"

"It's been a pretty dangerous job recently. Second thoughts?"

He shook his head. In the beam of her light, she saw on his face a small reflection of how she'd been feeling for weeks. Like the cold only started at the skin, and from there it just plunged deeper, carried in blood, filling up bones, reaching one frostflower at a time for the heart.

Which in Cameron's case had always been ice, hadn't it?

She stepped back so he could go into her room. At least the topmost layer might thaw.

018

William drank tea and huddled in his coat, leaning over his notebook as the orb glowed. Words vibrated out of the copper rings. Into three notebooks he had scrawled most of the history of The Altered. The cold pierced him, but still he wrote.

"Many years of development went into the super-soldiers, primarily focused on stabilizing their personalities. Unfortunately, their drive to follow orders was so strong that they were easily swayed, upon encountering a cunning enemy, to join them. It was determined that the next series would require more autonomy, while also having more fail-safes."

Cameron hovered in his mind. "The Twenty-Fours."

"Elmond and Lang, protected and assisted by The Altered who remained committed to them, spent thirty years developing Series Twenty-Four, taking all they'd learned—"

William gently spun one of the rings so that the voice halted mid-sentence. He thumbed back through his notes, looking at the tops of the pages, where he'd written the timeframes for everything that had happened since the day the Skylark Program began working on The Altered. The math did not make sense. "Elmond would have been almost a hundred and twenty five?"

He stopped and stared into the darkness around him for a few minutes. Then he wrote in his notebook, *Elmond would have been at least a hundred and twenty five.*

Was she the first Altered? Or was something else happening? Perhaps there was more than one Elmond? It was a small, strange thing but it struck him, because it felt like a glimpse of something larger and something stranger. Something he did not yet know enough to wrap his mind around. He tapped his pencil under that last sentence.

There was too much he didn't know. Every word that rose up out of the metal rings from that glinting orb was only a scrap on the floor under a table laden with an enormous spread of knowledge. He could smell the fine dishes in the air, but he could not see them, let alone reach them.

Scraps would have to suffice, for now. He spun the rings back into position.

"Elmond and Lang took all they learned from the failings of previous series, and used them to perfect Series Twenty-Four. They allowed for more variation in personality from one Twenty-Four to the next, within the confines of a carefully-designed algorithm. This made them more difficult for the enemy to predict. All, however, were given a strong propensity for logical reasoning detached from emotional states, and some mild physical enhancements to make them more durable. Most importantly, however, their ability and the instructions associated with it could only be activated in a lab, and used once before becoming dormant again. Otherwise, Twenty-Fours were scarcely different from those without augmentations.

"Their Alteration was the ability to change genetic code, and their primary purpose was to remove the powers of the most volatile

Altered, although if they gained full control of their ability and learned to work beyond those constraints, they could potentially give Alterations to those who had none."

"And no one thought that would end badly?" William's eyebrows rose. He was constantly waiting for someone in this tale to stand up and point out the potential pitfalls of an idea, but anyone who'd done so had been laughed away. This wasn't that kind of story, and he knew because he was living the aftermath of it.

"It was speculated that a Twenty-Four might judge someone as potentially helpful to their cause, and in that case, should be able to make that person more capable of fighting. Elmond and Lang had begun to acknowledge that their creations had been unpredictable in spite of their attempts to refine and perfect them, and saw the value of embracing human individuality."

The words drifted through the air, of the release of Series Twenty-Four. By that point, the survival of humanity was hanging in the balance, and The Altered had split into two distinct sides. One group declared the genetically-enhanced were the future of the human race, and they were bent on the systematic destruction of anyone without enhancements. They called themselves The Source. On the other side were those who believed The Altered were a mistake, and only those without Alterations deserved to be called human, and they called themselves Guardians. The Guardians were few in number, and given to self-sacrifice. Their cause was not helped by the fact that the most powerful and volatile Altered tended to join The Source.

The Twenty-Fours shifted the balance almost overnight. Their development had been kept a secret, so they felled the most powerful leaders of The Source before the enemy could grasp the implications of their ability. When realization dawned, the fight against the Twenty-Fours began. The conflict was desperate.

A Series 17 captured and learned how to control a Twenty-Four, and activate the ability from within (this William underlined and starred so much it would be impossible to miss) and the scientists counteracted this by giving Twenty-Fours a handheld device that could run their activation sequence. They soon found a constantly-activated Twenty-Four was a very different thing from one carrying the latent ability. The cold logic ran rampant, and soon Guardians, The Source, and even Elmond and Lang feared the Twenty-Four. A few Altered abandoned the sides they'd chosen, and fought beside the Twenty-Fours to finally end the conflict.

"Ultimately, Series Twenty-Four successfully controlled The Altered, but at great cost. Project Skylark was veritably destroyed, and the death toll was staggering. By the end of the wars, humanity was scattered, The Altered all but extinct."

William leaned forward and spun the rings, silencing the voice. It was late, or rather, early, and he was too tired to see what difference it made to know all this.

William carried a box full of what sounded like glass up the steep staircase to his mother's new apartment. Tristan was definitely leaving the heaviest boxes for him. At least when he was done he would have his house to himself again.

Tristan dashed by, carrying a stack of boxes labelled with things like "sheets" and "pillows." He elbowed William.

"Come on, Billy, you're falling behind."

William cursed under his breath.

"I heard that!"

Finally he achieved the fourth floor, then shuffled down the hall to the apartment, which was, of course, centered between the two staircases. Tristan passed him with another load of boxes before he'd quite reached the door, and he shut it right in William's face.

William swallowed some more expletives, then balanced on one foot, supporting the box with a raised leg and one hand, so he could reach the doorknob. It refused to turn.

"Damn it, Tris, open the door."

It was a long time before his cousin swung the door open. With an expression of contrived innocence, he said, "Oh my goodness, did I lock that door? I'm so sorry, must have done it out of habit. Be careful with that box, it looks heavy."

William finally heaved the box onto the kitchen counter. "What has gotten into you, Tris. Honestly, you're like a rabbit on too much caffeine."

"Cuz', don't be jealous I achieved enlightenment. It's available to you, too, once you accept that absolutely none of this matters."

"None of *what* matters?"

Tristan spread his arms. "*This.* That rug Auntie is rolling out, this box of glasses, which is good because at least half of them are broken, your very creepy office full of notes and all those boards with strings. Doesn't matter."

William looked over at his mother as she straightened the rug in the living room. She just shrugged.

"What in the world brought this on?"

Tristan had begun unpacking boxes and sliding things onto shelves. With a lot of leaps and excessive balancing on chairs. "I told you. I achieved enlightenment."

William turned his attention to unpacking the box of glasses. As he slid them onto a shelf in the kitchen, he considered all the other boxes and their contents. It wasn't all going to fit. The way the shelf bowed under the weight of the dishes wasn't comforting, either.

"Are you sure this is the right place for you, Mom? It's pretty small."

"It's not like I need much. I want to be able to do this myself, and I don't think I can if I try to live the way I have all my life. All those things. Like Tristan was saying, what did it matter?"

It was a lot easier to dismiss the importance of a stable life, complete with decent home and good furniture, when one had never gone without those things, but he didn't argue. At the moment, it appeared he was in the minority.

He and Tristan spent the morning unpacking boxes and giving opinions on where photos should hang. Tristan, of course, disagreed with all of William's suggestions. It was with an aching back and frayed nerves that he left after lunch for a meeting with Sean Ellis.

He arrived in the Military Quarter half frozen and in a foul mood. This was not improved when he found a messenger at his office door. The slight young woman told him that his meeting had changed locations. Instead of staying in the building, he'd need to walk across the square to the High General's Quarters. The messenger dashed away as soon as she'd said this. Whether because of William's scowl or because she was busy it was hard to say.

At least his annoyance took some of the bite out of the wind. The energy around him, which he could usually keep tuned out, whipped in golden streamers around him. He didn't try to dim them. They added interest to the barren trees, and the spinning eddies mirrored his irritation.

Finally he made it to the High General's personal quarters. He found three High Guards in the hall outside instead of the usual two. High Guard Brecht caught William's eye as he approached, and his expression made William slow.

Brecht jerked his head at the door behind him, which was open just a crack. William, hoping he understood the signal, stopped just at the side of the doorframe. He stared at the wall, listening. Ellis's voice, humming with fury, was clearly audible.

"—aren't being honest. Everyone knows why you allowed Armel too close. You just won't admit it."

"I made a mistake, Sir. It won't happen again." The responding voice was flat and weary. Cameron.

"The question is why. I have to know that you see it. You're no good to me if you don't understand it." The High General's voice could have pried apart welded iron.

"Sir."

"Admit it."

Cameron must have been very tired, or he'd been needling her for a long time.

"I loved him. He was my brother. I trusted him."

"If you could have saved him—"

"Of course. I would have."

"Even if it meant—"

"Sacrificing you?" She was quiet for several seconds. "No."

The High General gave a bark of laughter, though William couldn't see anything funny. "People think *I'm* monstrous. Because I'll sacrifice the lives of people I don't care about if it's for the greater good. Because I look at life and see the scales. But you. You sacrifice the people you love. People you care about, and who put their faith in you. And for what?"

Cameron didn't respond. William wished she would. He willed her to say something.

"I see your future, Kardell. I see the peace you long for slipping through your fingers. You will sacrifice everyone who is close to you, betray every friend, and you will gain nothing. You will live in the ashes. That is what your willingness to let your friends die will gain you. And you will turn cold. And you will kill countless more people, because they are against you, at first; and then because they are in your way; then because you aren't sure if they are your allies; and then because killing is all you know how to do."

"You can't predict the future, Sir."

"No? I already see it happening, Kardell. I know you feel it. Ever since you killed Erika. You fought it, but without Armel, you aren't quite human anymore. Am I wrong?"

William looked up to Brecht and mouthed, *Why?* Why would Ellis be doing this? Why would he try to unearth the weaknesses of the one person who'd saved him so often?

High Guard Brecht held his hands out at chest level, in fists. Then he snapped them apart, like he'd broken a stick. William saw, and understood.

With enemies closing in, Sean Ellis needed allies. Perhaps he'd seen in Cameron someone who might not stand with him. So he would make certain she obeyed.

Was she vulnerable enough for it to work? It was impossible to know what her long silences meant. But in one moment she'd lost

Ethan and Armel. She was strong, yes, but that would be enough to crack anyone.

"So. I'm not wrong," Ellis said triumphantly.

William looked at Brecht. *What can I do?*

Brecht smirked. Then he reached out, grabbed William's arm, and shoved him through the door.

The papers in William's arms flew up. He hit the ground hard, mostly with his elbows. At least it wasn't his face. Pages fluttered down all around him.

He felt something cold on his throat, and he stopped moving. A sword pressed against the soft skin just under his jaw. He looked up at Cameron. How could he have imagined she might be vulnerable? Tired, maybe, judging by the dark circles under her eyes, but her gaze was as hard as he'd ever seen it.

She said, "You tripped? Don't nod."

"It was an accident."

The sword left his skin, and returned to her scabbard. She stepped back next to Ellis, who smirked. William collected his scattered papers. Some had landed in the fireplace where they curled into ashes.

Brecht poked his head into the room. "It would seem Doctor Harfield didn't see my foot."

"Amazingly, we noticed. Since you're here, Doctor Harfield, would you like to begin our meeting?"

"I'm afraid I might have lost some of my data, Sir."

Sean Ellis waved a hand. "Somehow, I doubt that will make a difference. Unless, of course, the numbers were a critical part of your miraculous solution to our power problems."

"I'm afraid not, Sir."

The High General, never known for his patience, prowled around the room as William spoke, snacking on handfuls of his favorite almonds. Could he be absorbing anything William said?

At least the fire was warm, and the chairs were comfortable. William availed himself of an apple from the bowl on the coffee table then settled into his talk. Occasionally he glanced up at Cameron. She returned to her usual watchful poise. He hadn't realized just how upset she'd been until he saw her calm again.

What gave Ellis the right to torment the guards who defended his life? And out of all of them, Cameron deserved it least. Few other living High Guards had sacrificed so much.

Sometimes he still woke up at night, brought out of sleep by the memory of her struggling to breathe, her hand weak in his. She had been willing to give her life for this man now trying to tear her apart.

William looked down at the char on his paper. There was no way to make the numbers add up. Whatever he tried, the power would keep running out. Even cycling blackouts hadn't helped. How many people were freezing because of Ellis? How many were going to die so he could be safe?

"Doctor Harfield?"

William looked up. He realized that he'd stopped talking. A warmth blossomed in his chest that had nothing to do with the fire in the hearth. The bands of energy in the room were not flowing with their usual chaos. They wrapped and twined around his hands and arms, ready for him to pull. Cameron had a hand on the hilt of her blade. William knew that she would draw if he showed the slightest sign of losing control.

He swallowed. It didn't seem to help. He closed his eyes so he couldn't see Cameron's fingers tightening. He fought to keep his thoughts away from the fact that she was preparing to kill him. For Ellis. Always for Ellis.

I want to live. I don't want her to live with my blood on her hands.

He thought about the construction of wind turbines. The factories where all the parts were made, what types of metals were used and in what proportions. Where the ores were refined, where they'd been mined. Who the designers had been for each type, the arguments of the engineers while deciding if turbines in the lower hills were even viable, or how to install them in the dunes next to the ocean . . .

William opened his eyes, and cleared his throat. "Um, where was I?"

"You were talking about the balance of the electrical cost of expedited production versus power output of additional turbines. Although the engineers made more sense of it than you are."

"Frankly, sir, this is all outside of my area of expertise. I'm afraid that I wasn't able to find anything the engineers missed. It will take ten years to replace the power supply we lost when the north seceded."

"I don't know why I keep you on, Doctor Harfield," Ellis snapped. "You have no solutions, and you're a constant danger."

William thought about the careful balance of the turbine arms, the way they had been shaped to catch the energy of the wind. He remembered watching one spin, seeing the bands of energy flow around those great shining arms.

"Then why don't you just fire me, sir?"

Sean Ellis leaned forward, his eyes glinting. "Because, Doctor Harfield, these are lean times, and you might still have a use." His face lit up. "In the next ten minutes, let's revisit our strategies. Maybe there's something new we can dig up. If you have a specialty, I believe that is it."

Cameron didn't take her eyes off William for the rest of his stay in the High General's quarters. He tried to reassure her that he was striving to keep his emotions under control, but there was only so much he could communicate without words. She looked as grim as he'd ever seen her.

When he left, he carried with him several new books. Sean Ellis seemed to think reading on strategy would do him good. He spent a few hours in his office organizing his notes and considering what might be in the dusty corners of his brain that could save Cotarion.

He stopped by Tristan's house on his way home. He was stunned without knowing why, and he didn't know of anyone else he could talk to.

Tristan's buoyant mood seemed to have burst. William had expected to find him bouncing around as he'd been at his mother's apartment. Instead, Tristan greeted him with a scowl and a grumble.

"I see the enlightenment wore off," William said, dropping his bag on the chair by the door, divesting himself of hat, gloves, boots, and coat.

Tristan threw himself into a chair. "It didn't suit me. You look like someone who's interested in unburdening his mind."

William started helping himself to some tea. The steel and brick of Tristan's apartment looked cold when the banks of windows showed nothing but gray building and dim gray skies.

"I don't know where to start."

Tristan smirked. "I can do it for you. Once upon a time, there was a girl named Cameron Kardell."

William kept his hands busy with the tea. The back of his neck got hot. His stomach swooped like he'd been going downstairs and missed a step, like he was falling, hands flung out for the railing or a wall to stop him. He hadn't even known he was on a staircase.

"It usually starts that way, doesn't it?" He said it quietly, half-hoping Tristan wouldn't hear.

"For a while now. What is it this time?"

"Sean Ellis is torturing her. I heard him today, blaming her for Armel. He said she was . . . going cold, ever since Erika. That eventually she'll be killing for no reason."

Tell me, am I wrong?

Tristan considered. William strained out the tea leaves, and took his first sip. It was hot, but the mint cooled his mouth and throat.

"Was he getting to her?"

"Hard to tell. I couldn't see her, and she didn't talk much. When I did see her she was upset, but that might have just been because High Guard Brecht threw me through the door."

Tristan's eyebrows went up. "So, the other High Guards are worried? That isn't good. She's definitely been broody recently."

William folded his hands around his mug. "That's what I thought. And she was just letting him say terrible things. I know she's a High Guard, but is it in her job description that she has to let him walk all over her?"

"Billy, have you ever known her to do anything without good reason?"

"No."

"Then I'd say don't worry about it. She and Sean Ellis are playing some kind of game. They're each trying to gain some kind of advantage. It's best for both of us if we stay far, far away from it."

This didn't do much to satisfy William's sense of fair. Although, on thinking about it, getting worked up on Cameron's behalf seemed ridiculous. She could take care of herself, far better than he could ever hope to.

"Hey, I've been meaning to ask for a while now. You see electrical energy, as well as all the world kind, right?"

William refrained from making a technical correction, and nodded.

"Can you check my place for anything that doesn't belong? I've really got to track down this supposed spy. The Agency is breathing down my neck about it. There's condensation on the hair back there."

William suppressed a sigh, put down his cup, and proceeded to poke around. Tristan followed just behind him wherever he went, which was unnerving. There was little to see, as the power was out and Tristan's décor was sparse.

He went into the corner of every room. He lifted pillows and peered under couches. He scooched chairs. He looked into cracks. He slid clothes around inside closets. As he finished up in Tristan's bedroom, he grew desperate. He really didn't want this to get serious.

Finally, as he replaced the blankets, Tristan said the dreaded words. "The roof."

They climbed the iron stairs up to the heavy door that led out onto the top of the building. The hinges creaked as it swung out. Tristan still managed to lower it gently.

Up above, there was a small table and chairs, which had been added when Mel was dating Tristan. Some pots scattered around held the twigs of long-dead flowers. There was nothing more than a ghost of some summer night spent laughing, air perfumed by, what were those, some kind of rose?

William peered in every nook, moving quickly. Once the sun dropped over the horizon the wind scoured the rooftop. He finished his survey without noticing anything strange.

"Sorry, Tris, I don't—wait a minute." He had glanced over the railing to look at the street below, and he'd caught the faintest glimmer of . . . something. It was as miniscule as a single falling snowflake. He squinted. It flickered again.

Tristan leaned over the rail, his gaze following William's. He pulled on a pair of black gloves, reached over the wall, and groped in a cranny of the building's cornice.

What he pulled out was much smaller than anything William had anticipated. It looked like a rectangle of glass. But the opacity was strange. Sometimes it glinted like a fish scale. Every now and then he saw a tiny flash of power run through it.

"What the hell is this?" Tristan breathed. His silver eyes were wide, his hands unsteady as he passed it over to William.

It was so light. William turned it in his hands. When he focused hard, he saw filaments of power, like glowing spiderweb. But they all spiraled in. He couldn't get a grip on any of them.

"I can't turn it on. It's wound tight."

He and Tristan stood in silence for several frigid moments.

At last Tristan spoke. "That's the scariest damn thing I've ever seen."

019

WILLIAM REFUSED TO have the meeting at Tristan's, even though it was by far the most spacious place. He was entrenched in the idea that carrying all his notes and diagrams would simply be too risky. And then what if someone asked about something in a notebook he'd left at home?

Tristan made sure to get his retribution by whining about the location as often as possible. As well as the fact that he'd been turned into a messenger boy.

"Tell me where Melanie lives and I'll go tell her about the meeting myself," Will snapped. Tristan slouched off to do as he'd been bidden. At least his bad mood ensured that he wasn't tempted when Mel flirted.

He knew he was surlier than normal. Everything he'd once believed about his ability to see lies, to know whether he could trust someone, was now cast into doubt. Melanie, simple and soft, a retreat from a harsh world, now seemed more dangerous than an asp.

What good was he, if he could be beaten in combat, if he couldn't read someone? What was his purpose, if he could be fooled?

He met Cameron as she left the Military Quarter. There seemed little point in pretending that he wasn't guarding her from assassins.

He'd nearly drained his personal bank account to pay The Agency for the time he spent on it, but it bought him a little more breathing space from Red.

She didn't roll her eyes when she saw him, but her lips thinned as he fell into step beside her.

"They aren't giving up?"

Tristan gave her his best grin. "The one that gets you could retire and live like a king. Brecht's price is excellent, too. Thea Clemens is worth the most, though. Probably why she hasn't left the Military Quarter in weeks."

Cameron's eyebrows were a low line. Good. She should worry.

They made small talk on their way to William's house. That had grown easier the past few months, mostly because Tristan had learned not to expect too much. When a silence rose, it was he who filled it. When she grew grim, he joked.

Three Sides handed out coffee and tea. The line wrapped around the block. The skies above had been heavy with snow for days. The whole city seemed to be holding its breath. When it started to fall, things were going to get desperate. Niko had said that some of his friends had begged him for recommendations to The Agency. They would do anything for a warm place to sleep when the streets were freezing and the shelters full.

"It's getting bad," Cameron said in a voice so low only Tristan could hear.

"Yeah, sweetheart." Normalcy wouldn't hold much longer. Tristan hoped Cameron had a plan for getting her distance from Ellis, soon. Was this loyalty to some code of honor, or did she enjoy playing dangerous games?

They arrived at William's house without incident. Corkboards covered in papers filled the living room, punctuated by a single blackboard for note-taking. The smell of cookies and coffee wafted over them. Cameron smiled, a ghostly upturning of her lips that vanished almost as soon as it had appeared. William entered the living room from the kitchen, ruffling his hair.

"I swear, I know this looks insane," he waved a hand at the boards, "but it's not. It's just a lot of information, and I wanted to make sure we could all see it."

"It's fine, Will. No one thinks you're crazy," Cameron said.

"Speak for yourself." Melanie flopped into a chair with a cup and a cookie. "You guys are obsessed. This is not normal."

"One could argue that we aren't in a normal situation," William said. "Cam, Tris, do you want any coffee?"

They all settled in, although not without some stilted commentary on the weather. Cameron took a chair beside the fireplace and perched there eating a plate of cookies, looking more at ease with each bite. Melanie hummed a song, which Tristan recognized as one of Ethan's. Cameron did a splendid job ignoring that, or maybe she just didn't recognize it. Tristan roosted on the back of a chair. William kept sitting on the couch across from the fire, then hopping up to rearrange a board, then sitting down again.

Finally, when her cookies were reduced to crumbs, Cameron said, "All right, let's get started. Will, if you could do a very quick review."

William at once engaged a mode Tristan had never seen before. He'd never known his cousin to stick to the realm of solid facts without wandering off into his own conclusions and suppositions. His time as an advisor seemed to have focused him.

"So far, we are certain that the following people are Altered: the four of us, Ellis, Niko, Finch, and Erika. Tristan encountered another suspected Altered who fled with Doctor Maikon. We've located two hidden bunkers, one laboratory, and an information repository. Cameron encountered a third suspected bunker, and I've mapped the locations of eight more potential bunkers. The most vital of the information I found in the historical archives were in the papers I sent out last week, which I assume nobody read." No one objected that they had. "So. Does anyone have anything to add?"

"Ellis might not be a reliable source of information. I doubt he will tell me who The Maker is without some serious compromise," Cameron said.

William pulled one of the blank blackboards forward. "That's our focus. Maybe together we can figure out who it is. Personally, my money is on Ellis." He wrote an "E" on the board, and began a list of evidence. Chalk dust rose as William scrawled. He might as well have been printing, "He's a bastard," repeatedly.

Cameron said, "He's scared. Indecisive. And I don't think The Maker would want to be a 24, if they could choose anything."

Tristan nodded. "Not to mention his position gives him very little freedom to work."

William's heart rate went up a few ticks. "He had no reason to make me an Advisor. I'm terrible at it. That only makes sense if he's The Maker, and he's keeping us all close."

"Finch said Ellis wants to fight what was done to us. If that's true, then keeping other Altered where he can see them makes perfect sense," Cameron said.

William didn't continue his arguments, but he wrote out Cameron's points in silence, his nostrils flared. "Any other suggestions?"

"Reese," Tristan said. "He's about the only other person who's had direct contact with all of us. He knows more than he should." He kept a close eye on Melanie, but she was fanning out her purple-tipped strands between her fingers, looking for split ends.

"Not as much as he believes, though," William said, starting on a second chalkboard labeled "R." "Those books he lent me turned out to be useless—"

"No. Because of those books we found the Compendium. You'd never heard of it before."

William paused, and wavered. "It's a thin thread, if he wanted us to find that book."

Cameron sat forward, her eyes sharp. "But it helped us prepare. Made us more certain. The book you found that reference in, was it common?"

"It wasn't unique. There's a copy in the library at Gates. I hadn't read it because it's one of the driest historical texts known to academia, and that's saying something." William ruffled his hair again. "He did flag the pages that mentioned the Compendium, but they weren't the only ones."

"If he was The Maker, though, wouldn't he have done more for Erika? She was his star student," Cameron said. "What do you think, Melanie? He knew you were Altered for a while."

"He didn't really say much. He gave me books, like he did William. Encouraged me to volunteer at the clinic in Brook's Cove. The day he called me to patch you up, Will, was the first time he'd personally asked for my help." Her voice was even. Her heart rate remained low.

She noticed Tristan staring at her, and favored him with a smile. Her pupils widened. If it was all an act, then it was a convincing one.

"He's never acknowledged that I'm Altered at all," Cameron pointed out.

"If not Reese, or Ellis, then who do you suspect, Cameron? I know you have theories." William said this with his face primed for an expression of incredulity.

"A few. I strongly suspect that it's someone we haven't met yet. If it were me, I'd stay hidden. With Ellis still mucking around, especially. Of the people we do know," her eyes went to William's face, "I'm beginning to think it could be Seat Member Conrad Harfield."

William let out a loud, "HAH!" But then, very slowly, the amused smile fell away, to be replaced by a blank horror. "Wait. Why?"

"I've never seen anyone, even the other politicians, maintain control as well as he does. The way he's been nudging Ellis around has been masterful. His connections to all of us equals that of Reese or Ellis. The more I see him in meetings, the more I think he has a much larger purpose."

William and Tristan both sat in shocked silence. Oh, Cameron. She couldn't help but deliver it with cold rationality, could she? Each sentence like some kind of hammer, cracking apart their worlds. There'd been times they hadn't loved Conrad for what he did, but still, he'd been a father to them both.

"Do you work at being frigid, Kardell, or does that come naturally?" Melanie asked.

"You should be able to tell, as hard as you work at not giving a shit," Cameron snapped back. Tristan stared in wonder at her flushed cheeks and the flashes of fury in her eyes. William stood oblivious in front of a blank board, rolling the chalk between his fingers, afraid to write. Tristan laughed, and everyone stared at him.

"I see now why we didn't do this sooner. Billy is going to fret for weeks that everyone he meets is The Maker, you two are going to kill each other, and then there won't be anyone left to tell me what to do."

Cameron was already regaining control of her emotions. She stood, took the chalk from William, and wrote out the arguments in favor of Conrad as The Maker. "There are some counterpoints, of course. Why didn't he do anything to help Erika?"

"He never showed much interest in what we could do, either, unless it could be used to give him some political advantage," Tristan said. His uncle might be clever, but his primary ambition in life seemed to be gaining political influence.

"Until he told Erika to use her telepathy to encourage Armel to marry her," William said.

"I'm sorry, what?" Cameron said. Then she waved a hand as William opened his mouth to explain. "Nevermind. Later. Try not to get too worked up. I think it's much more likely that we're looking for someone we've never met. Tristan, did you have any luck finding Doctor Maikon again?"

Tristan shook his head. "She's a ghost. Finding her even before she knew we were looking was a hell of a job. And did I mention that I almost died doing that?"

"A few times, actually. So, do we have any other names to throw in?" William looked particularly at Melanie, who shook her head. She was wedged into her chair, one leg hooked over an arm, the other swinging like a pendulum along the front of the chair.

"Can we agree that there's no clear frontrunner?" Cameron asked. Everyone did. She straightened up to her full height, her eyes sharp. A sure sign of trouble. "This is my plan: I'm sticking as close to Ellis as possible. Hopefully he'll be vulnerable enough soon to start talking. Assuming he actually knows something. I'm also calling Reese to see if I can dig anything up there. I think we need to check into some more of these bunkers, too, and try to get something new."

Tristan sighed. "Which one do you want me to check first?" Of course he would be sent all over Cotarion, chasing down flimsy hints.

"I was actually thinking that all three of you might go looking. If you each go out for about a week, we could cover them all."

"Ha!" Tristan said.

"I'd have to ask Ellis for time off, and right now I can't imagine—"

"What money am I going to travel on—"

"—car is in terrible shape—"

"I don't even have a car!"

Cameron wasn't perturbed. "One week, and we can find out if these places are even accessible. Melanie, I'll give you the travel funds and my bike—"

"A bike! In this weather?"

"—or you can take Tristan's car and he can take my bike."

"I'm sorry, did you just volunteer Hestia?"

Melanie laughed. "Shut up, I forgot you named that thing."

"Work it out, however you need to. This is the next job on the list. Because we have to find out who did this, changed our lives without asking. It's no accident Niko and Tristan have both become trained killers, that Erika and I were soldiers, that William calls fire when he's angry, that you, Melanie, keep coming when I call. Some choices were taken from us," Tristan heard, just then, Melanie's heart rate rise, "and they're being taken from others, too. We can put a stop to it, but it's going to mean chasing down every lead. It's going to mean giving up certain comforts and disrupting our normal lives. But if we succeed, it will be worth it." Cameron's eyes were dark and hard. For the first time in weeks she looked alive.

Even Tristan found it hard to dredge up a smart-ass comment about this speech.

Melanie sighed. "I would like to argue, but I can't. I'll talk to the shift manager and see how much time I can get off."

William cleared his throat. "This plan of yours is leaving you alone in Advon with assassins everywhere. Not to mention Ellis, who we know wanted to kill you."

Cameron smiled. "Are you worried you'll come back and find I've taken care of them all? I promise to keep my sword under control while you're away."

William made a face that might have cowed a lesser being, but Cameron was no mere mortal. Wisely, Tristan thought, he kept silent. His concerns were valid, but she wasn't in the mood to listen. Was she ever, really?

"So," she said. "We don't know who The Maker is, the doctors we were tracking petered out, and we are following up on the bunkers. What else is there?"

Tristan had nothing to contribute, William had too much to pick just one thing, and Melanie looked restless. Cameron grabbed another stack of cookies, spent a few minutes looking over William's boards while she ate them, then announced it was time she left.

As she pulled on her coat and boots (she never bothered with a hat or gloves, however bitter cold it got) Tristan saw the spark drain out of her. A mask fell over her features. The armor she wore, against the world she lived in.

She glanced up. For a breath it fell away again. "You've done well collecting and organizing all this information, Will."

Tristan's cousin grinned. "Thanks, Cam."

Melanie caught Tristan's eye, and made a face of exaggerated shock. The door clicked as Cameron left. The scent of snow wafted through William's living room, then was gone.

William collected a couple of the boards and carried them up to his office. Melanie stood, stretched, and sauntered over to Tristan, all warmth. Yes, there was invitation in the sway of her hips.

"What's up with those two?" she asked. "Last I knew they were growling and snapping like cranky seals."

Tristan watched her. "Seems they're getting over it."

"I saw you staring at me. You have something on your mind?"

He sighed, putting as much feeling into it as he could. "Nothing worth mentioning, Mels." He stood. She drew a little closer. She'd worn that perfume, the floral stuff she'd only worn when they were dating. His heart raced. It had always felt good, to draw her into his arms.

You know better.

"Why do you have to keep me all to yourself?" She pouted, as beautifully as she ever had.

"Oddly, I just like to know whether or not you'll be around. The sometimes there, sometimes not, showing up unannounced. It gets old."

She smiled, a gleam in her eyes. Anytime she wanted him, she would have him. She reached out a hand.

Tristan was ready. He pulled the rectangle of glass he'd found on his rooftop and pressed it into her fingers.

She looked down, confusion creasing her face.

Then her lips turned white as her eyes flashed wide. She'd done so well for so long, but he'd taken her too much by surprise for her to hide that she recognized the thing in her hands.

It didn't feel much like triumph. He'd never wanted to believe it was her. All those days and nights they'd spent together, every moment of joy in an otherwise grim life, it had all been a lie. Every moment shriveled, bittered.

She reached for his hand, but he jerked back.

"Who are you, Mel? Really? And who are you working for?"

She didn't answer. She'd regained control of her heart rhythm, but the expression on her face remained horrified.

"I didn't have a—"

"—a choice? Meanwhile, Cameron and William are servant to a man they hate just for the slightest chance at learning something. I have killed, and lied, and thieved. I watched my cousin die for this, you watched her die, all because we didn't know enough! And all that time, you knew. And you spied on me." He yanked the piece of glass out of her hands.

"Either you talk now, or you leave."

For just a second, she seemed about to speak. Her throat worked around the words, her lips parted. But then she changed her mind. She put on her coat and boots and the hat with the bobbles on it, and left.

Tristan sank down onto the coffee table. William, who had been standing on the stairs for a while, said, "Ah. So . . . "

"She got me, Will. She really did." Tristan pressed his hands against his forehead. How had he messed up everything so much? How had he turned out to be so useless and weak? "I never suspected a thing. And you know, I still love her? Damn." He looked up at his cousin, tremors running through him. "Please tell me you have something I can drink."

The drinks didn't help, so Tristan walked. The heavy snow clouds finally let loose. The first flakes fell, small and delicate and innocent.

What would he tell the Agency? If they knew Mel was the spy, they would have him kill her. But he couldn't pin it on someone else, either. Unless it was someone already dead.

He prowled the sidewalks, as he hadn't in a long time. Towers of brick, concrete, steel rose up all around him. He moved among all the citizens of Advon trying to pretend their lives were normal. Like it was normal that the power kept going out, that their country was at war for no discernible reason. Some people pretended better than others. Tristan didn't feel like he was pretending very well at all.

What do I want?

William wanted to know everything there was to know. Cameron wanted to stop The Maker. His uncle wanted to rule the world. His aunt wanted to be normal. His parents wanted to forget.

Once, all he'd wanted was his tower. Now that didn't seem important. But he wasn't sure what was.

Helping Niko. The boy was a chance at keeping someone so much like him from making the same mistakes. If he could figure out how to stop him getting sucked into Agency business, if they could, like Cameron said, stop The Maker, maybe Niko could live a freer life.

Eventually the snow seeped through Tristan's coat, and he turned to his apartment. He didn't feel any less heartbroken, but at least he had a goal, one that was really his.

His apartment was dim when he returned, no surprise since evening had begun to fall. He threw together a sandwich, and took a few bites. Then he realized that the familiar smell he'd caught didn't belong. Not anymore. Flowers. Nights on the rooftop. Mornings at markets. Lies of warmth and softness and safety. His heart contracted.

"Mel?" He saw a shadow change shape, there in the hall that led from the living room to the bedroom. Melanie stepped out of the gloom, her eyes wide, a glint of metal at her throat. Behind her was Red. He grinned, his teeth as bright as the dagger he held.

"I found her sneaking around when I dropped in for a status update. Imagine that. Your spy."

Tristan held his breath, heard his blood roaring in his ears. She had some nerve, coming back to his place. But just now, it was hard not to feel sorry for her. And he definitely didn't want her blood all over the floors. It would never come out of the hardwood planks.

"Good job, Red. But how do you know it was her?"

"She was trying to access your personal files."

Tristan sighed. "Seriously, Mels? Even for you, that's audacious."

"Wow, a three-syllable word. Where'd you pick that up?" she snapped back. Her voice trembled.

Red rolled his eyes. "You know the rules. Are you going to kill her, or should I?"

Tristan remembered Niko. He needed to set a good example, didn't he? If he really wanted to help that boy, he couldn't have his former girlfriend's blood in the cracks of his floors all the time, reminding him what a loathsome creature he was. "I'm not murdering for the Agency anymore."

Red's lips couldn't stretch any wider. "So after her, I get to kill you. This day couldn't get better." He gripped Melanie's chin, tipped her head back, the dagger pressed hard—

Then Red's body jerked. His face contorted in agony. He dropped the dagger, pushed Melanie back as if she'd stung him, and clutched a hand to his chest.

"What—"

Melanie wrapped one of her small hands around Red's throat, her face alight with rage. Shadows wrapped around her legs, her arms, but every moment her face was in a silver moonlight streaming through the windows. The assassin's body jerked again, he made a strange sound, like nothing Tristan had ever heard before. He fell, awkward and stiff. He groaned, his face a blank mask. Then he was still.

Tristan stood rooted to where he'd been the entire time, half a sandwich still in his hand. Melanie wheeled around, her eyes shining, trembling all over.

"You were really going to let him kill me!"

"He was too far away!"

She looked so small. He told himself not to touch her, told himself she was dangerous. She'd just killed Red. But she was shaking.

He reached out to her. She walked right into his arms. He held her, told her not to be afraid, kissed the top of her head until her trembling ceased.

He was in so much trouble.

020

THE LIGHTS IN her parents' house were bright. Music drifted out, and laughter, and talk. Cameron went lightly up the steps. Winter Solstice wasn't exactly her favorite holiday, but the warmth and the joy tugged at her, irresistible.

When she opened the door, Owena flew to her first. William, across the room next to her father, looked up and smiled. He took a step in her direction without thinking, then stopped himself. He looked away, his face a little red.

Oh, stupid Will.

"How are you feeling?" Cameron asked Owena.

"Fine, really. Super emotional, you would hate it. I walked past a little girl selling kittens in a box the other day, and I cried."

"That sounds awful."

"Especially when my job is listening to the problems of a school full of nine-to-twelve-year-olds. Last week I had no fewer than three break-ups to deal with. Then there was a fight between these two kids who have been best friends since they were six."

Cameron raised her eyebrows. "How do you even deal with something like that?"

"Mostly I listen, and help them come up with solutions. But you know, at that age they're not always great at putting them into practice."

"My friends and I always used to hit each other with sticks when we were mad. It worked pretty well."

Owena laughed, but she didn't really think it was funny. Cameron saw the look on her face. It wasn't hard to read.

As kids you hit with sticks, as adults you shoot with guns and cut with swords. So Armel is dead.

What Owena said instead was, "I'm glad you're here, too. Amazing that the High General could spare you. I better go see how Nana is doing."

Much more amazing that Nana was there than Cameron. How old was she, now? Closing in on a century.

Cameron drifted over to where her father still stood with Harfield. She endured hugs from sundry aunts, uncles, and cousins along the way. By the time she achieved her goal, her skin crawled and every nerve ending tingled.

"I'd ask for a hug, but I can see you've had enough," her father said. "But here, you can have a drink instead."

"They're really good," William said, a little too loudly.

Cameron smiled. "And you've had a couple of them, I guess?" She took a sip. It was sweet, fizzy, and a little spicy. "Dad, everyone is going to be falling over by the end of the night. This is a dangerous thing you've made."

"Dinner will be soon, and things will settle down. With everything in Advon so tense, I figured everyone needed to take the edge off. But speaking of dinner, I have to go make some sauce. It's good to see you, sweetie. William, if you'll excuse me."

He left, looking guilty. Cameron clutched her glass. Why would he feel bad about leaving her alone with William?

"Can we agree not to talk about work?" he said.

"Of course."

"In that case, I have a question. Your family is so normal and they seem so nice, but you hardly ever spend any time with them. Why is that?"

Cameron raised an eyebrow. He smiled. It wasn't accusatory, just gentle curiosity. "You could have just talked about how cold it is."

"Where is the fun in that? I desperately need to learn something interesting that doesn't involve wind turbines or politics."

"I'm not sure the answer is that interesting. I don't fit in. They love me, I'm sure, but they don't understand me."

"Where *do* you fit in, though? Even the High Guard seems to prefer some toned-down version of you."

That was true. No one liked the practicality with which she did her job. Cut someone down for honor, and everyone understood. Do the same for considered reasons, and everyone acted like you were a monster. Even Armel hadn't liked her way of weighing life and consequence, though he'd accepted it. "Nowhere, I guess."

"Not even with Tristan?"

Oh. So that's why her father had felt bad for walking away. That little hint of interest, the thousand unspoken questions behind that single sentence.

William Harfield was *interested*. In *her*. He could not have picked a worse time.

"Least of all with Tristan. He's not very trustworthy." She took a gulp of her drink, let the peppery spice fill her mouth. "Of course, I am the one spending the Winter Solstice with my family. What's going on with your parents that you aren't there?"

"Well, Dad's at the High General's feast, and Mom is visiting my aunt and uncle. Tristan's parents. Tristan has been weird recently, so who knows what he's doing."

Cameron's mother approached, with the glow of a parent with children at home. Cameron braced herself for the inevitable hug. "Hi Mom. You look nice."

"Thank you. And this blue suits you, much better than all that red. William, you're as dapper as ever. I was just thinking as I came over, well, I'm glad that the two of you have settled your differences. Armel always thought it was a shame you didn't get along better."

William started coughing, leaving Cameron to respond. "I don't know what you mean. William hates me just as much as ever. Don't you?"

"I'm sorry to say, Mrs. Kardell, I find your daughter abrasive and difficult."

Seren rolled her eyes. "Clearly you've both already imbibed too much. Thankfully, dinner is ready. Cameron, your father would like you to sit beside him at the table."

William started to laugh before she'd even turned away.

"'Abrasive and difficult,' how many of those have you had, anyway?"

He stared at the bottom of his empty glass. "I swear, it's only been two."

Cameron's mother announced dinner to the rest of the room. In the rush, Cameron had to throw a few elbows to get the place beside her father at one end of the table. One of her cousin's kids wedged in beside her. Poor William paid for his dearth of aggression with a seat between Uncle Filbert and Nana. As Nana kept up an unceasing string of chatter and Uncle Filbert hacked and wheezed, Cameron mouthed, "sorry." Then the girl beside her knocked over a glass of water, and William laughed.

Cameron's dad made sure she ate well. Crispy potatoes, roast beef, hot rolls, sautéed brussels sprouts all went through her hands first. When he wasn't directing food, he talked. She'd almost forgotten what it was like to have a conversation that wasn't guided by purpose. When he asked how she'd been he wanted to know.

"I'm okay, Dad. Just lonely. Being around other High Guards all the time, well, we're a grim crew."

"I'm sure. Things seem serious."

Cameron dolloped some sauce onto her niece's plate. "It's always serious."

"Owena told us you broke up with Ethan, months ago. Were you worried that he might be in danger?"

"He would be, but that's not why. He wanted a commitment, which would mean I'd have had to leave the High Guard. I think, after this summer, that he really wanted me to leave the Sentinels entirely. Anyway, I'm sorry I didn't tell you. Armel died that same day, so it didn't seem worth mentioning."

He touched her hand, lightly. She wished she could return his smile in full. "I cannot tell you how proud I am to have a daughter so courageous. Even we were hard on you, then."

"You had good reason to be. I should have been the one to tell Owena. I thought it would be easier if it came from someone else, but that was wrong."

She endured one last smile, before he turned back to speak with Cousin Traci on his other side. Cameron took a long drink of the wine now on the table.

Everyone else around her thought she didn't care, and her father thought she was brave. She saw no other way to be. There were jobs to do. There were obstacles that she couldn't allow to stop her. Forward was the only way. How was that bravery?

The dinner lasted a long time. Eventually, all the chatter started to rise around Cameron, like a wave of meaningless sound. Each response was harder to drag up than the last. When the children got restless and started running around the table, shrieking, Cameron looked at her father. He nodded.

She escaped through the kitchen, where her mother and Uncle Henry were putting dessert on plates. Cameron stole a slice of pie. She went upstairs, past lines of family photos, to her old room. It wasn't much different than when she left. The bed was instead a couch, the paint a subtly different shade. Cameron sat in the deep windowsill, ate her pie, and savored the silence.

The talk downstairs became rhythmic background noise. Snow fell on the sidewalks and houses and shrubbery outside, softening them all into pale blurs.

Movement behind her. She wheeled. A knife slid out of her boot. Metal flashed in the darkness.

William sat on the couch, his arms raised, his eyes wide. Cameron cursed, and turned away from him. Sweat prickled her neck, face, and arms. Her hands shook so much that she struggled to return her knife to the holster.

"I'm sorry," William said.

"Why the hell were you sitting in the dark, anyway?" Somewhat composed, she turned back to face him.

"Just taking a break from the noise. And you?"

"The same."

"I'll leave, if you want me to."

She sat back on the windowsill. She held her hands out. Steady again. "I don't mind that you're there, as long as I know about it." Two years ago, she'd been unshakeable. Now she jumped at rustles in the dark. "So, do you come hang out in my room all the time when you're over here?"

"Not usually. Your mom said she thought I looked tired, and this was a good place to rest a little."

Cameron smelled interference. Normally, this would have annoyed her, but for once she saw all the concern and felt . . . gratitude. A little. Mixed with annoyance.

She didn't like it, though, that little flicker of interest in William's face. They were all so close to the High General, and people around that man tended to end up on the ground, gasping their last breaths. There was danger here, for both of them.

"I know we said we wouldn't talk about work, but maybe consider this more of a personal warning, okay? You've got to control your temper around Ellis."

William sighed. Normally he would have looked away, but this time he met her eyes. They had the hard glint of emeralds.

"He will tear everyone around him to pieces, Cam. I'm watching him do it. So he can stay safe. You, Armel, the High Guard, his advisors, all the people of Cotarion."

His anger was like an arrow, flashing out, seeking a target. She could turn it, use it.

"Do you think I'm so different from him?"

He leaned forward, and though a whole room stood between them, Cameron felt as if the distance had collapsed to almost nothing. His eyes still burned, but in a different way. "You are not Sean Ellis."

"We are different in some ways, but not in this. To find and stop The Maker, I'll break you, William, to make you better. To turn you into the kind of weapon you need to be. Tristan, Melanie, anyone else who follows me, too."

He didn't lean back, even though the words had struck him with all the force she'd meant them to have. He held himself in place. It showed in his eyes, which had gone all cool and reserved. "Why?"

"Because we weren't given a choice, and we don't know how many more are out there who lost that same freedom. Because in Palisade children died, and even the monsters suffered. Because Erika deserved better. We all do. I will take us to the ends of the earth if I must. I will drag you through the worst hells, if I must, sacrifice your happiness, even your life, to rid the world of people who direct our lives on their whims."

At last William leaned back. Everything she'd said was true. He must know it. He stared down at his hands.

An orb of light winked in and out of existence over his palms. Cameron watched for a little while in silence, then looked back at the snow piling up outside. Her walk back to the Military Quarter would be a slog.

William spoke, too quietly to hear. Cameron looked back at him. "What?"

"I said that I'll follow you. Wherever you go, whatever the price, even if that's my life." The light in his hands was bright, his lips slightly upturned. The fervor on his face took her breath away, even though it demonstrated that she had failed utterly.

It would be easy to cross the room, lean in close, put her face near his, watch his eyes go soft. He would welcome it. For a moment she could forget all the weights she held in precarious balance. The grueling fight with Ellis, the assassins hunting High Guards, their search for The Maker.

And she would feel. That was by far the greatest temptation. The last time she'd felt anything had been there with him, the night she'd wept for Armel. The way he'd held her . . .

She'd had too much to drink. The stakes were too high. A distraction now could cost her all her advantage over Ellis.

"I know you will. You're good at following."

That at least was enough to wound him. It would hold him off for a little while, to have his pride struck when his guard was down. But it wouldn't last for long.

A door below opened. Cameron looked out the window, and saw some of the family leaving.

"I have to go say goodbye to Nana."

She grabbed her plate and escaped.

How was it possible that she'd lifted a veil over her thoughts, shown him what she was, and his feelings had only intensified? That had always driven people away. Even Ethan had pulled back if she didn't keep her deepest intentions sequestered away. The most compelling of her motivations belonged to her alone.

But William had heard the truth, and vowed to follow her.

Cameron said goodbye to her grandmother and the group of aunts, uncles, and cousins leaving with her. When they'd left, all the children and half the adults were gone. Cameron went to the kitchen to help with the cleaning. Owena was already there, directing the team's efforts. William washed and rinsed with a ponderous, thoughtful slowness while Cameron's father dried.

"—so there I was, holding this enormous order of lobsters, and the things are escaping because the claws weren't banded. Everyone's slipping on the water on the floor, and yelling at me, but I couldn't put down the pot, because lobsters are still flopping over the side, but I had to get the ones on the floor. So I put them down in a sink, at the exact moment Chef Hand went to drain out some cooked pasta."

William and Owena groaned. Cameron took over rinsing the dishes.

"That's the exact second I was fired from my first job. Poor lobsters. Poor pasta."

Cameron took a plate from William. His shoulders were stiff, his eyes uncharacteristically withdrawn from her. Still, she stared long enough that he returned her gaze, and she mouthed, *sorry.*

He shrugged one shoulder. Cameron passed the dry dish to her father, who took it with raised eyebrows and a subtle nod at William. Cameron glanced over to Owena, who made a smooching face.

Cameron frowned and shook her head.

A half an hour later Cameron's father put the last dinner plate on the shelf.

"We did not break any records with that wash session, kids," Owena said, "but a good effort and at least you were thorough. Cameron, we might've finished ten minutes ago if you hadn't kept handing back plates to be scrubbed again."

"It's not my fault William sent them to be rinsed with food still stuck on."

"I couldn't even see some of those supposed particles. I maintain that you were inventing them to slow me down."

Owena grinned. "Watch out, she'll call you paranoid."

"Excuse me if the idea of putting a dirty plate on the shelf is gross," Cameron said. Then she grabbed one last drink and left the kitchen.

She found her mother sitting in the living room, playing a raucous card game with the few remaining adults. Cameron picked a book off the shelf and sat next to her. She read for the next hour while the house emptied of guests.

When everyone was gone besides Owena, William, and her parents, she put aside the book and joined the game. They teased her for waiting so long, but she ignored them.

Cameron played with her usual quiet efficiency. She won so completely that the rest might have been ashamed if they hadn't known her so well.

"And that's why you didn't join before," her mother said, smiling with a mixture of pride and irritation. "Uncle Nick wouldn't have been able to stand losing, you know."

"He bluffs very aggressively. You can tell he's lying when he won't stop smiling and making eye contact," Cameron stood. "William, I think you have an early meeting with the High General."

He groaned, but stood too, even as Cameron's family protested that they could stay a little longer.

"Any later," Cameron said, "and we will be late for our jobs. Everything was very nice, Mom and Dad. I'll come back for a visit soon. Owena, take care."

Farewells followed her all the way to the front door. She put on her coat, then waited while William did the same, with the addition of gloves, a scarf, and a hat. Her mother stole one last hug.

"Be careful, Honey. The game you're playing is dangerous, to everyone."

She pulled away. Cameron searched her careless, happy smile for any hint of the words she'd spoken. She saw nothing.

A moment later Cameron and William slogged through snow piling up on the sidewalks. The dark and the cold enveloped them, but Cameron felt warm behind the barrier of her coat.

William talked with an easy energy, as if once he'd started he found it difficult to stop. He wasn't shy, it turned out. He just needed to build momentum.

They walked together, William chatting, Cameron listening and responding as necessary. They reached the intersection where they needed to part ways. William stopped and looked up and down for cars, even though the streets were empty. Cameron laughed at him as she turned away.

His hand brushed her elbow, and she stopped. He looked terrified. He opened his mouth, but no words came out. Cameron shook her head.

"You trust me, right?"

"Of course."

"Keep your head down. Let me deal with things, okay?"

He pressed his lips together. Fat snowflakes stuck to his striped hat, swirled in the air between them. "I'll try, but—"

"No. You will."

She turned and walked away, glancing back just once, but he had left the corner and vanished into the curtains of snow.

Cameron woke too early. In spite of three pairs of socks, her feet were cold. She scrunched her toes together, and tucked her legs up to her chest. Maybe she'd fall back asleep if she could get warm.

After several minutes she gave up and rolled out of bed. The floor was frigid, the water jetting from her sink like ice. She washed as quickly as possible before pulling on her uniform.

A fire blazed in the common room. A clock struck the half hour, reminding her just how little she'd slept. Master of the High Guard Clemens sat near the fire reading the morning newspaper. She looked up, their eyes met, and Cameron looked away quickly. Clemens's expression had been too raw to bear for more than a moment.

Cameron huddled as close to the fire as she safely could. Her extremities thawed rapidly. She'd just warmed up enough to consider moving away when Thea pushed the paper into her hands.

The headline read, "Lithring Destroyed. Hundreds Dead, Injured, or Missing."

Cameron glanced up at Thea, who watched as she read. Yes, it was as bad as the headline suggested. Cameron returned to the paper.

"Late last night, unknown forces attacked Lithring. Reports suggest that the number of attackers was no more than thirty, but they possessed advanced weaponry. With it, they were able to destroy entire buildings and homes. In spite of the brave actions of local Public Safety Officers, the town was defenseless against the attack.

"'They wore armor and carried shields. Officer Wen's guns couldn't do anything. Some of them had gloves, when they pointed them at walls, they just crumbled. Like everything was just sand. Others had rifles that shot fire. No one could get away, and everything was on fire or falling. It was like vengeful gods everywhere,' reports one survivor.

"Investigators insist that eyewitness reports, particularly in times of trauma, are notoriously unreliable. They are continuing to seek answers, and have not yet determined whether or not any unusual weaponry was used in the attacks."

Cameron leafed through the paper. There were several more articles about the attack: theories on who had done it, where their weapons had come from, what the response should be. Cameron folded the paper and handed it back.

"What do you think?" the Master of the High Guard said.

They'd had reports for weeks of Varcove troops moving closer to Advon. Small, skilled groups. All along they'd assumed that their goal was the capital, was Ellis. Were they attacking smaller towns first, as a warm-up? If so, it was a dangerous game. They could be caught before reaching their goal. Or was there some other aim entirely?

"I think there's more going on here than we know. This doesn't make a lot of sense."

"Will they strike at Ellis next?"

Master of the High Guard Thea Clemens had never asked for Cam's advice before.

"I don't see the danger first because I can predict it, Ma'am. I see it first because I assume that it's always there."

Clemens sighed. "I'll prepare the senior High Guards."

Cameron remained in the common room for as long as she could stand. As other members of the High Guard woke up and got their hands on the morning paper, she found the conversations around her increasingly cyclical.

No one seemed interested in the weapons the attackers had used. They all dismissed that part of the report as exaggerations. Standard explosives and flamethrowers could do the same, right?

Perhaps Cameron had seen enough strange things to believe it possible. The world wasn't all it appeared. Had the town been destroyed by advanced weaponry, though, or were the attackers Altered?

When she'd heard the phrase, "such a tragedy," for the fifth time, she abandoned the common room. The warmth wasn't worth it. She had over an hour before her shift began, so she went up two floors to the sparring room.

It was already in use. Sean Ellis was there, destroying every illusion that Gordon Palmroy knew how to fight. Poor Gordon. He'd always relied on misdirection to get him through sparring sessions. That combined with the fact that everyone liked him too much to hit very hard. Ellis was ruthless, unyielding, and apparently in a foul mood.

Cameron winced as Palmroy took a brutal hit to his lower back, almost fell. A fight that uneven only made Ellis angrier. Cameron took a deep breath and went inside.

The High General turned. He grinned. Cameron picked up a training blade from a rack, and the grin broadened.

"You're free, Palmroy." Gordon limped out of the ring as Cameron stepped inside it. "So, you read the papers, I'm sure." He swung his blade, keeping the muscles in his arms warm.

"Have you ever seen anything like it?" she asked. He would understand. Weapons so destructive, or such a large group of Altered.

"No, never." They bowed, and settled in on their opposite sides. His face said it was true, and that he was afraid. Then he fought it down, and Cameron prepared.

When he attacked, he was merciless. But then, so was she.

021

WILLIAM'S HANDS SHOOK as he read the paper. What was the point of attacking that town? It had no military value, it wasn't a production center. He'd learned enough about tactics to know that it provided no strategic value.

If it was the mercenaries from Varcove, then they'd just made their target harder to reach. The security around Ellis and Advon would tighten. Did they have another objective? William cast around for reasons. He might have missed something.

He paced, the paper crumpled in his hand. Caesar followed him, his nose bumping the back of William's legs when he paused. After a minute, he stopped, and Caesar circled him, tail wagging.

No, he hadn't missed anything. They wanted Ellis to turn himself over. The citizens of Cotarion had become hostages, their deaths blackmail. Calling for assassins to pick off the High Guard hadn't worked as well as they'd hoped. The security around the High General still remained too heavy to break through.

Ellis himself, however, had weaknesses. Stubborn pride, a well-known temper. If they ensured his utter failure as High General by wiping out towns just off his doorstep, maybe, just maybe, he would leave his fortress and go to them.

The mercenaries probably didn't know that Sean Ellis already used his position as protection from those who wanted him dead.

How many more innocent people would die for him? Already they piled up, unbearably high.

William closed his eyes, and raised his hands. Between them, he spun a complex orb of energy, like a weaver bird's nest. Then he pushed it, spun it. The threads wrapped tight—

He opened his eyes. The light between his hands was a mere speck.

Let me deal with things.

That was before whole towns burned.

He looked up at the clock. It was time to go to work. William ran his hands through his hair, rubbed his forehead, then smoothed his hair back down.

The snow had stopped falling, and William was well defended against the cold. He wore a pair of his grandfather's boots, lined with sheepskin, and heavy pants over his work clothes. With a scarf and a hat, only his eyes were left exposed to the freezing air.

Advon lay still and white under a foot of snow. Shop owners cracked through the layer on the sidewalks, shifting it away one inch at a time, but roofs, light posts, mailboxes, and tree branches had all been made round, soft, and white.

Some sidewalks still lay under a deep blanket. William tried to revel in leaving prints in the crisp surface, but even cutting through fresh snow didn't do much.

Just a few miles away, hundreds lay dead. No childish thrill could make an impact on that.

The walkways inside the Military Quarter were all clean. Soldiers had probably spent their Solstice celebrations shoveling. William's boots clomped over the concrete.

A messenger stood outside his office door, with her hands clasped behind her back. She bounced on the balls of her feet, as Erika had done when she was nervous.

"Doctor Harfield, there's something in your office I need to pick up right away." All the words ran together.

William shifted his bags around to find which pocket his keys were in. "All right, I'm here, I can get it for you in just a second."

The woman's face paled and her voice dropped to a mutter. "I'm sorry, sir, but by order of the High General I have to get it myself."

William paused. Did the inside of his office belong to him, or the High General? William doubted he had any right to privacy inside an office that stood within the Military Quarter. It was why he'd never brought any of his research into the Altered or The Maker.

He let the young woman in. She scurried to the desk and picked up a thick piece of paper. William discerned quite a few words before she stuffed it in her pocket.

. . . do not allow your citizens to suffer . . . brings us Ellis . . . remembered as a hero . .

"Thank you, Doctor Harfield, have a nice day."

Had all the advisors received the note, or just a few? What about General Ellis?

Even if he knew the terms, he wouldn't turn himself in.

William, running on instinct, pulled off his winter gear. He changed into his office shoes, straightened his tie, and failed to flatten hair made wild by his hat. He unpacked his bag, then tidied his desk. He made a cup of coffee.

When it was time for his meeting, he picked up his notebooks and walked to the High General's office. The High Guards in the hall looked sterner than usual. Or maybe that was his imagination. Cameron was not among them.

The previous meeting ended just as William arrived. Advisor Sands left. She nodded at him, but she didn't smile. Not today.

"Come in, Harfield."

William's feet carried him inside, but his mind still seemed stuck in his office. Clemens and Brecht were on personal guard. William let go of a breath he hadn't realized he was holding.

Sean Ellis's desk lay under stacks of photos taken from the attack. Burned buildings, bloodied corpses, rubble, and soot. The High General stared at them, his face so still that he had to be hiding something. William looked away, but it was too late not to see more than he wanted to.

"Your opinion of this event, Doctor Harfield?"

Event? Disaster was more accurate. "I think you already know what they're hoping, sir."

"I have some evidence, some theories. Brecht, Clemens, wait outside."

The two High Guards left. When the latch clicked, Ellis brought a handful of photos to William. He looked. He knew better than to refuse. The High General might appear to be in command of himself, but that rarely lasted long.

The images were not terrible, mostly of the attackers rather than the victims. They all wore dark clothing. Helmets shielded their faces. Some carried large rectangular packs on their shoulders which connected to tube-like rifles in their hands. Others wore padded gloves. Most had shining armor protecting their bodies, jointed for quick movement. They reminded William of the scorpions he'd seen in the desert.

William couldn't interpret a lot of it. The figures blurred as they ran through the grainy images. One might have shown a person blasting fire across the front of a house, but the flare of light rendered the image as silhouettes without detail. Still, it was enough to make some guesses.

"They weren't Altered," William said at last.

"No. But their weaponry is too advanced for Cotarion or Varcove. There isn't anything like it made on this continent."

William handed back the photos. "What are you going to do?"

Ellis smiled. "I have weapons of my own."

They stared at each other for several breaths. That cunning gleam in Ellis's eye, meant that William was supposed to know what he meant.

What could meet with weapons that wiped out an entire town in one night? Nothing William knew of had that kind of power. Erika might have been able to match them, had she been able to get close enough, had she been able to force them to turn their weapons on one another.

And who had stopped Erika?

"No. I will not fight for you."

Ellis thrust another photo in front of him. Of course there had been children, there wouldn't have been any avoiding it. "How many will it take, Doctor Harfield? You can stop it."

William knocked the High General's hand aside. "You can stop it more easily than I can. Just turn yourself in."

"I will not negotiate with people who do things like this. You won't let Sentinel Kardell go by herself. I doubt even she can handle them without help."

William's hands balled into fists and heat burst in his chest. "Don't you think enough good people have died for you?"

The smile, so assured and superior, was too much. "I survive. Whatever it takes. If you would only listen, you might survive as well."

"How many times will you throw her in front of you? She's not a shield, she's a person, and a far better one than you."

Ellis dropped the photographs back on his desk. His gaze was sharp. "Doctor Harfield, you care about her? That's incredibly stupid of you."

The heat was there, all around, ready. Could he fight Ellis? Would it make a difference? Nothing else he'd done had made any impact. The High General still watched him.

"Hold your temper. You'll regret attacking me."

William let his fingers relax, and then the fire was there. And it was so very easy, in the end, to throw it at Ellis.

Ellis dodged. The piles of photographs became embers and ash, the top of the desk scorched. William sent more fire at him, enough to keep him from rising up and firing his gun.

Then Ellis's foot lashed out from under the desk, catching William's shin. His grip on the energy shattered. Ellis leapt over the desk, and in a flurry of powerful motions brought William to the floor. The way he twisted William's arm back kept a steady spark of pain running up his shoulder.

The office door burst open. Brecht hauled William to his feet, while Clemens stared at him, her face lined with rage.

Ellis smoothed his coat. It was with a fierce joy that William saw scorch marks on the edge of the fabric. Bits of smoldering paper drifted through the office, a perverse imitation of the snow outside. Sean Ellis coughed even as he made his pronouncement.

"William Harfield, I find you guilty of treason. You are hereby exiled from Cotarion."

"Sir. An attempt on the High General's life is worthy of execution." William had always thought Clemens fair. Now she suggested his death.

Ellis smirked. "I'll send him to The Crag. As good as an execution." Already he signed a piece of paper sealing William's fate. "You could have helped, Doctor Harfield. It's a shame you threw away your talents."

"Someone had to do the right thing." It would have sounded better if his voice had been steady.

"Brecht, take him to the Special Criminals division. Tell them to treat Doctor Harfield as extremely dangerous."

Brecht (how often had he smiled and told William jokes?) clamped his hand on William's shoulder. As he was steered out of the office, Sean Ellis walked beside him.

"You remember the beasts in Palisade? There are more where you're going. With any luck, my failures might destroy one of my enemies. There's something poetic about that."

William turned to face him, but Ellis had stopped walking while Brecht pushed on. So, the monsters were Ellis's fault, too. If only he'd been faster, bolder . . .

The door at the end of the hall opened. Cameron walked through. Ah.

Everything in his body and in his mind and in his heart went numb. He stumbled. Brecht pushed him.

For just a moment she looked surprised. But then her eyes narrowed, her mouth formed a tight, angry line. Her eyes were as dark as the bottom of a stormcloud.

"You missed the show, Kardell," Ellis called down the hall. "I hope you won't pine for Doctor Harfield too much."

Her face was still, other than a slight twitch at the corner of her mouth. Like a smile suppressed.

"One less thing to worry about, sir."

Did Brecht make that strange sound, like a half-formed protest cut short? Or was that William, the noise forced from his chest as his heart contracted?

The door shut behind him. And William began to tremble.

Many hours later, he still shivered. It seemed he might never stop.

He sat in the back of a car, his hands bound, his shoulders aching and his wrists numb. The guards in the front spoke only to each other.

The anger having worn away hours before, William rode in the company of nothing but dread and thoughts of his own stupidity.

He understood more fully with every mile that opened between him and Advon why he'd done it. A single image rose through the tumult of his thoughts: Cameron gasping for breath, her pulse weakening as blood drained from the wounds in her body.

The moment Ellis had suggested sending her in to fight his enemies once again, William had committed to action. How could he have done otherwise?

If only he hadn't hesitated. He might have had a chance, but his resolve had wavered. Now Cameron was in just as much danger as ever, and William didn't even know where he was going.

One less thing to worry about, she'd said. She'd had to, though, to assure Ellis she didn't care. Surely she hadn't meant it.

But she was so careful, so logical. Maybe having William out of the way was a relief.

He stared down at the darkness where his feet vanished into shadow. The sun had set long ago. For a long time he swayed in the back seat as the roads twisted, trying not to think. Trying only to observe the trunks of the trees that flashed by in the headlights, the occasional outcroppings of rock.

He failed, of course.

Hours later the car stopped. William waited, thirsty, hungry, in desperate need of the bathroom. The guards got out of the car, and a moment later pulled William out. He stumbled in snow that lay in knee-high drifts around him. So that explained the all-terrain vehicle. In its headlights he saw crags rising all around. They were in the Crescent Mountains. A bitter wind howled, drawing the breath from his lungs and drowning out everything the guards said. They communicated with shoves.

Would he be left in the snow to freeze to death?

They pushed him forward through the drifts, until they came to a sheer tumble and a cliff face. William halted, but one of the guards pulled him forward, and the other pushed from behind. They would all fall over the side . . .

Then William found he was on a set of stairs carved into the rock, with crags brushing his left shoulder and wind tugging his right. He banged his shins on the edges of rock. His feet slid on patches of ice. His boots still sat in his office.

The climb felt as if it lasted for hours. Finally they arrived at the end of the staircase, the last twenty steps sheltered by spires of rock on both sides.

In the open space beyond, snow rose and fell in drifts. The guards let go of William's arms, and unbound his wrists. Then they left, vanishing down the stairs.

William was alone.

He counted five uneven breaths, inhales and exhales. Then he lifted his numb hands. He envisioned light in the space between them.

The light didn't come. He would die here in the cold and snow. Sean Ellis had won, and won easily.

Not if I live. If I live, then he loses.

A small flicker of light appeared between his hands, then guttered out. He breathed again, and light flared once more. He fed it. He would live. He didn't let his mind wander to the how. He just would. With the glow cupped in his hands, he slogged over the snow, pushing through drifts, seeking anything that might provide shelter.

He found a low wall of rough-hewn logs, which came up to his knees. A slope of snow rising above it suggested a roof. A cabin, maybe, half-buried.

He found the top half of a door, the handle just visible. He let the light go out. Darkness drew around him for only a moment. Flames leapt to life in his hands, their warmth prickling against his skin. The snow around the door melted when he held his hands forward.

When he'd cleared a pocket of around the door, William pulled it open and stepped through.

He exchanged flames for light. It was more efficient, and flickered less.

The interior walls were as rough and dark as the outside. The cabin had a stone floor, a woodstove, a bed, a table, and chairs. Hooks by the door held equipment: a coat, boots, snowshoes, an axe, a hunting rifle, a shovel. There were enough logs in the stove and piled beside it to last a few days. William lit the fire, and tended it until it roared. By its soft glow he continued his inspection.

A cabinet in one wall contained cans and packets of military rations. They had no expiration dates; they also bore no resemblance to food. William ripped open a bag of stew, which Cameron had always argued was the least offensive of all the options. He tipped it straight into his mouth, and shuddered. Maybe it was better warm.

He remembered his bladder. How had he forgotten it? The cabin had no facilities. He put the ration near the woodstove to warm, grabbed the coat and boots, then went back into the snow. He burned a short path away from the cabin, emptied his bladder, then rushed back. Hadn't he latched the door? It stood open now, swinging against the cabin wall while wind swirled inside.

William cursed and pulled the door shut behind him, making sure to slide the bolt home. Whatever warmth the cabin had gained was gone, but at least the fire in the stove still burned.

He picked up the bag of stew and continued eating as he inspected the stocked cabinet. For exile, it could have been worse. Enough rations for three months, socks, undergarments, ammunition, paper, pens, pencils, string, rope, wire, nails. He might survive. And he'd thought for a moment that Ellis had just given him a slow, agonizing execution.

Something growled in the darkness. The sound reverberated, evidence it came from an expansive throat and chest.

William turned. A pair of eyes glowed in the shadows beside the bed. The hulking shape behind them shifted in the firelight.

Weariness rolled over William. He'd used up a great deal of strength clearing the door and summoning light. Did he have the strength to create enough fire or electricity to kill the thing?

It shuffled forward, and its teeth glinted. William's chest tightened. He could not draw breath. He reached into the shelf behind him, never taking his eyes off the monster. His fingers found the box of bullets. He flipped up the lid, and grasped one small metal torpedo.

He wove strands of energy around the projectile. The creature crept closer. Its shape was familiar, much like the thing Cameron had killed in the mountains so many years ago, the monster more human than not. William could smell it. He'd never tried anything like this before. And his aim had never been good.

Of course, at this distance if he missed then he deserved to die.

The energy wound tight, the beast reached out. William threw the bullet.

022

Tristan stood under a light so bright even he couldn't make out the shapes of the people in the shadows. He heard their voices, though.

They were not happy.

"Our investigation shows that Frank Boyles, more commonly called 'Red,' died of a heart attack. His body was unmarred, and no poison was found in his blood or his tissues."

Tristan flashed his best smile. "I told him all the time that he needed to relax."

"Boyles's records also show a unique obsession with your work and movements. He expressed concern that you misspent The Agency's resources, in spite of no explicit evidence of wrongdoing."

"We all need our hobbies."

"We're surprised you didn't file a complaint, considering such a blatant misuse of authority." This was a new, colder voice

Tristan spread his hands. "I figured he would get bored eventually, move on. Why launch a months-long inquiry when he'd be pestering someone else in a few weeks?"

"His records also contain frequent mention of a young woman named Melanie Stillwater. A former sexual partner of yours, it seems. He believed she is an accomplished spy."

"Doubtful. She's cute, but short, both literally and in brains. I told Red, sorry, Frank, that she couldn't have pulled it off—"

"And yet she disappeared on the same day that Red died."

Alarms sounded in Tristan's head. They wouldn't know that unless they'd gone looking for her. And that tone. They knew something. Or at least suspected. The Agency knew Red's death wasn't an accident.

They couldn't prove it, though. Tristan would already have been taken to some dark place where people vanished. Like William.

Was that the destiny of Altered? Did the world eventually turn on every single one of them, casting them into pits where they would rot?

"Maybe she went back to Brook's Cove."

"We checked. We have, in fact, scoured the continent. She is gone. Which is difficult to explain, unless she really was an agent. Or had help."

Tristan's smile didn't waver. "I think I see where this is going."

"I should hope you do, Mr. Rush. You'd have to be incredibly stupid not to. So, the question is, where is Melanie Stillwater, and what did she do to Mr. Boyles? Before you deny knowledge, you should know we have a witness who saw Ms. Stillwater in your apartment with you and Boyles the night he died."

Hell, was all of Advon able to see through his windows?

But the power had been out that night. It would have been impossible to see into his apartment from the outside. Only someone with eyes as good as his . . .

Oh. Like Niko.

"Mels and I weren't on good terms. I've got no reason to help her. Am I being charged with something?"

It was The Agency, so proof wasn't necessary for them to dispose of him and the trouble he'd caused. But an unwarranted execution was in poor taste. Assassination was an honorable business. Taking life without money or reason made you a common murderer.

The darkness rustled as his inquisitors changed positions.

"We do not charge one of our own without proof. We have already lost one skilled assassin, and we are in no hurry to lose another. Without reason."

"The Agency recommends you watch your step, Mr. Rush. Your work is erratic at best. Your connections are suspect. Mr. Boyles may have been misguided, but not entirely unreasonable."

Tristan bowed. "Of course, I shall follow your wise council, ladies and gentleman."

One of them laughed out loud, and a few stifled their chuckles. A couple were silent. The coldest voice said, "Good day, Mr. Rush."

After several moments of silence, the lights came on. The small amphitheater in which Tristan stood was empty besides him.

Tristan spent the next twenty-four hours behaving like a good boy. He met with a client, delivered a few unremarkable messages. He met with his distressed aunt, who, upon William's banishment had inherited the townhouse. She seethed with a fury that could have matched her son's.

"If Conrad hadn't pulled him into such an important political position! He had to know William wouldn't stand for the awful things that happen. He never could. The arguments he had with his tutors, even when he was only eight."

She put her hand to her mouth. "Tris, I should have been stricter. Maybe if he hadn't had his way so much."

"No, Auntie. Nothing would have changed this. Billy's always had a big heart. He didn't like to see people hurt. That was why he tried to do something." The town, of course—and how much of it had been for Kardell?

Teague dried her eyes and smiled, but it was bitter. "At least he isn't dead. It could have been much worse. Most exiles are reprieved eventually. You don't exile someone unless you think you might need them again in the future."

"Of course." Poor Auntie. If she knew William had been sent to one of the most dangerous mountains in the Crescents, she wouldn't so optimistic. But that knowledge had to remain Tristan's burden. Why should two of them lie awake at night, imagining William with eyes rimmed in frost—

Tristan went home, slept, then worked for a few hours. Just before lunch he decided it was time he lost the young woman who'd been tailing him all morning.

He went to a marketplace. Oh, to be one of the masses, with no greater concern than the quality of a bulging bag of onions. He wove through the clusters of people, bought bread, cheese, meat, and lettuce. His tail did an excellent job, sticking near the front of the store by the cash register. The things she bought even made sense. Her basket of fruits, vegetables, nuts, and fresh juice were just the choices of a health-conscious, single woman.

She slipped in line behind him. With a practiced air of unconcern, she flipped through a magazine.

Tristan paid for his sandwich ingredients, and joined the crowds leaving the store. The timing favored him. He flipped his coat inside-out, showing the well-finished gray interior, yanked a knitted hat on, and folded into the crowd.

She would be close behind. He hunched his shoulder and tucked his head, adopted a stiffer walk. For several blocks he stayed with the busiest eddies.

When he was sure he'd lost all the tails, he ducked down an alley and rushed to the Arts District. On Opal Street he stopped at the side door to a theater which held sporadic shows.

The interior smelled of moth-ridden costumes and stage fright. Tristan slipped through the shadowy props, the tangles of ropes and weights, the twisting hallways of the backstage world. Then down into the basement, then past the heating and cooling systems, then to a semi-forgotten prop room.

Niko sidled up just as Tristan put his hand on the doorknob.

"The improv group has been more fun than I thought. And the Agency agreed that I need to work on my acting. Apparently I don't have the right sort of teeth to pull off that smile you do."

Tristan nodded. He didn't look over at Niko, whose desperation for approval radiated out from him. "They know Mel was there the night Red died. I think they had a report from someone who saw everything."

Niko didn't respond for one, two, three heartbeats. Ba-bum, ba-bum, ba-bum.

"I was delivering a message, sir. But Red had an apprentice, and Mala has been acting weird ever since he died. He wouldn't talk to me in our test prep sessions at all, he lost weight. Maybe he saw something."

Tristan looked up. Where was the street urchin who'd begged to be trained? The young man beside him stood tall and broad, a gleam of certainty in his eye. He'd learned that posture from Cameron. Mel had made him healthy. Tristan was the one who'd taught him to lie and to live in a moral gray area.

There could be no trust between people. At least in this career that fact was out in the open. Tristan didn't live with any illusions that Niko would be loyal.

"You don't believe me?"

Tristan smiled in the way only he could pull off. "You've done good work. Take a few days off, all right?"

Niko looked hurt, for just a moment. Then he shrugged it off, and slipped away.

Finally, Tristan opened the door.

The prop room was a graveyard of painted backdrops, wood carved into candlesticks and cheaply gilded, shells of boats, and glass gemstones. Melanie had made a bed out of stacked stunt mats, with drapes as blankets.

She juggled some faux fruit when he walked in. Her lovely face was set in concentration. "That wasn't very nice, Tris." She dropped an orange, then threw aside the rest before plunking down on a creaking bench in front of a cracked table. Tristan dropped the bag of food. She attacked it at once.

"Still no magazines? I'm going to have to start juggling knives and torches for entertainment."

"The tail was right behind me in the checkout line. I think she'd have noticed."

Melanie didn't answer, as her mouth was full of sandwich. Tristan perched on a giant horse statue and watched her eat. She glanced up at him occasionally and smiled. She knew him far too well. Especially when he didn't know her at all.

"So, are you waiting around to ask who The Maker is?"

"Gave that up."

"What, then? Other than the consuming loneliness that is your sorry life."

"I don't have to bring you food, you know."

She smiled. "Yes, you do. If you don't, then I'll have to leave. Then they'll find me, and they'll kill me, and then you will be very sad because you're still desperately in love with me. Poor, stupid boy."

"I only love you because you *made* me."

She shook her head, her hazel eyes alight. "Did not. That was all you. And favorable circumstances. I did feel bad about that, it wasn't fair to pick you off in the midst of your cousin's death."

Tristan looked away. If he'd learned one thing from Cameron, it was how to be silent. Most people yearned to fill up the quiet with words. And now, Melanie was the lonely one.

He counted the seconds while he traced the grooves of the horse's mane with his thumb. Melanie stood and paced the room, weaving around the objects she'd arranged into something like a home. A painted mural of a stormy sea hung on one wall. She stared at it for a long time.

"I didn't want to lie to you. You treated me better than anyone else ever has, like I mattered. Well, Mom did, too, but she needed me. I was the only thing standing between her and certain death."

She stopped, swallowed, her head bent. "We can't have kids, you know. Not on our own. And I've known I wanted children for a long time. After my mom died I made a deal. I spy on you, pass along information, and The Maker lets me have a family of my own."

She looked back up to him, her lips in a tight smile. She might be small, but she was not fragile. And her eyes held all the wild power of the painted ocean waves behind her.

"I won't get that, now. The Maker will be hunting me, instead. The Agency, too. Will is lost. Kardell tied up in duty. Erika is dead. So that leaves us." She stood in front of him. "What will we do, Tris?"

He slid down off the horse. They were so close, almost touching. He felt a grin break out on his face. How could he stop it? "I've never really been great at plans. I follow orders. So, what do you have?"

"A whole lot of nothing. Let's think about it, okay?" She was so near that he could feel her breath warming the hairs on his face, prickling against his lips. He could hear her heart racing. She enjoyed taunting him, pulling him along, knowing the whole time his strength. That, at least, was the same.

Then she stepped away and sat at the table again to have another sandwich.

Tristan returned the next morning with breakfast. A plastic dome full of fruit, buttery pastries, coffee.

He wouldn't let her soothe away his irritation today. Whatever her reasons—and what a stupid reason, having diapers to change and puke in your hair—she had betrayed him. For years she had lied. He had to remember that he didn't know a thing about her.

She threw off her blankets when he walked in, and scrambled for a hiding place. When she realized it was him, the corner of her mouth quirked up.

"Angry again, I see."

"Shouldn't I be?" He sat on the edge of the boat while she tamed her hair. She shuffled to the bag of food.

"You're just upset that I tricked you, wounded your professional pride. You aren't angry about anything personal. Mmm, fresh stuff. I am aching for vitamins."

"I don't know what was real with you."

"You enjoyed the time we had together?"

"Yes."

"Then it was real. Don't overthink, Tris." She stabbed a strawberry with a fork. "What is important now is to figure out what's next."

He pressed his hands together. The boat was no good, either. Too low to the ground. "Did you ever care about me?"

She sighed, put down her fork. "If I didn't like you, you'd have figured out that I was playing you a long, long, long-long time ago. Love? Maybe a bit. As much as you loved me? No way. How could I? I couldn't be honest. And damn, you sank like an anchor."

It was something, at least. It could never make up for all those years of lying. But she cared.

"Does that really make you feel better?"

"The only times I didn't feel like scum were when I made you happy. Every other part of my life has been dishonesty, and trickery, and inflicting pain on people."

Melanie scooched over. She patted the clear space on the bench. Tristan sat beside her. She ran a hand through his hair, and the muscles in his neck and shoulders unwound. Without the perfume he smelled only her, skin and hair, and it was strange, and new. He didn't mind.

"I know who The Maker is, but not where. I know this person is obsessed with Cam, so as much as I hate to say this, she might be our only way forward. Have you still been watching out for her when she leaves the Military Quarter?"

"Yes."

"Good. I think if she dies the rest of us won't be far behind. Of course, I'm probably already marked." She took a bite of pastry and swallowed. "The problem is, Cam wants The Maker dead, and I don't. At least not until I get what I want. And she is like a pillar of granite. Or maybe basalt. Sharp edges."

"How are you planning on getting Cam to leave Advon to find this person? It seems like The Maker won't go near her as long as she's close to Sean Ellis."

"She'll leave on her own, eventually. The trick will be making sure we're there when she does."

Tristan might have laughed at her certainty if she didn't look so serious. Kardell would not leave her position. She was a Sentinel, down to the bone. "You really think you can hide what you want from her? Or convince her not to do anything she's set on doing? Will tried that, once, and Erika still ended up dead."

Melanie smiled up at him, a glint in her eye. "She'll take me where I want to go, because she wants the same thing. And she'll underestimate me, just like you did, because you people with your swords and knives don't understand how much power there is in making people like you. Cam can keep her blade. I'll win people."

She rubbed a hand through his hair again, her fingers light on his skin. Tristan yielded to the gentle pressure, and bent his head until their lips touched. Her kiss was as painful as it was pleasant. He knew she would never love him as much as he loved her. But that had always suited him. He didn't deserve a happiness complete.

She pulled away. Whispered, "You'll help me?"

"Of course."

The softness in her eyes was warm and familiar, but tinged now with knowledge. He realized that he was seeing her for perhaps the first time. And she would rule him, guide him.

She pulled him back into her embrace, and he gave her all she wanted. He might be a fool, but at least he was a happy one.

Two days passed. The weather warmed. His tail, probably frustrated at how often he'd slipped out of sight, abandoned subtlety in favor of proximity. But he could wait. Eventually everyone let their guard down.

Then she was gone. He walked several blocks before he realized the prickling sensation that came with being followed had vanished. He glanced around, saw nothing.

She would lose her career for that. Pity.

He stopped to get food, then walked to the theater. He was with Mel again, and it felt like breathing again.

He opened the side door, and gagged on the smell of blood. For it to be that powerful—that was death.

Tristan's feet carried him to the prop room. The door stood open. A body lay on the floor. Too slender to be Melanie. Dark hair.

No, no. Not Niko.

Tristan knelt at his side. Cuts peppered the boys arms, face, and torso. He still breathed, but only just. So much blood.

No one in The Agency could have bested Niko in close combat. Cameron had made the boy as good as Tristan.

The Maker?

For the first time, rage at their creator swelled in Tristan's chest. He stood, a dagger in each hand, and stepped into the prop room. Melanie's scent hung in the air, but it was hours old.

A clanking footstep behind him. Tristan spun, threw one dagger at the approaching shape. It hit metal and rebounded, almost slicing his shoulder. He leapt, bringing a dagger up, where the gap would be under the breastbone, all the while pulling a third dagger out of his jacket.

His blade skittered across metal again. Arms clamped around him. He stared into a smoky plastic visor. Behind it, unseen, was the face of whomever had killed Niko. Tristan kicked, and jabbed with the daggers, but every strike glanced off.

"Where is Melanie?" the person inside the armor said. The voice was filtered. But Tristan grinned. She'd escaped.

"I don't know."

Tristan felt unseen eyes on him.

"Then you will suffice."

One metal arm released him. Tristan levered the other open enough to slip out of the metal grip. He'd taken one step when a hand snagged his jacket.

Pain in his shoulder. It spread, rippled out.

Not pain, ice. It hit his brain, and everything went dark.

023

CAMERON WAITED IN Thea Clemens's office. Staying still had become so hard. If she wasn't training, or sparring, or reading, her mind wandered to burning cities and freezing mountainsides and Armel. Armel lying on the path, wind scouring his hands and face as he looked to her.

At the time, she'd believed that her attention had been on her surroundings, nothing else. But why, then, did she remember looking down at him? It had only been for a moment. That was enough to sear into her mind his black eyes which seemed to try to say to her a thousand things at once, none of which she could understand. Would someone else have known? Would a better person have seen in that look his love for Owena, or the raising of one last glass?

None of the other High Guards spoke to her anymore. The only one with any reason for this was Brecht, who'd liked William and hated her for not caring that he was gone. The rest just followed his lead. They all came at her during training with a vengeance, but all their fury just made her even sharper.

If only she could get out of the Military Quarter and see Owena. Or anyone, really.

Something was missing. She could feel it, but could not place it. Feelings weren't sense. It should have lifted after a month or so, but it wouldn't go away.

Armel, obviously. Ethan, too, although she had to be over that, it had been months.

Of course, every time his new song played on the radio, a High Guard cranked up the volume to ensure she heard it. It was called "House of Stone." If it was in reference to her, it was not flattering.

There was William. But he'd done it to himself. How often had she warned him? She had no reason to feel bad about that. He was the one who'd attacked Ellis. Stupid.

She rose and paced in front of the desk, even though her feet ached from standing guard.

Failures mounting. And Ellis would not yield. Not to the attackers, not to her. Eventually the soldiers would move on Advon, and the High General would die before she learned The Maker's name. Most likely, she would die defending him.

That would be an end to things, wouldn't it?

The door opened, and Clemens entered. So, Cameron wasn't the only one losing sleep. They both sat. The Master of the High Guard avoided Cameron's gaze for a long time. She shuffled stacks of papers, the way William did when he was nervous.

"I have an assignment for you, High Guard Kardell." Her hands shook as she picked up a bundle of documents. She slid them across the desk. "These are copies of the Sentinel's Oath, the High General's Oath, and the official list of duties for both. I would like you to review them for anything irregular."

Cameron caught the implication at once. *Find out if we can rein in the High General. Discover if a High Guard has a responsibility to stop him if he isn't acting in the best interests of Cotarion.*

Surely Clemens had already combed it through, and found nothing. Otherwise she would have acted.

Cameron took the papers.

"Are you sure I'm the right person for this job, Ma'am?"

Clemens's lip twitched. "As usual, Kardell, you are the only person for the job. Isn't it nice, being indispensable?"

"Not really."

The Master of the High Guard laughed, more out of nerves than because it was funny. "You're dismissed, Kardell."

They exchanged salutes. Cameron went to her room, changed into civilian clothes, laid the papers on her desk. She left the Military Quarter by the main gate. If assassins were bold enough to hover around the front entrance, then the side gates were surely covered.

She didn't see Tristan or Niko on the rooftops. Without their protection, she was vulnerable. She walked quickly, kept her eyes open, counting on the evening crowds to offer protection. She took a route that had become, of late, so very familiar.

William's mother opened the door of his townhouse. Cesar tried to leap right over her and reach Cameron.

"Sit, Cesar," Cameron said as she slid through the gap in the door. The retriever plopped his rear on the floor, though his front feet still danced. Teague took Cameron's jacket.

"You won't be in trouble for coming here?"

Cameron shrugged. "There aren't any rules against visiting the parents of an exile.

Teague smiled. "I think they're implied."

Ah. So William had inherited the urge to correct. "I didn't see Tristan out there. Is he away on business?"

Fresh worry in her eyes, piled on top of pain. "He didn't say he'd be gone. Every day since William was sent away he's come to see me, but not the last two days." She bit her lip. "He seemed really happy his last visit. I wondered if maybe he'd starting things up with, oh, what was her name, from a couple of years ago . . . "

Cameron caught her breath. "Melanie?"

"Why is that bad?"

Cameron raised an eyebrow.

"You've seen my husband. If I could read him I can read anybody. You're good at everything but the eyes. They're very expressive." Teague didn't look the least bit self-conscious about saying such a thing. "So, what's wrong with Melanie?"

"I'm just not sure if she's friend or foe." And if Tristan had gone back to her, she couldn't be sure about him, either.

"I'll get you some refreshments. You want to look in his office again, I assume?"

"Thank you."

Cameron went up the stairs to the spare room. The word 'office' hardly applied. There was a desk, true, and books, but also microscopes, blackboards, and boxy machines that clicked or hummed when turned on. It was more laboratory than anything else.

Cameron sat in the chair behind the desk. She didn't have a lot of time, she never did, and the number of notebooks was staggering. Little flags of paper marked random pages. Any system he had, she could not discern.

She hunted for scraps. Any piece that might be a link to The Maker. Something William had recorded without understanding its significance.

The closest notebook had several loose papers jammed in it. One was a flier for Advon's dog agility club. Several more were part of his work for Ellis. One was a page torn from a book of fairytales.

Asterisks stood to the side of some notes, but these were usually personal, things like, "Buy coffee! Pick up laundry! Throw away gloves with holes!"

Who needed to write that down?

Teague came in with a tray of tea and crackers smeared with peanut butter and jam. Cameron shoved the notebook back, ignored the tea, and ate a cracker.

"Not going so well?"

Cameron swallowed. "He writes down everything, and I don't even know what to look for."

"Here's the thing about Will. Even here, in his house, in his office, he would have squirreled the most important things away. The good stuff is not going to sit on top of the pile." Teague lifted a stack of papers and notebooks. Cameron pulled out the slim, leather-bound journal that had been at the bottom. It was, compared to the other books, pristine.

Inside were lines of bulleted notes, in meticulous print, very unlike the scrawl in the other books.

> – *Tristan unable to make connection past Dr. Maikon. Must seeks answers from SE, or trace through code.*
> – *OF explained abilities of Series 5. See pages 15–27 of blue book.*

- *Dream of SK cutting out my heart recurs at regular intervals. I suspect it is a message left by Erika. But why? A warning? Could she even plant dreams?*
- *Explanation of light orb stability:*

Which was followed by complicated diagrams and equations that ran on for several pages. The notebook had been half-filled with more notes in the same style.

Cameron put it down then checked the underbellies of more piles. She found the referenced blue book, as well as red, green, and gray volumes. A rifle through the pages showed they contained information about each type of Altered, excluding Twenty-Fours.

Teague, who'd been searching, too, became very quiet. Cameron turned. She stood in front of the bookshelves, another black book in her hands, this one smaller. She read with wide eyes, her lips pressed together. It was some mixture of horror and amusement.

"Is it important?"

Teague looked up. She passed the book over, pages splayed open.

Big Picture

Question: *What are we trying to achieve, looking for answers to all this? I like to think that we are trying to put a stop to it all. That we are putting a stop to the things that happened to Erika. That even if we cannot achieve freedom from all this for ourselves, that at least there will be a chance at freedom for Niko.*

Is that even possible? We don't know anything. I can feel it; we are ants in a hill, too small to even understand the scale of what stands above us.

Cameron seems to think so. Or at least that's what she says. I wonder, though, if she will ever be able to act. She has molded herself to the uniform she wears. Worked her entire life to wear the Sentinel's Eye. Surely at some point, if we survive long enough, this quest for answers will call on her to shed her duties.

Can she?

And if she can't, what will become of me?

Cameron closed the book. She should not have read even that much.

"Can you?"

"Yes." Cameron said.

Teague stood unbreathing. "Were you there, when they took William away? Could you have stopped it?"

Cameron's hand lay still on the notebook. "I don't know how to answer that question."

"I might never see my son again. Shouldn't I at least know that much?"

"That isn't fair."

"Life isn't fair. I've lost both my children. I'm asking for one scrap of truth in all this."

Cameron turned away. She picked up a photo on the desk, of William and Erika, posed, but with happy smiles. No, that made it harder. She put it down. Rested her hand on the hilt of her sword.

"If I'd been there when he went after the High General, I would have stopped it. By the time I arrived, they were taking him away. Could I have struck down two High Guards, freed him, and helped him escape? Of course not. We would never have made it out of the Military Quarter. Could I have tried?" She looked up at William's mother. "Yes. I could have tried."

She stopped, because she felt just then all the weight of all the miles between Advon and the Crescent Mountains, and all the times she'd paused, every day, and wondered if he was still alive up there. It was more than she could afford to carry. And yet, there it was.

Cameron swallowed. *Can she?* William wrote. Could she set aside the uniform, her duties, Advon, Cotarion, for answers that might not even exist? To go fight other forces that might be unimaginably powerful?

Teague wiped her eyes, and then squeezed Cameron's hand. Cameron regretted saying as much as she had.

Cameron took a deep breath. "Let's put all these together, so when William needs them they'll be easy to find. I have to get going, but hopefully I'll be able to come back soon."

"Do you always leave when things get personal?"

Cameron smiled, at how much William had seen, at how little she'd been able to hide, at how it was far too late for any of it, now. "Yes."

After seeing Teague, Cameron visited Owena, who had developed a noticeable bump. Cameron talked about Armel, especially, which Owena seemed to enjoy. Cam found leaving strange. Or perhaps painful? Memories of her friend hovered in that home. They vanished when the door closed.

The streets as she walked were cold and dark. The feeling of loss faded quickly, replaced by the chill.

Then she heard a light hum, and an arrow struck the street several feet away. Cameron saw the movement on the rooftop. She ran to the top of the fire escape before the assassin could nock a third arrow; the second had rebounded off the metal grating at Cameron's feet as she rounded one of the landings. Up close, it wasn't anywhere near a fair fight.

Cameron wiped the blood from her blade, her breath coming in quick gasps. Not fear. Not from the run. Anger.

Another figure moved a few rooftops away. Cameron met the woman's eyes and bared her teeth. "Try me!"

The shaped paused, then vanished, like a mountain cat slinking back into trees.

Cameron walked back to the Military Quarter, and no one else dared strike at her. For now.

Cameron's study of the codes yielded nothing. Sentinels swore to defend Cotarion, but the High Guard's oath superseded it, and they were sworn to defend the High General. They had no hope of being in the right if they tried to move against him. Whatever wrong Ellis might have done, it was their duty to protect him.

Cameron trained in the morning, alone. After lunch she stopped at Clemens's office for the run-up prior to her shift.

She opened the door.

Everything was wrong. For a moment she stood frozen, her fingers tingling.

The Master of the High Guard lay across her desk. Blood dripped over the edge of the desk and onto the floor. Cracks spiderwebbed out from a hole in the window. Something moved in a building across the quad.

Cameron lunged forward and slammed into the wall under the window just before the glass cracked again. A second bullet struck the wall next to the door.

Thea Clemens dead.

William Harfield probably also dead.

Towns burning.

Armel dead.

Her own body bore the scars of the High General's quest to remain safe, whatever the cost. It was time. Time to do something.

But first, the assassin. She pulled out her pistol.

Cameron was at a significant disadvantage. She needed several seconds to line up the shot. The assassin knew exactly where she was going to appear when she stood up.

Unless she moved to another room.

The door was still open. If she stayed very low, it might work.

Cameron crawled along the floor, inching her way across the room, until she reached the doorway. Once in the safety of the hall, she dashed two doors down. The door was unlocked. Swiftly, swiftly, Cameron opened it and crept to the window. Her eyes found the outline of the assassin. Her hands followed.

She lined up her shot, breathed in—

The assassin's rifle shifted towards her.

—let it half out. Pulled the trigger. The pistol rocked hard in her hands.

The assassin fell. So lucky. That shouldn't have worked, with a small firearm at this distance, not with Cam's marksmanship. The rest of her work, at least, would be in close quarters.

Cameron leaned back against the wall, and caught her breath.

Then she moved on to step two.

Back in Clemens's office, she checked the day's schedule. Brecht and Palmroy. Damn. It could go either way, but it would have to do.

She ran up to the High General's office. The guards in the hall stared at her. Did she reek of gunpowder? Was her intent written on her face?

Into the office. She shut the door, and before Brecht could consider leaving his post, she said, "Thea Clemens, Master of the High Guard, is dead."

She watched as it hit them, even Gordon who hadn't known Clemens for long. Ellis sat back in his chair, and stared at something very far away.

Cameron cared, more than she really thought was wise. And so did he. But Cameron understood that she cared, and he didn't. That made all the difference.

Finally, in a voice that seemed to come from about the same place where he'd set his gaze, Sean Ellis said, "Sentinel Kardell, I name you Master of the High Guard."

"I'm sorry, Sir, but you can't. A Master of the High Guard must have served in the High Guard for at least fifteen years."

"Brecht, then that leaves you. Go get to work."

Cameron met Brecht's eye, and he paused. Cameron said, "Sir, if you don't mind I'd like him to stay for a few minutes There's a conversation we need to have, and there have to be witnesses."

Ellis sat up straight. His eyes honed in on Cameron. "Master of the High Guard Brecht, arrest High Guard Kardell for treason."

"Can't, Sir. She hasn't spoken a word of treason. There are some rules."

Ellis slammed a hand on his desk. "You've been the one making her a pariah for weeks!"

Brecht smiled, just a little. "That's because she's been half-dead for weeks. Right now is the first time in a long time I've seen High Guard Kardell alive and well. And I want to hear what she has to say."

Cameron laid her sword and pistol on the desk in front of Ellis, then sat across from him. She looked over at Gordon. "If I say anything that could be treason, you can shoot me." Gordon nodded, just once.

She met Sean Ellis's eyes. He was more annoyed than frightened. For so long, the High General had refused to see the inevitable. Cotarion was at risk only as long as he remained its leader. This wasn't a war between two countries, and it wasn't a secession. It was all about Sean Ellis. It was past time to lift the veil from his eyes.

She began. "You understand what this means. One of them got into the Military Quarter."

Ah, there, a flicker of doubt. Then the line of his mouth hardened. "They're closing in."

She nodded. "What are your options?"

"I'll fight to the last. It's what Cotarion deserves."

Cameron flipped over the newspaper on his desk, spread it to the front page. Another town in ruin. How would he fight a band of attackers that could do that? They'd even been prepared this time. There had been Sentinels on guard there.

Ellis remained still. He couldn't admit that he was the target. Or that he and he alone had the power to stop it.

"What do they want, Sir? When will they stop?"

Brecht and Palmroy watched, still as statues. Probably wondering what the hell Cameron was trying to say. Cameron's gaze met Ellis's. They were both certain, unyielding.

"Varcove isn't doing this," Ellis said.

Cameron didn't answer.

And it was Brecht who said, "What do the attackers want, Sir?"

"Me," the High General said. "They want me."

Ellis rubbed his face, and only the smallest of twitches served as warning. He lunged, snagging Cameron's sword, pulling it clear of the scabbard just enough to expose a few inches of the edge.

Cameron caught it along hilt and scabbard, leaned forward enough in her chair to stop it from tipping. He was above her, on top of the desk, and she just barely held him back. She wouldn't last long. Her shoulders already screamed.

Neither Brecht nor Palmroy had moved. They didn't know whose side to take.

Somehow, Cameron formed words. "Killing me won't stop it, Sir."

"I never thought you'd turn on me."

Her arms shook. It was like holding up a brick wall. "You can sit and wait for them. Or you can act. Make things happen on your terms."

"I'll die either way."

Which was her point. The edge glinted, and drifted an inch or two closer. It was her neck he wanted, but under the circumstances he didn't have to be close.

"You make a real choice, people will remember you. A damn long time."

She'd caught something there. He saw it, the accolades, the books about his bravery, his selfless sacrifice. A better way to go than huddled in his office, while Advon lay in ruins around him. One way, glory; the other, a failure forever.

The pressure on Cameron's hands eased, the sword drew back. Hilt and sheath met. The High General sat back. He stared at the newspaper a long time.

Cameron risked a little further nudging. "If you stay here and wait, you'll be recorded as the High General who lost Advon. That will be your legacy. If you turn yourself over, you'll be the man who selflessly saved Cotarion."

"It's the best way, isn't it? I'll be a hero. Dead either way."

Cameron said nothing. It wasn't done yet.

Then the spark rose in his eye. "On one condition. You'll come with me."

"Yes, Sir." There. The last thing. He wouldn't go without at least a small remnant of his shield.

He jumped to his feet. "Let's not waste any time, then. If we're going to our deaths there's no sense in waiting around."

Cameron stood, too. She returned her pistol to its holster, her sword to her belt.

"Brecht, in about two hours I'd like you to call Seat Member Harfield and my advisors. Tell them everything you just heard. I doubt they'll be sad to see me go." He grabbed his sword, which hung on the wall behind his desk. A grim excitement gripped him. "Is there anything you need before you go, Kardell?"

"Gordon, come up with something nice to tell my family. And Brecht, make sure you send someone down to Clemens." Both men stared in shock. Brecht at least managed to shake off enough to pull Cameron in for a quick embrace that included a thump of her back.

"I'll push for Doctor Harfield's reprieve, too."

"That would be good," she said. Brecht winked.

Ellis grabbed some food he kept stashed in his desk, maps, and water. He even had coats for them both in the room's small closet. When he'd stocked up to his satisfaction, he shook hands with Brecht and Palmroy. As they left the office, Palmroy said, "What the hell just happened?"

Cameron kept her hand on the hilt of her blade as they walked through the building. Ellis's grin unnerved her. He strode in a snappy way that she hadn't seen in a long time. It was as if he'd been waiting all this time for someone to suggest running right into the jaws of the beast.

They arrived at the garage, where Sean Ellis showed his identification, though it was hardly necessary. The nondescript armored car he requested was ready in minutes. He threw the jackets on the back seat and handed Cameron the keys.

Twenty minutes later the car swept past the outskirts of Advon. Ellis propped his feet on the dashboard, a map spread across his legs while Cameron drove. He ate salted almonds.

"You didn't sign a resignation," she said.

"Do you know what I hate more than paperwork? Nothing. Let someone else deal with all that. Want an apple?" She shook her head.

"You never know where your next meal might come from. Most captives get slop to eat, even important ones like you and me."

"You really doing this without a fight, Sir?"

He looked up at her. "I've been halfway to doing it for two weeks, now. Clemens was a damn good Sentinel. I'm not going to sit behind my desk and let that stand. It's time I got out here and faced the enemy. Between us, we might get a chance to give them hell. If not, like you said, we'll be heroes. A lot better than going down as the High General who lost Advon to a bunch of punks with flame-throwers."

024

Sean Ellis directed Cameron down back roads for several hours, keeping an eye on the dashboard clock and the maps as they went. Finally, he told her to stop at the end of a rutted dirt road in the middle of a pine forest.

They both pulled on coats and set off into the woods. Cameron finally accepted an apple. They made good time over the clear ground.

Sean Ellis hummed "House of Stone" as they went. Cameron ignored it. He wouldn't be satisfied with such subtle needling for long.

"I'm curious, what did it for you?" Ellis said. "Was it Armel? The towns? Doctor Harfield? Clemens?"

"All of that. None of it. There's right and wrong. You've been wrong a long time." She glanced over at his map, tried to predict where he wanted to end up. They had maybe two hours of daylight, and then it was going to get cold.

He sneered. "That's a lot of judgement from you. How many people have you killed to defend me, for no reason other than that one little scrap of information that I still haven't given you?"

"Fewer than have died because of The Maker."

Ellis barked with laughter. "So you've got the scales of justice in your hands. Let me guess, you're okay with throwing out that crusade because by some mysterious calculation, the loss of life tipped too far. More died because of me than The Maker."

Cameron didn't answer. Ellis walked in silence for a long time. They crossed streams, stripping off boots at one bank, pulling them back on at the other. Ellis stopped trying to share his food.

They scared several herds of deer. Each time they paused to watch the flash of tails and the high-flung hooves until they were gone.

Finally, Ellis stopped. He put his pistol and his sword on a fallen log, then sat on a rock. Cameron put her weapons next to his. She remained standing, off to the side. The whole thing felt familiar.

"Old habits die hard, don't they?" Ellis said. Cameron raised an eyebrow. "You're standing right where you would if we were in my office."

He tossed her a pack of almond butter from a ration. She wrinkled her nose, but tore it open anyway.

"If you live through this, you really need to start eating better, Kardell."

She rolled her eyes. "You don't think Varcove is behind this anymore?"

"Not entirely. The weapons are from somewhere else." He rubbed his hands together. "I've seen things you can't imagine, and still I know only a fraction of The Maker's resources. Across the ocean, they have tech I can't explain. Vehicles that float in the air, glass towers that touch the sky, weapons that can make a person vanish like they were never there."

Cameron's brow furrowed. That didn't make sense. People with tech like that would cross the ocean easily, wouldn't they? Cotarion hadn't seen a ship from that part of the world in over fifteen years, and that little raft was famous for being far too small to make the journey the occupants claimed it had.

"Who is it? It won't matter if you tell me, now."

Ellis shook his head. "It might matter more than ever. They're coming."

Cameron saw them, too. Advance scouts, just visible through the trees. Their armor glinted with gold in the slanting evening light. She longed to have her sword where she could grip her hilt.

Had there ever been another way? No matter how she turned all the alternatives, she saw only this, or death some other violent way.

"Any regrets?" Ellis said.

"No."

"Lucky you. I regret that I didn't stay with Ami. She told me I should. I promised I would go back, but I never did. I would have left eventually, of course, and it would have been ugly, by then.

"I regret the Hevan Desert, too. I got a lot of good Sentinels killed that day. Sent them down the wrong damn ravine. You sure you don't have any?"

Cameron considered. She should have taken Reese's advice and left Erika alone, maybe.

She could have kissed William on the Solstice, but then that moment in the hall after he attacked Ellis would have been so much worse. Better that she hadn't.

"I hurt William Harfield. A lot. He deserved better than that."

One armored man stopped a few feet from them, his weapon trained on them. Two more closed in. Their faces were all cold, and they seemed unsurprised.

"Yeah, he did. And I'm saying that as the one who exiled him."

"Put the hands top your head," the man said, the words heavily accented. Cameron and Ellis both complied.

In a few minutes many people, some in heavy armor and some entirely without, but all carrying weapons, surrounded them. One young woman held their swords. Conversations buzzed around them, some of it in Varcove, but some in another language Cameron couldn't understand.

One young man stepped forward. He was short, lightly armed, and so familiar that Cameron was sure she must know his name, though nothing came to her.

"Who are you?" he asked. His Varcove accent was light.

"I am High General Sean Ellis of Cotarion, and this is High Guard Cameron Kardell. I heard you were looking for me."

The young man looked at Cameron when Ellis said her name. His eyes. They were just like hers.

"Cam?"

"Siv." Cousin Siva, who had spent summers at her grandparents' in Varcove. He'd always been eager to learn her language, couldn't understand why she saw learning his such a chore. They'd built a dam in the creek once and flooded Uncle Luke's vegetable patch. Another summer they'd made their own fort in the woods, complete with handcrafted weaponry. No one had minded until they'd hit Cousin Helen with the trebuchet.

Siva's grin faded fast. "I was afraid you'd be with him when we found him."

One of the armored men snapped at Siva in the language Cameron didn't understand. Siva responded in the same rhythmic syllables.

A lot of people started shouting at once. Some whooped at their success, but some voices rose in fury. One soldier stormed up to Cameron, breaking the circle. She flinched when he yanked her jacket and undershirt up, exposing her skin to the chilly air.

He pressed the barrel of his gun to the scar on her side. His finger trembled on the trigger. The metal jabbed between her ribs. She fought the urge to grab the rifle, turn it back on him.

"Sister," he growled. Cameron frowned into his fury-lined face. Siva shouted at him in Varcove, telling him to put the weapon down and step back.

Oh. His sister was the one who shot her there. Which meant Cameron had killed her. He was going to pull the trigger, given a few more seconds. Would she survive a second bullet to the lung?

She had expected a quicker death, something more like an execution, with less gasping and expecting each ragged breath to be the last.

Then a loud voice interrupted all the rest. The words were unfamiliar, but the tone commanded. The soldier dropped his gun and Cameron's shirt. Before he stepped away, he spat, very deliberately, on her face.

A moment later another soldier gripped Cameron's hands and bound them behind her back. The commander stopped in front of her. He was dressed like all the rest, but his head gleamed. His only hair grew from small patches just in front of his ears, and this was long enough to brush his shoulders.

He wiped the spit off her face. "Cameron Kardell. My warriors call you the Gate Demon. A reference I'm sure you do not know, but there is as much respect in it as fear. Your loyalty is remarkable. For that, you have earned a very honorable execution."

He turned to Ellis. "High General Ellis. The Guardians send their regards. Your escape has become legendary. If The Maker had not asked me to keep you safe, I would kill you myself."

Sean Ellis bared his teeth. "Do they talk about how I slid down that building on my ass? I couldn't sit down for weeks after that. By the way, I don't recommend you kill Kardell, at least not until you've talked to The Maker."

The commander raised his eyebrows. "Ah. That would explain some things." He turned to the soldiers, and gave more orders. When the commander was done, Siva translated everything into Varcove. Most of the soldiers broke away from the ring and hustled off to set up an encampment. Cameron and Ellis stood, bound and under guard, until enough hard-sided shelters had been erected to place them each into one.

A soldier bound Cameron's foot in a shackle. A chain ran from it to a large magnet that locked onto the shelter's metal wall. The magnet hummed. Cameron tugged at the chain, but it didn't give.

The soldier laughed as she left Cameron alone.

Darkness fell. Someone brought a tray of food. It was a slushy gray-hued pile that smelled vaguely moldy. Cameron drank the glass of water and drew stick figures in the food.

She kept her mind busy with thoughts of what she would do if The Maker did show up and let her live. Would this person want her to make more Altered? That seemed to be the entire point of a Twenty-Four. When the ability was turned on, would she be able to stop herself from using it?

If she did manage an escape, which would require more resources than she had on hand, she would need to find The Maker herself. Ellis hadn't been a good source of information. Maybe Melanie knew something and would be more forthcoming.

Outside the shelter, the Varcove soldiers talked about finally going home. She couldn't tell anything about the others. Where had they come from? There seemed to be no more than ten or twelve. Their language was completely unfamiliar, so they probably weren't from countries to the south or the east.

Maybe they'd come across the ocean, as Ellis had suggested?

Siva was the one who took her tray of food away. He didn't say anything, but he smiled at her. The expression was tinged with sadness, and Cameron knew he didn't expect she would live much longer.

He didn't leave anything behind, not even a scrap of paper. If it had been her, she would have found a way to be helpful. They were family, after all.

Had he known when he signed up that part of his job would involve killing civilians? Or was he just a translator? In an operation this small, she doubted it. Altogether she estimated forty men and women. Everyone in the group had certainly taken life.

She inspected the electromagnet again for a way to switch it off, but of course there was nothing. She ran her fingers along the bench, checking for any sharp edges or loose portions to grip, but the welds were smooth. Much like the metal doors in Lab 9.

That was it. She would just have to wait until circumstances changed. In the meantime, she leaned back against the wall.

She'd settled into an uncomfortable half-doze when the door of the hut opened. Two mercenaries entered, one small and round, the other gangly. Both pulled protective wraps away from their faces.

Niko and Melanie grinned at her, for just a second, before they went to work. Niko put his back to the door while Melanie knelt at Cameron's ankle and fiddled with the cuff.

The cuff popped open. Melanie hopped to her feet.

"Ellis," Cameron whispered.

Melanie shook her head. "No way. I'm not risking my skin for him. He is way too heavily guarded."

"Then you and Niko go, I'll meet up with you when I get him out."

"You are finally free of him. Why would you save his sorry ass?"

He had nothing to lose, now that he wasn't High General, and he had no love for The Maker. As long as their goals aligned, he would be an asset. And he had experience and knowledge none of them could dismiss.

"What he knows might keep us alive."

Melanie cursed. "Fine. I'll help. If I get shot, though, you gotta promise to feel bad about it for the rest of your life. Or else I'll haunt you."

They shook on it.

"I'll distract them," Niko said. Then he slipped out.

Cameron and Melanie waited for long, quiet minutes. Melanie inspected her nails and pushed back her cuticles, more out of nerves than vanity.

Shouldn't Tristan have been there? Even stranger that Melanie was helping Cameron. She wanted something, and this was her offering.

The camp lay quiet. Hopefully Niko didn't kill Sivan out there. Or vice versa. Cameron's fingers itched for a sharp weapon. Her pulse quickened at every pass made by one of the guards.

Then a roar of sound, so loud it stunned Cameron, who had been expecting something, but not that. She grabbed Melanie's arm, and out they went.

Niko must have found a way to ignite some fuel. Whatever it was, the light it cast was bluish-green and seemed brighter than the sun.

Every one of the soldiers ran away from it. The hairs on Cameron's neck prickled. Hopefully, Niko had not been close to the explosion.

No one looked at Cameron or Melanie for more than a second as they ran alongside the mercenaries. And there, dragged along by two soldiers, was Ellis.

Cameron hooked a foot around one man's shin, and they all went down. The one furthest from her raised his gun, but Ellis brought his manacles hard against his head.

The nearer rolled and brought her gun up, but Cameron got a grip and shoved it down, though wresting it away was not so easy.

Abruptly, the young woman twitched, then went limp. Cameron rose to a crouch with the weapon as Melanie took her hand away from an exposed wrist. Mel's grin could be clearly seen in her eyes.

A second explosion rocked the encampment, filling the world with light. Cameron grabbed Melanie by the elbow again. They stumbled on behind Ellis. They left the encampment and entered the forest, where everything was lit by a green light.

Melanie dropped her pace to a jog, much to Ellis's irritation. Niko hadn't yet reappeared. A metallic odor hung in the air.

Cameron opened her mouth to ask where Melanie and Niko had left their vehicle when Melanie shrieked.

Cameron wheeled in time to see the commander throw Melanie to the ground, then dance away. He knew what Mel could do, which probably made him more knowledgeable about Altered than Cameron was. He pointed an oddly-shaped rifle at her. Cam pointed her stolen weapon right back at him. The beads on his hair tendrils flashed in the green light.

"You hit me in the limbs, and I'll recover. The slightest glance by this—" he nodded at the weapon in his hands, "—and you are, what is it, a dead cat."

"If you want me to come along quietly so you can deliver me to The Maker, then you're talking to the wrong person."

"It was polite to at least offer." He pulled the rifle in tighter, took aim. So did Cameron—

Niko appeared through the trees behind him, Ellis's sword in his hands. Melanie gasped, the commander spun and changed targets as the blade swept down.

A brilliant blue blast emitted from the rifle into the trees. Niko's blow was true, but didn't have quite enough speed to kill.

In the opening, Melanie jumped up and pressed a hand to the commander's head. His eyes closed. A mercy, considering the gaping cut to his torso. Still, he breathed.

Ellis shouted, "Your jacket boy, take it off."

Niko slipped his jacket off and tossed it on the ground. One arm of it had a small circle of blue glow, which became a hole with glowing blue edges, which just kept growing. Another small circle of the blue light spread on Niko's shirt. He pulled that off, too.

The blue, a tiny patch, was on his arm as well.

"Damn. Hold still." Ellis pulled a knife from Niko's boot, grabbed the boy's wrist, and sliced away a small divot of Niko's forearm.

The young man yelled, shoved Ellis away. Cameron reached out, Niko held out his arm again, and she peered at it. When she dabbed the blood away, she saw only exposed flesh.

"What would it have done?" she asked.

Sean Ellis's face had gone very stormy. "Let's get out of here. Faster than a jog, Ms. Stillwater. Where is your car?"

Niko led the way through the trees, into the deep darkness away from the fires and the soldiers.

025

THEY CHANGED CARS twice on the way north. Cameron and Ellis swapped their uniforms for civilian clothes Niko had stashed in the second car. He provided them with fake IDs as well.

"Did Tristan set all this up, Niko, or did you do it yourself?" Cameron asked.

"I did it. Tristan's been taken by The Maker."

Melanie grinned at Cameron while she hacked off her hair and threw hunks out the window. She would have bet good money that Mel had picked an ID with a recent date and a photo of a short-haired woman just so Cam would have to chop hers off. "And we're going to get him back."

Cameron frowned. "Why?"

Niko didn't take his eyes off the road, but he glared at Cameron in the rear-view mirror. Melanie's eyes glinted.

"Excuse me?"

"It's not as if Tristan is vitally important, especially if we have Niko. He's just moped ever since that other Twenty-Two beat him. I don't see what part he plays in all this that can't be fulfilled by someone else."

"You made me save *that* bastard!" Melanie jabbed a finger at Ellis. "What good is he? He's a failed Twenty-Four, as well as a terrible High General, and a horrible human being."

Cameron ignored the increasing volume of Melanie's voice. "He's a brilliant large-scale tactician, and he's had close contact with The Maker. He has more experience in tight corners than the rest of us combined. So, what does Tristan do that's so special?"

"He's your friend!"

"So was Armel."

Melanie ground her teeth together. "Niko, stop the car and kick her out!"

Niko kept driving. Ellis sat back in his seat with one hand over his mouth as if trying to hide amusement.

"Maybe it's not just skill that matters. Maybe it's the fact that he actually cares about you, and William, and Niko, and me. He doesn't have to care, in fact he'd rather not. It's better than you deserve, but he does. And he's just a dumb puppy dog that's been kicked a few times, but he's our puppy. And I care about him. And he loves me, and all of you, really. Well not *you*." This to Ellis. "But you owe him better than to ask why we should go after him. Seriously, you know, he wouldn't hesitate to help you."

Cameron leaned forward, putting her face very close to Melanie's. "You really care about him? You've been stringing him along for over two years."

"If I hadn't cared he'd have figured out I was lying. Are you going to help or not?"

"Of course I will."

Melanie's nostrils flared. "You were *testing* me? You wanted to know *my* reasons?"

"You've been misleading us all for a long time. I'm well within my rights to find out your motives."

"You could have just asked."

Cameron raised an eyebrow. "What fun would that have been?"

Apparently that was a step too far. Melanie growled—actually growled—then whipped around to stare out the front window. She sat there with her arms crossed, and huffed. Even Niko frowned.

Cameron checked the issue date of the license again, tugged at the hair on her forehead, and sighed. She cut until she had the same slanting bangs.

"You're off to an auspicious start as leader of this little crew, Kardell," Ellis said.

Cameron savored the right to ignore him.

Niko bribed the guards at the bottom of the mountain, which would get them up. Coming down, he said, they'd have to move fast, and change cars again.

Rain misted down as they climbed the rough-hewn path that twined its way up the mountain. Glaciers, rocks, and trees drifted in and out of the mists, as If the Crescent Mountains weren't sure of their own existence. The air smelled of pine resin.

Cameron squeezed through a rift in a cliff face, scrambling over jumbles of loose rock. She came out into improbable slice of gentle hillock in an otherwise daunting landscape. In the middle of the fresh green patch of grass stood a cabin, built of stone and timber.

No smoke rose from the chimney. The ground was too soft, all the footprints unclear. That curve might have been the edge of a boot imprint, or a large hoof.

Sean Ellis marched to the cabin door and pushed it open. He returned from within a moment later, shaking his head.

She would not call his name. She would just find him, or not.

On the crags behind the cabin, rocks clattered. Loosened by frost and rain, or a mountain goat. Cameron went towards the noise. Ellis held up a hand.

"That creature you killed in Palisade, I made that. And those weren't the only ones. Some of them might still be around here."

Cameron's stomach clenched. Everything Palisade had suffered was because of him. He sighed and looked away.

"Judge me all you like, as long as you're careful. Even my fate hangs on yours, now."

Cameron drew her pistol, which seemed to alleviate his fears. Then she edged around the side of the cabin. More rocks clattered as she moved forward. The curtains of rain thickened.

She rounded a boulder at the same time William did. Startled, he raised his rifle at her. She froze with her pistol trained on him, the safety off.

He didn't recognize her for several long, breathless moments. She saw it in the crease between his eyebrows, the tight line of his shoulders. Rain dripped off his broad-brimmed hat, and a month's growth of beard glistened. A rabbit and a pair of ptarmigans hung from his shoulder.

Then the rifle dropped. Cameron lowered her pistol, and breathed again.

"Cameron?" he said. He cleared his throat and tried again. "Cameron?"

"Who the hell else would it be?"

Then he dropped the rifle, the rabbit, the birds. They met in the space that had once been between them. He wrapped his arms around her, and she wrapped her arms around him. William shook. Cameron pressed hard against his back and shoulders. Maybe he wouldn't notice that she was shaking, too.

At last William let go and stepped away. He couldn't have grinned wider, but his eyes glistened. He took off the hat to run a hand through hair gone wild.

"Are you ready to go?" she asked, at the same time he said, "Did you get exiled, too?"

He paused. "What?"

"Things changed. Get your stuff and I'll explain on the way."

026

Niko and Melanie told the story of Tristan's capture, followed by their rescue of Cameron and Ellis in with so many interruptions, backtracking, and corrections, that William had no idea what had actually happened. Sean Ellis's snide comments did little to clarify.

Weeks of solitude and cold and scrapping with the mountain to live had suddenly become a warm seat in the back of a car, with people talking all around. He'd eaten three apples before Melanie snapped at him that they had to conserve their resources.

Cameron sat beside him, silent. When he glanced over, he saw the smallest of smiles, but she reined it in when she noticed him looking. Her knee pressed against his, more, he thought, than it absolutely had to.

After they changed cars, Cameron fell asleep, her head bobbing down to William's shoulder. Melanie leaned around him to stare at this, one eyebrow quirked up.

"The Maker has Tris?" he said. It had been so long since he'd talked to a person that he could almost feel the words in his mouth, like rocks.

"Did you hear anything we just said?"

"I caught bits and pieces. Look, it's a lot to absorb after spending weeks with mountain goats."

"We're going after Tristan, yes."

"So, will we finally be let in on the secret of who The Maker is?"

Ellis turned in the front seat to look back at him. "I'd have thought it was obvious."

"Everything is obvious when you have the answer key."

Ellis smirked his aggravating smirk. "Reese, of course."

Melanie laughed, even in the face of the dark look Ellis gave her. William didn't think he'd have that much courage. "And he just let you believe he was the only one, did he? You really think one person could run this whole program?" She looked at William, her expression too complex to put a name to. He realized, with considerable shock, that he was seeing her for the first time. There were old wounds on her face, knowledge she'd never let show, fears that ran back to the beginning of her memory. "Reese is just one of the agents working on the Skylark Program here in Cotarion. The leader of the program is my father. And he, I'm certain, has fled to Gemini."

"Which is?"

"It's the city where I was born. We just need to get to the coast and find a boat—"

"That can cross the Quellan? That's suicide."

"That's what they want you to think."

So he'd been pulled out of exile to chase conspiracy theories. Was that an improvement? He supposed as long as he was warm he shouldn't complain. It couldn't be too bad, if Cameron was part of it. Of course, she might not have had much choice.

"We might have just lost Doctor Harfield," Ellis said.

Melanie sat back. Her voice was . . . fearful, or mournful? "He'll see, soon enough. A whole continent being used as a testing ground. It's completely insane until you see what things are like over there."

Ellis said, "You were two when you left."

William let his mind disengage from the ensuing bickering. He didn't understand most of it, anyway.

The sun sank towards the horizon, shining full into his face. Usually he'd be finishing up outside at this time, doing what he could to patch the leaks in the cabin's roof during the last few minutes of daylight. Maybe moving firewood inside to dry for the next evening, or replenishing the stack against the cabin's wall. He'd developed a rhythm there, once he'd taken care of Ellis's beasts.

Darkness fell. He leaned back against the seat, folded his arms against his chest. He let his head drift back. Cameron's breath brushed his hand. The in and out was smooth, rhythmic.

She wouldn't lead him into too much trouble.

Clinging to that, he fell asleep.

He jerked awake what seemed like a long time later. He blinked up into Cameron's face.

"We have to hustle," she said. "Melanie found a boat, but the tide is going out."

William grabbed his bag (Melanie and Niko had stopped by his house before leaving Cotarion, so it was heavy with notebooks) and followed Cameron.

He smelled the ocean air and the tarred wood of the docks. Warehouses stood all around, hulking in the light of huge lamps.

William's throat tightened as he walked behind Cameron down the pier. Her hacked-off hair curled along the back of her neck. Nothing quite seemed real.

They stopped in front of one of the smallest vessels bobbing beside the dock. In the guttering lamplight, William read the name. Barnacle's Song. Well, the crusting of white on its side suggested this was accurate, if lacking in romance.

Melanie talked to the captain on the deck. He glared down at William.

"Well, on board now! Time to stare later, the tide won't wait."

A moment later he was on board. He'd barely stowed his gear at a tiny bunk when the boat lurched away from the dock.

William went up on the deck and watched home pull away. The lights of the docks bobbed up and down as the boat rocked. It wasn't, as last looks went, the patch of shoreline he'd have chosen.

Cameron sidled up beside him. She put her hand on his, then threaded her fingers between his. He looked over at her, seeking a clue in her expression as to what this meant.

"Can you forgive me, for not stopping him from exiling you?"

"Hmm. Maybe after I've had a few more warm meals. And a shave."

She tugged on his beard and smiled. "You did get a bit wild."

"I very nearly took half my chin off with the straight razor in the cabin." He flipped his hand over, so they could press their palms together. Her hand resettled in his, like a bird come home to roost. Amazing, how such a small thing could feel so important.

"And Erika? Can you forgive me for that?"

His breath left him. He looked away from her, not trusting his face. Her fingers loosened, and he felt her pulling away, but he retightened his grip. She remained.

"That was never your fault, Cam." It was easy to admit now that they'd begun their pursuit of The Maker. Now that all their ties in Cotarion fluttered loose. He turned back to her, and her expression, lit now by the impending dawn, was strange. She smiled, her eyes bright. "So . . . where do we stand, you and I?"

She quirked an eyebrow. "On a boat called Barnacle's Song heading west out of Port Ellicott."

All his nerve failed him. He laughed, but couldn't work out the words he needed to carry on his point. Cameron took a deep breath, and bumped her shoulder against his. "I know what you meant. But why ask when we can just find out?"

She leaned in. So did he. The pitch and roll of the boat seemed to slow as their lips met. Small shocks raced through him. Everything in his mind shuddered to a halt.

Cameron transformed in that moment from some monolithic figure to something warm, human. He held her, a person of flesh and blood and mistakes and triumphs. As her fingers wound ever tighter between his, as they both pressed closer, he understood the precipice on which they stood. Both of them were only alive there because of determination and luck.

He savored her warmth, the sweetness of the moment, in light of this fragility.

Eventually they both eased back. William felt his heart pounding. Cameron smiled with a ferocity he'd never seen before. As if she'd achieved some long-held goal and found it an even greater triumph than she'd hoped for. How long had she waited for this? In his memory rose the Winter Solstice, all the moments she'd warned him, the night they'd sat in front of a fire before Erika found them. On each occasion he'd seen a moment of rising hope, soon extinguished.

So often he'd been so cruel, and all that time she'd been waiting for him to turn a corner.

"I have been a total ass," he breathed.

She opened her mouth to respond, but was cut off.

"So," said Ellis from a few feet away, "you couldn't wait twenty-four hours to risk the whole enterprise. Really, Kardell, I am appalled."

Cameron didn't drop William's hand, but the warmth fell out of her face. She wore the cool, clear expression she always did when facing Ellis.

"It's not a risk unless I let it influence my decisions, which I won't," Cameron said.

Ellis smiled his cold and knowing smile, the same one that had brought William to the point of lashing out. Why he was even with them he still couldn't understand.

"And we all know that he definitely will be influenced."

Cameron nudged William before he could respond. He looked at her, and with a tip of her head she indicated that he should go. He scrunched up his nose, but nodded. She kissed him again. There was nothing perfunctory about it.

He found himself wishing he'd stopped being angry with her a long time before.

Ellis cleared his throat and they separated. Cameron gave his hand a reassuring squeeze, then let go.

William walked by Ellis, making sure to scowl as they passed. The former High General sneered. It was shaping up to be an excellent working relationship.

"We're going into a chaotic situation, Kardell, one you can't begin to understand."

William looked back when he was out of earshot. Cameron's face was a mask, her eyes dark as Ellis talked. The sky behind her brightened by the moment, and Cotarion was a wedge of land at the horizon. She looked over at him, and her expression cleared for a moment.

She was human, after all.

READY FOR MORE?

Megan Morgan lives in Baltimore. She can be found on most social media platforms as *@mmmwrites*, where she posts writing updates and discusses all sorts of random topics that the algorithm doesn't understand. Don't be afraid to say hello! You will probably find she's just as nerdy as you.

Keep an eye out for the next books in *The Sentinel Quartet*, and more to come after that.

MORE GREAT TITLES FROM CLICKWORKS PRESS

www.clickworkspress.com

Death's Dream Kingdom

Gabriel Blanchard

A young woman of Victorian London has been transformed into a vampire. Can she survive the world of the immortal dead—or, perhaps, escape it?

"The wit and humor are as Victorian as the setting . . . a winsomely vulnerable and tremendously crafted work of art."

"a dramatic, engaging novel which explores themes of death, love, damnation, and redemption."

Learn more at clickworkspress.com/ddk.

The Dream World Collective

Ben Y. Faroe

Five friends quit their jobs to chase what they love. Rent looms. Hilarity ensues.

"if you like interesting personalities, hidden depths . . . and hilarious dialog, this is the book for you."

"a fun, inspiring read—perfect for a sunny summer day."

"a heartwarming, feel-good story"

Learn more at clickworkspress.com/dwc.

Black Velvet
The Erin O'Reilly Mysteries #1
Steven Henry

When an art heist at the Queens Museum leaves an officer down, Erin and her K9 partner face criminals, art dealers, and obstructive detectives in a race to capture the killers—and maybe bring closure to a 75-year-old crime.

"This book kept me going from start to finish . . . Can't wait to follow more of their adventures!"

"A must read! Love it!"

Learn more at clickworkspress.com/erin01.

Share the love!

Join our microlending team at

kiva.org/team/clickworkspress.

Keep in touch!

Join the Clickworks Press email list

and get freebies, production updates, special deals, behind-

the-scenes sneak peeks, and more.

Sign up today at clickworkspress.com/join.